W9-BNO-400

QUEEN B

QUEEN B

Laura Peyton Roberts

delacorte press

Published by Delacorte Press
an imprint of Random House Children's Books
a division of Random House, Inc.
New York

This is a work of fiction. Names, characters, places, and incidents either are the product of the author's imagination or are used fictitiously. Any resemblance to actual persons, living or dead, events, or locales is entirely coincidental.

Text copyright © 2006 by Laura Peyton Roberts
Jacket photograph copyright © 2006 by VEER

DELACORTE PRESS and colophon are registered trademarks of Random House, Inc.

www.randomhouse.com/teens

Educators and librarians, for a variety of teaching tools, visit us at www.randomhouse.com/teachers

Library of Congress Cataloging-in-Publication Data
Roberts, Laura Peyton.
Queen B / Laura Peyton Roberts.— 1st ed.
p. cm.
Summary: Now dating Kevin, high school sophomore Cassie struggles with her insecurities and learns some lessons about friendship and dating, while also trying to direct the school talent show.
ISBN-13: 978-0-385-73163-8 (hardcover) — ISBN-13: 978-0-385-90201-4 (GLB)
ISBN-10: 0-385-73163-9 (hardcover) — ISBN-10: 0-385-90201-8 (Gilbraltar lib. bdg.) [1. Interpersonal relations—Fiction. 2. Talent shows—Fiction. 3. Family life—Fiction. 4. High schools—Fiction. 5. Schools—Fiction.] I. Title.
PZ7.R5433Qr 2006
[Fic]—dc22
2005022682

The text of this book is set in 12 pt. Goudy.

Printed in the United States of America

July 2006

10 9 8 7 6 5 4 3 2 1

First Edition

For Wendy,
editor extraordinaire and friend
through thick and thicker

To B, or to Bee?
A life hangs on two letters.
Trust me: spelling counts.

I'm in Big, Big Trouble

Whoever said "the show must go on" probably had a decent show. Or else he wasn't in charge of it. He definitely wasn't the second act. If his curtain had been about to go up on a disaster as big as this one, he would have had to rethink that whole motto. We're about to flop so hard, they'll hear the impact in New York. Geologists will measure us on the Richter scale. I'll be the laughingstock of the school—again—but nobody cares about that.

Why did Mrs. Conway put me in charge of this nightmare? I can guess why she had to bail, but what did I do to deserve this grief? I mean, what did I do to *her*? She could at least have shown up for moral support.

Maybe she's out in the audience, but I don't dare peek through this curtain again. Mom, Dad, and Grandma Smythe are part of the record crowd packing our school auditorium, and the last thing I want to risk right now is accidental eye contact. It must be killing them to sit there next to each other, and since I begged them not to come tonight I can only assume they're doing it to punish me. It's been a war zone at my house lately, with Mom barely speaking to Grandma and not speaking to Dad at all. Unfortunately, Dad's speaking to me every chance he gets, like it's my fault Grandma's here making his life miserable.

Okay, that is kind of my fault, but it was an *accident*. How many times do I have to say it?

I hope Mom at least gives up on saving that empty seat for Trevor. There's no chance he'll sit there. He'd avoid the indignity of being seen with parents even if he *weren't* in the middle of a major hissy fit about cheap polyester, stuck-up high school girls, and the general unfairness of life. Which reminds me: I really ought to go see if he finished fixing that cape.

It's just that I'm kind of paralyzed here in the wings.

Fear will do that to a person.

I would love to run crying to Kevin right now. If he weren't so mad at me. Boyfriends are supposed to be there for you in a crisis, right? Assuming he's still my boyfriend. I could definitely use some support right now, and I'm not going to get it from Hayley. If she stalks by one more time with that self-righteous look on her face . . .

All right, so I should have told her! Excuse me for not wanting to brag about the most boneheaded thing I've ever done. Is it my fault Quentin has a big mouth?

Well, maybe a little.

But still.

Oh, no! Principal Ito is dimming the lights.

The show's about to begin.

In My Own Defense . . .

The first thing you ought to know is, I never set out to direct Hilltop High School's first Student Talent Showcase to Benefit Cancer Research. I'm not crazy—usually—and what normal person signs up for something like that? Besides me, I mean, because I swear I'm completely sane. At least, I was before all this started.

Just forget about everything else for a minute—whose mental health *wouldn't* be touch-and-go after six solid weeks of up-close-and-personal time with Fourteen-Karat Carter? Oops—pretend I just said Sterling Carter. Ever since I vowed to stop hating the girl, I've been trying to break myself of calling her Fourteen-Karat, but that's no easy deal, believe me. The not-hating-her part, I mean. She's been obnoxious since the day we met, but ever since the winter formal, where she beat me out for Snow Queen and I stole Kevin Matthews from her, she's been a truly epic pain in the butt. It's a full-time job just trying not to stoop to her level.

Because let's face it: I'm mostly nice, but I'm no saint. And even an angel would lose her wings if she had to spend any quality time with Sterling. The girl is heinous—sneaky, snarky, and a world-class soc. She's also a truly bad singer.

Someone ought to at least clue her in on the singing.

Someone other than me, I mean. Because even if I *have*

gone crazy, I'm definitely not suicidal. Where's Simon Cowell when you need him?

"Stuh-ling . . . ," he'd say, in that smug British accent. "I don't want to be rude, but in what universe could that be called singing? It's going to take a lobotomy to get those sounds out of my head."

A few seconds from now, when Sterling opens our talent show with her rendition of "Wind Beneath My Wings," every member of the audience will probably get in line right behind him. She'll make a total fool of herself—which I'd obviously enjoy a lot more if I weren't in charge of the show. People will think I tricked her into singing because I'm jealous that she got Snow Queen and I only got second place.

1. I only wish I were that clever, and
2. I was *thrilled* with second place.

Considering everything that happened leading up to that dance, I'm lucky Principal Ito even let me in the building. Besides, I'm used to coming in second. It's a special talent of mine.

Taking second place is my gift—or my curse, depending on what mood I'm in. Lately I've dedicated myself to seeing the bright side of every talent, but when you consider all the other possible talents in the world—and the fact that some people get to be amazing singers and actors and painters—it's hard not to feel ripped off by being the queen of second place. I have to keep reminding myself that while some gifts may *seem* more glamorous, under the right circumstances every talent is beautiful. I honestly believe that.

At least, I believe it most of the time.

Anyway, talent is kind of an obsession of mine—which I just this second realized is probably the reason Mrs. Conway put me in charge of this show. If I survive my impending heart attack, I'll have to be way more careful what I say to adults from now on—especially the ones who pay attention.

Emily Conway might just be the sharpest teacher at school, and her tongue can be even sharper. It turns out she has good reasons for her mood swings, but if she ever found out that I know *anything* about her personal life, I might have to explain how I learned it, and believe me, that wouldn't be pretty.

Privacy's like a religion to her.

Which, personally, I don't get. How are people supposed to help you if you won't even tell them what's going on? I mean, they *might* help you, if you trick them into believing that a student talent show benefiting cancer research is an altruistic act of charity.

Then again, they might not. Hayley's my best friend and I'm still not completely certain she's going to perform tonight. If I could tell her why I care about this show, she'd cooperate like crazy. But I promised to keep Conway's secret. Even though doing that makes no sense to me. I guess Mrs. Conway doesn't like life to get personal, but that's how life is.

Everything's personal. You just can't take it that way.

I mean, if I took things personally, the fact that Kevin

and I have been together for over two months and he still hasn't said "I love you" might make me feel kind of bad. In fact, if I took that omission personally, I might start wondering what's wrong with me, and why he bothers to hang out with me, and if he even cares. Then I'd probably start wondering if anyone will ever love me or if I'm destined to spend my entire life as a bridesmaid and never a bride, because, you know, that would really tie in with the second-place thing. And—taking all of this personally—I *could* start getting paranoid about some random girl and acting a tiny bit crazy, which might eventually lead to the type of stupidity that only I am capable of.

Oh, wait.

That's pretty much what happened.

I'm Doing It Again, Aren't I?

Jumping all over the place when I ought to be telling you things in order. On the other hand, if you insist on showing up in the middle of my messes, how do you expect me to remember what I've already told you and what you've missed? I'm under some major stress here.

Don't get me wrong—I'm totally glad to see you again. But it's not like I don't have other friends to talk to if you're going to keep disappearing. I have an absurdly hot boyfriend, don't forget, not to mention Hayley. Plus there's Fitz and Quentin—and, unfortunately, Ros Pierce, but let's not go there yet. If I got really desperate, I could talk to my parents, or even my annoying younger brother, Trevor. But I like talking to you, because then I can talk *about* all those people and you don't tell them what I say.

So I guess I'd better back up and start at the beginning. Right?

Seriously, don't take this the wrong way, but if you could check in more often, it would really help me out.

Once Upon a Time . . .

I'm just kidding. No need to go back that far. Christmas vacation should be far enough. Or maybe a teensy bit further, just to fill you in.

Let's see. . . . You remember the Snow Ball, right? Well, after Kevin and I got together at our school's winter formal, the guy of my dreams and I enjoyed two whole weeks of uninterrupted bliss. Well, mostly uninterrupted. Because as seriously as I'd love to report that Sterling Carter evaporated like a bad smell after the dance, she was alive and well and back at school on Monday. Not only back, but she'd rebounded from Kevin's dumping like a Super Ball on speed. You couldn't go anywhere without seeing her and Tate the Great making out.

You must remember Bryce Tate. That immensely muscular, semipopular, football-playing loser who showed up drunk at our formal? He passed out in the landscaping and Ros Pierce lost her date. That was when *my* date, Quentin, and I agreed to go our separate ways, so that he could pursue his true crush, Ros. And even though I'd never actually believed that Quentin and I might finally become more than friends—okay, I thought *maybe*—the timing was still a bummer. I was bummed right up until the second I found myself with Kevin, the guy I'd been in love-at-first-sight with since October.

Of course, that left Kevin's original date, Sterling, on her own. . . .

Do you see where this is going?

It's completely unacceptable for a soc like Sterling to be solo at a formal—that's kind of the antonym of *social*—so by the end of the night she had Tate the Great sobered up and acting like her thrilled new boyfriend. I say *acting* because of what happened later, but we're doing this in order now, right? And after the formal those two were totally lovey-dovey.

Lovey-dovey barely scratches the surface of how I felt about Kevin. I normally don't have much luck in the romance department. In fact, being the queen of second place means I usually end up with the *friend* part of *girl+friend*. But this time—at last—I'd come in first.

I can't even explain how amazing first felt.

Love at first sight.

First love.

Desperate crushes don't count anymore once you experience the real thing.

Luv Story

School let out for winter vacation and two more weeks slipped by like a dream. Every day was filled with all those romantic boyfriend things I'd always wanted to do and never could before: ice-skating with Kevin, exchanging silly gifts, making out under the Christmas tree while our faces turned holiday colors beneath the twinkling lights. . . .

Bliss.

The only teeny, tiny fly in my ointment was the way Kevin signed his New Year's card:

> *Dear Cassie,*
> *Happy New Year! It's so amazing*
> *knowing you. You are a very special girl.*
> *Luv, Kevin*

Granted, he'd followed that up with a stroke-of-midnight kiss that's making me blush just thinking about it. But still . . . *luv?* That's how I signed my Christmas card to Quentin. Everyone knows *luv* is a safety net, a way of saying you care about someone without saying you actually *love* them.

"You're stressing over two stupid letters," Hayley told me, watching the Rose Parade from a pillow on the floor in our den.

"Technically three, if you want to count the *u*."

"And, of course, you do." She rolled over to give me an impatient look, her face framed by dozens of dark brown ringlets. "Why can't you just relax and enjoy having a boyfriend for once? I'm starting to think you've got something against being happy in the moment."

She might be on to something. The problem with being happy in the moment is, moments never lasts. Things change whether you want them to or not, which makes it only smart to keep looking ahead. That's how people avoid getting hit by cars.

"He's obviously crazy about you," Hayley said. "And you've only been together for, what? Three weeks?"

"Three and a half," I corrected.

"Have you told him that you love him?"

"He's the guy. He should say it first."

Hayley sighed and returned her attention to the TV, where a giant, petal-covered dinosaur was trying to make that killer turn onto Colorado Boulevard. "Give the boy a break."

I figured she was right. She usually is. And by the time Sunday night rolled around, I was so caught up in deciding what to wear for the first day of the new semester, and how I'd force my hair to cooperate, and whether the glitter eye shadow I'd bought for New Year's Eve was too flashy for school that I pretty much forgot about luv.

Pretty much.

After all, this new year was my year to shine. For the first time in my life, I had an actual shot at being someone at school. I've always been more of a Queen B than a Queen Bee—you know, B as in not A. Second tier. (Fine, if you have to get technical, sometimes even lower.) But this year, out of nowhere, I had a chance to be a real Queen Bee.

Not that I intended to be snobby, or cliquish, or any of the other rude things sometimes stapled to that label. I certainly didn't want to be a soc.

I just wanted people to love me.

(With the *o* and the *e*, not the *u*.)

Second Semester

The best thing about changing semesters is getting all new teachers. Or, in my case, mostly new, because students in sophomore honors English serve a two-semester sentence. Principal Ito says that's because Mrs. Conway is the only instructor teaching the class, but I can't help suspecting my lifelong lack of luck has got to factor in.

"Same seating chart as last semester," she announced as Kevin and I walked in.

We dragged our feet down the aisle to our old seats in back. "It could be worse," I said. "She could have split us up."

But when the bell rang a few seconds later, things started looking less sunny.

"Welcome back," Mrs. Conway said. "I trust you all had a nice break."

I sighed with the rest of the class. You know your fun is over when teachers refer to your vacation in past tense.

"I won't be issuing new books this semester," she went on. "We're going to continue working in *Modern English Grammar*."

Sighs turned into groans, partly because people had been hoping to kill time passing out books and partly for the obvious reason: *Modern English Grammar*. Conway treated us to one of her patented eyebrow lifts and the room fell instantly silent.

"However," she continued, "we won't be jumping right back into grammar. We're going to kick off this new year with something completely different."

Kevin leaned closer to my desk. "I doubt we'll be writing any more plays," he whispered, smiling.

I made a face at him. Did he think that was funny?

"We're starting a section on poetry, specifically Japanese haiku. The form is deceptively simple—only three lines. A first line of five syllables, followed by one of seven, then a final line of five. But you'll be amazed how much you can cram into that tiny package."

Somebody snorted.

"More importantly," Conway said, glaring, "*I'd* better be amazed."

She spent a lot of time explaining the history of haiku, and how each poem traditionally includes at least one word related to a season of the year. There was something called cutting that had to do with dashes, but by then I'd become so hypnotized by the second hand on the clock that I'd stopped paying attention. When she finally got around to reading some haiku, the words washed over me unheard.

"Your homework for tonight," she said, bringing me back to earth, "is to write three haiku on any subject. I'll collect them tomorrow morning."

Then the bell rang and Kevin and I rushed out at the back of the class, happy to finally be free.

"Can you believe her?" he griped as we walked down the hall. "Our first day back from vacation and she's already loading us up."

"She's one of a kind, all right."

I wasn't any happier about having homework than he was, but it felt disloyal to bad-mouth Conway. Knowing her husband was fighting cancer while she worked to support them both made it pretty hard to hate her.

Of course, Kevin *didn't* know that, so he had no loyalty issues. "I can't believe I signed up for another semester of this."

"Thanks a lot! You'd transfer out of the only class we have together?"

"Not to get away from you. Be serious, Cassie. It's not like last semester was a picnic for either one of us."

Which has to be the understatement of all time.

"It's just a haiku," I said, determined to keep the past behind me. "Seventeen syllables."

"Yeah, times three. How much is seventeen times three?"

I don't generally multiply by seventeens, so I smiled and changed the subject. "I'll see you at lunch. You're sitting with us, right?"

He leaned over and kissed me, letting his lips linger on mine. "Unless you want to ditch this place and run away together."

Believe me when I tell you that I could have been convinced. "Where would we go?" I asked.

"I don't know. We could join a haiku-free commune in the hills and become vegetarians or something."

"Mmm," I said, kissing him one last time. "Get back to me when your plan doesn't involve a lifetime without pepperoni."

So painfully bored
The clock ticks but time stands still.
Geometry kills.

A Soc Among Us

Haiku is easy! Don't tell Kevin I said this, but it's even kind of fun. Math, on the other hand, is obviously not my subject. My new third-period geometry class makes an hour feel like a week. It might help if Mr. Beyerson didn't drone on as if he's half asleep himself, but in the unlikely event my life ever hangs on my ability to label acute and obtuse angles, I'm totally going to survive.

On the brighter side, I now have art fourth period instead of Western civ, and considering that Ms. Lane lets us talk the whole time, that class goes by fast. As soon as the bell rang I ran outside to find Hayley and the table she'd promised to save us.

Last semester we usually ate by ourselves on one of the benches edging the quad, but now Kevin and Fitz eat with us almost every day. Quentin usually joins us, and with Rosalind Pierce tagging along, we need to grab a table.

Ros Pierce. I guess this is as good a time as any.

Ever since the dance, Quentin and Ros have been inseparable. The only time she isn't glued to him is when Sterling demands her attention or Quentin goes to his new job bagging groceries at MegaFoodMart. Because now that he has a girlfriend, Quentin says he needs money for dates and stuff. I say if he's running through that much cash, he ought to ask Ros to pay sometimes; everyone knows the Pierces are loaded. But he won't. Quentin's old-fashioned that way. Or maybe he's just proud.

Anyway, when she's not hanging out with Sterling, Ros is part of our group these days. And she's not hanging out with Sterling nearly as much as she used to. Ros insists they're still best friends, but anyone can see that they're not as tight as they were. After all the stuff Sterling did to keep Ros and Quentin from getting together, I guess Ros feels like she has to choose between them now when she's deciding who to hang out with. Which doesn't bother Sterling as much you might think, because she's plenty busy with Tate the Great. Those two are together nearly as much as Ros and Quentin. It's kind of weird, when you think about it, how we all got boyfriends at the same time.

Anyway, my life was definitely less complicated when we all thought of Ros as Sterling's empty-headed sidekick. But Ros is nothing like we thought.

For one thing, she's smart. (So sue me for assuming that anyone who actually likes Sterling isn't setting IQ records.)

What's more surprising is, she has a sense of humor. Even more surprising? When she's not hanging out with a certain bad influence, Ros is hardly soc-y at all.

(We agreed on the definition of *soc* last time, right? One of the *so*cially elite snobs who think they run the school? Well-dressed evil in heels? Picture Sterling Carter, then extrapolate a pack of clones.)

So, getting back to Monday, I ran outside to the quad and found all my friends and Ros already crammed in around a table.

"There she is!" Quentin greeted me, his arm around Ros's shoulders.

Here's what I've decided: if money can buy hair like Ros's, then being rich is worth the hype. Anyone can tell the difference between her salon-tinted tresses and, say . . . mine.

Luckily, Kevin likes crazy red hair. "Hey!" he said, grabbing my hand and pulling me down to sit next to him.

"Hi," I replied breathlessly.

"Don't get comfortable," Hayley butted in, "because if we're buying pizza, someone has to go get it."

Sometimes Hayley's just too practical. She says she's in love with Fitz, but whenever anyone else is around they act more like buddies. Which doesn't say much about their relationship, in my opinion. I mean, it's not really love if you can switch it on and off. Not true love, anyway.

The way you know you're truly in love is, you can't breathe when the other person's not there. And you can't breathe when he is. Basically, you just can't breathe.

It sounds bad, but it's heaven.

"Ros and I'll get the pizza," Quentin volunteered. "With maybe one more person, to help us carry stuff . . ."

He looked my way, but I didn't want to leave Kevin.

"You two can handle it," I told him. "Use trays."

Hayley shot me a put-out look, which I aimed right back at her. If carrying lunch really took three people, there was no reason she couldn't go.

"*I* got the table," she said, reading my mind. Looking for someone to take our sides, we both accidentally glanced at Fitz. He started to stand up.

"Never mind!" I cried. "Kevin and I will do it ourselves."

I yanked Kevin to his feet before Fitz could get up. Constantly coming in second *is* a gift compared to Fitz's talent: every line he stands in either slows to a crawl or stops dead. That's a gift with surprising uses—but buying lunch isn't one of them.

"You don't want any help?" Fitz asked dubiously.

"Ros and I'll still come," Quentin offered.

"No need," I said, waving them back into their seats. Mostly I just wanted to prove that they could have done the job themselves, but the truth is that those two as a couple can be pretty hard to stomach.

Have I mentioned the baby talk?

Kevin and I collected everyone's money and joined the shorter of two lines behind our school's outdoor fast-food kiosks.

"This is going to take forever," he predicted, gauging the distance between us and the register.

"No, forever would be if we'd let Fitz help." I laced my

fingers through his, content to wait. There's really no down-side to killing time with the cutest guy in school. I don't want to brag (okay, maybe a little), but ever since the Snow Ball, pretty much everyone recognizes me and Kevin and knows how we got together.

Which obviously drives Sterling crazy.

I could see her and Tate at the edge of the quad, Tate talk-ing to some of his football friends while Sterling put on a show, laughing and tossing her perfect blond hair every five seconds in case everyone wasn't already staring at the way she was kneading Tate's glutes through his jeans. I felt my ir-ritation rise despite the fact that I've vowed to ignore her a million times. If a girl could buy a neon sign that floated over her head flashing LOOK AT ME, Sterling would get two. Not that she needs them. Between her hair, her miniskirts, and the way every shirt she owns seems about to burst at the crit-ical button, she's got attracting attention down to a science.

"Do you think she even likes him?" I asked Kevin.

He followed my gaze across the quad, sighing when he spotted Sterling. "Do you care?"

"No. It's just . . . I can't see how you stood her. She's so fake!"

Kevin tensed; he hates it when I mention that Sterling is his ex. "Everyone makes mistakes," he said.

What I *wanted* him to say was that he didn't see how he'd stood Sterling either, that he certainly couldn't stand her now, and that he had absolutely no intention of ever standing her again.

Not that I thought he did, but a girl likes to be reassured.

"What are you doing after school?" I asked, moving to safer territory. "I was thinking maybe we could do our homework together in the library."

Kevin laughed, his face tilting up into the January sunshine. His tan had faded since October, and most of the blond highlights had grown out of his spiky hair, but somehow he kept getting cuter.

"As thrilling as that sounds, I'm going to have to pass," he said. "It's bad enough being back at school without turning it into slow geeky torture."

He was right, of course. The library on the first day of a new semester? Definitely not the place for a Queen Bee.

Or even a Queen B.

But if we went to my house, Trevor would bother us. And Kevin's mother only works mornings, specifically so she can be there when he gets home.

"I just want to be alone with you," I admitted.

"And you are," he said, grabbing me playfully by the waist. "You have me all to yourself right now and you're not doing a thing about it."

Which wasn't exactly true, since we were standing in the middle of the crowded quad. Still, I laughed as he swung me in a circle, not wanting to seem like a bad girlfriend.

I *am* a bad girlfriend, but I didn't know that then.

I had no idea.

Badminton

I might as well admit it: when Hayley and I got the idea to sign up for badminton this semester, I thought we were total geniuses. I mean, okay, Hayley probably *is* a genius, but that's beside the point. The point is that we finally landed a totally easy sixth-period PE class that actually takes place inside the gym. The *gym*, where there's no track to run, the weather is always nice, and the entire world doesn't see you wearing those hideous blue shorts. If you're not on one of the sports teams, that's as sweet as PE gets.

Hayley and I arrived at the locker room early that first day, but we still got assigned new lockers in the back of nowhere. I was irritated until I discovered there were only a couple of other girls dressing in our little alcove. I'm not a privacy freak, like Conway, but I don't need a crowd when I'm changing clothes. Or showering. Hence my preference for taking PE sixth period, so I can skip the showers and go straight home.

We got dressed and walked through the locker room into the gym, where a bunch of other blue-shorted girls were hanging out amid a half-dozen badminton nets. A few had already removed delicate, long-handled racquets from a rolling equipment rack, and others were examining the weird, plastic-feathered objects we'd soon be hitting through the air.

"This is going to be fun!" Hayley said.

"If you say so." Last semester's tennis improved my hand-eye coordination, but let's just say the Williams sisters aren't shaking in their Nikes.

"Where's our teacher?" she asked.

That was when the gym door opened and my worst nightmare walked in.

Sterling Carter was in my PE class.

"I see her," Hayley said before I could even open my mouth. "Promise me you'll ignore her."

"Me!" I protested. "She's the one who always starts it."

"And when she does, you can't leave it alone." Hayley grabbed my arm and pulled me over to the equipment cart. "Just pretend she isn't here."

"Right. Ignoring her always works," I said sarcastically.

Snatching up a racquet, I swung it in sullen arcs. Running the track was pure joy compared to spending all semester in an enclosed space with Fourteen-Karat Carter. I was still swinging when a familiar soc-y voice drawled at my back.

"Nice tan, Howard. We could turn out the lights and play by the glow off your legs."

I'll let you in on a little secret: anytime you see a red-head with a tan, you can be certain something is fake. Either her hair is dyed or her skin is. *Every* time. Guaranteed. Tan redheads don't occur in nature.

I turned to face Fourteen-Karat, stoically clenching my teeth against the many clever retorts that came to mind. All right, fine—nothing clever came to mind. For reasons I still haven't figured out, Sterling has a paralyzing effect on the comeback portion of my brain. But trust me on the teeth-clenching part. Her blue eyes taunted me from a flawless tan face. Her sleeveless white T-shirt was tight in all the right places. She even made those awful shorts look good.

"It does go with your hair, though," she allowed. "Orange and white . . . like a human Creamsicle."

"Stop it, Ster!" a new girl beside her giggled. "You're so *bad*!"

Which is too true to argue with. Unfortunately, this girl meant it as a compliment. Pretty, petite, and brunette, she wore her long curls tied back with a perky blue bow and her cap-sleeved shirt even tighter than Sterling's.

I had no idea who she was, but I already knew we weren't going to be friends.

Picking up a racquet, Sterling tossed a last mocking grin my way and sauntered off across the gym with her fellow debutante.

"Lord help us," I moaned. "They're multiplying."

"Can you spell *soc*?" Hayley echoed.

"I don't have to spell it. I can smell it."

Then the gym door opened again and Sterling's new sidekick was forgotten. Our badminton teacher was a man.

"I'm Coach Crawford," he said, motioning for everyone to gather around. He wore blue shorts too, but his looked nowhere near as ridiculous as ours. In fact, they looked kind of . . . hot.

"He's young!" I heard someone whisper.

"I wonder if he's single," her friend whispered back.

Hayley and I exchanged glances, and I could tell we

were thinking the same thing: badminton was about to become a highly competitive sport.

"It's going to take me a while to learn who you are," Coach apologized, opening his roll book. "I'm not good with names, so please bear with me if you're all 'hey, you' for the first few days."

"You'll remember *my* name," Sterling assured him, tossing her long ponytail. "Everyone does."

"Yes, um . . . okay." He gave her an unsettled look before returning to his book. "Let's see. Abby Anderson?"

"Here." A girl in glasses raised her hand.

"Kari Buchanon?"

"Here."

"Sterling Carter?"

"Here!" Sterling's smile telegraphed her belief that he'd never need to ask again. And here's the nauseating part: she was right. People *don't* forget her name.

Especially male people.

The roll call progressed through the alphabet. I spoke up at "Howard" and was about to resume fiddling with my racquet when a new name grabbed my ears.

"Tiffany Hughes?" Coach called.

I knew just from the way that name sounded—before she even raised her hand—that Tiffany had to be Sterling's new buddy.

"You can call me Tiffi," she said, with a suggestive lift of one well-plucked brow. Her full lips went extra pouty beneath their glimmer of rose-colored gloss. "All my friends do."

"It's official," I whispered to Hayley. "Sterling has found her long-lost twin."

"They look nothing alike," Hayley whispered back.

"Not on the *outside*." Any casual observer could see that Tiffi and Sterling were made of the same stuff. Tiffany Hughes had soc attitude oozing from her pores.

"Maybe she's just sucking up to the teacher," Hayley said.

"Uh-huh. Or maybe she's pure evil."

Looking back, I have to admit I jumped to conclusions. But that doesn't mean I was wrong.

Ice Cream. Headache.

When I got home from school that afternoon, I was not in the world's best mood, and seeing Trevor in a great one didn't help at all.

"Only one semester left!" he crowed as I walked into the kitchen to cheer myself up with ice cream. "I'm nearly out of that place!"

Trevor's completing eighth grade to join me in high school is not a prospect I'm thrilled about, but right then it barely fazed me. "Hooray for you," I said, sinking my scoop to the bottom of the rocky road.

"So . . . any good parties this week?"

"No," I said irritably. "I told you I'd let you know."

"You said that all through Christmas vacation and nothing happened," he whined, getting up from our computer in the den to come bother me over the breakfast bar. "You promised, Cassie."

"I also said it could take a while."

"You're not even trying!"

Rolling my eyes, I stuffed a spoonful of ice cream into my mouth. It's not like I'm in charge of scheduling every party in Hilltop. Or any of them, for that matter.

"What about Julie?" he pressed. "Did you talk to her today?"

"About what?"

"About *me*."

"I thought I wasn't supposed to mention you."

"You're not." His gaze followed his thumbnail as it scraped something stuck to the counter. "So have you?"

Trevor's freshman crush, Julie Evans, and I hardly know each other. And while I had promised to sneak him into a high school party where I could casually "introduce" them, I still hadn't figured out how I'd accomplish that. For one thing, I had no idea what parties Julie might actually go to. For another, the whole plan reeked of a setup. And finally, even though Trevor had been in love with Julie for a year, I was willing to bet she couldn't pick him out of a lineup.

"I haven't mentioned you, Trevor, because I've barely said two words to Julie since I left middle school. If you want this ridiculous idea to work, you have to let me do it my own way."

He looked up from the counter, his eyes narrowing suspiciously. "You'd better not be weaseling out. A deal's a deal, Cassie."

"Whatever."

Picking up my bowl, I headed for my bedroom. The last thing I needed just then was more Trevor time.

Not that my day had been all bad. In fact, overall it had been pretty good. But PE was still fresh in my mind, and anytime Sterling is stuck in your head it's a guaranteed headache. Wedge Tiffi Hughes in there with her, and no wonder my temples were pounding.

They ought to make a pill for soc-induced migraines.

Holiday Hangover

At dinner that night, it was my dad's turn to be in a bad mood.

"I don't know what you're complaining about, Hal," my mother told him. "Personally, I'm glad the holidays are over. Now we can settle down and get back to work."

"When did we *leave* work?" he retorted. "I must have blinked and missed it."

"Don't exaggerate," she said.

"I'm not exaggerating! One day off for Christmas, one day for New Year's . . . We didn't even get Christmas Eve!"

"That's because Christmas Eve isn't an official holiday."

My mother, the lawyer, is very big on "official" holidays. If it were up to her, there would only be about three. It's not the festivities she objects to—she just doesn't think her company should have to pay people to take a day off.

My dad, on the other hand, seemed convinced that that

was exactly what his firm should have done. "We had that day off last year," he said stubbornly.

"With pay? What day of the week did Christmas fall on?"

"What difference does that make?"

I wondered the same thing, but I didn't care enough to listen to her explanation. Reaching across Trevor, I grabbed the salt. He gave me a snotty look, to let me know I still owed him a party.

"If you wanted more time off, you should have used vacation days," my mother concluded.

"That's what they *want* us to do!" Dad protested. "They set this whole thing up so we'd *have* to use vacation time."

"Don't be silly. That's what vacation days are for."

Dad looked as if he had an entirely different opinion on that subject, but he swallowed it with some mashed potatoes. The only interesting thing about the whole conversation was the fact that he'd started it at all. My dad generally avoids any discussion that might turn into an argument.

"Anyway," my mother said, "if that's your biggest problem, you've got nothing to complain about. I sent my new secretary to pull a case file today, but he couldn't find it. So I took him back down to Archives, to show him how it's done, and the place looks like a landfill—all that's missing is the seagulls. I had to fire our librarian, and now I don't know who'll straighten out that mess. How complicated can it be to shelve boxes in numerical order?"

"Mmm," said my dad, retreating to safe ground.

I pushed my food around while Mom continued her rant

about archival incompetence. Unlike my father, my mom *loves* to argue. It's not just her gift, it's her job and her hobby. When no one wants to debate her, she's fully capable of carrying on by herself.

"What's the matter, Cassie?" she asked at last. "You're not eating much tonight."

"Not if you don't count that half-gallon of ice cream she scarfed down after school," Trevor the Snitch supplied.

"I'm just not hungry," I said, kicking Trevor under the table.

Mom gave me a probing look. "Why not?"

I sighed, knowing she wouldn't understand, then took a shot anyway. "Sterling Carter's in my PE class."

"And?"

"That's not enough?"

"Did she say something to you?" Mom pressed.

"Only that my legs are so white they glow in the dark."

Milk snorted out of Trevor's nose, showering his side of the table. Mom and I both gave him dirty looks.

"Hey, that's just the truth," he muttered, wiping up with his napkin. "You can't blame me for that."

Mom's glare lingered before she turned her attention back to me. "Sterling is probably as unhappy about this as you are. I imagine she'd rather avoid you, too."

"You don't know Sterling," I told her.

"I know you're dating her old boyfriend, and that's got to sting. Keep your distance and see if she doesn't do the same."

I could have pointed out that Sterling's human Creamsicle crack was completely unprovoked. But if Mom was right, perhaps that gibe was just Sterling's desperate attempt to put me down before I could get to her.

Which made my pathetic lack of a comeback seem almost virtuous. Cool, even.

"I have to keep reminding myself that everything's different now," I admitted. "I'm practically a different person."

"That's my girl. Name it and claim it," my father said.

I had no clue what he was talking about. He seemed to be encouraging me, though, so I nodded.

After all, did it really matter if Sterling was in my badminton class? I'd simply pretend she wasn't there. The fact that she'd been impossible to ignore in the past was in the past.

There was a new queen in town.

Queen B.

If she's the queen, then
All her bizzy friends are drones.
Social little bees.

Show and Tell

Tuesday morning I trotted the last few blocks to school, hoping to meet up with Kevin before classes started. I spotted him waiting out on the lawn, his hoodie hanging unzipped despite a shimmer of frost on the grass. My breath came out in little white puffs as I hurried over to join him.

"Look at you!" he said. "You're all pink!"

"It's the cold," I explained, blushing until my cheeks matched my new down jacket.

"It's adorable," he said, putting an arm around me.

Wait till my nose starts running, I thought, but I obviously didn't say that. Instead, I snuggled into Kevin, feeling on top of the world that he'd waited for me in the cold.

Just inside the main hallway, Hayley, Fitz, Quentin, and Ros were staring at a banner strung above their heads.

Hayley saw me and pointed. "Hey, Cassie! Check it out."

HILLTOP HIGH SCHOOL

STUDENT TALENT SHOWCASE.

SIGN UP NOW. REHEARSALS START MONDAY.

I shook my head. "Who'd want to be in some cheesy school talent show?"

"I was thinking you," Hayley said.

"Me?" I said, shocked. "What would I do in a talent show?"

"You tell me. You're the one who's so obsessed with talent."

"That's because I don't have one worth mentioning. If anyone ought to perform, it's you. At least you can whistle."

"You should!" Fitz urged her. "Represent for the rest of us!"

"Be serious," Hayley scoffed. "No one wants to hear me whistle."

"I do," Quentin and I said at the same time.

"You can whistle?" Ros asked.

"Hayley's an *awesome* whistler!" Quentin always sounds overcaffeinated whenever Ros is around. "You should hear her. Go ahead, Hayley. Whistle!"

"Maybe later," Hayley said uncomfortably.

"Besides, you already heard her at the Snow Ball," I said. "That was Hayley whistling 'Charge!' "

Ros gave me a blank look. Quentin's was more of a glare.

"Oh, right," I said, realizing my mistake. "I forgot you and Bryce showed up late."

"Sorry to hear I missed something good. Next time," Ros added, with an inside smile at Quentin. He got that annoyingly gooey look right away—we were headed straight for the baby talk.

"The problem with talent shows is, they're too narrow," I said, eager to steer the conversation to less nauseating ground. "If I *were* going to be in a talent show—which I'm not—it would be an all-talents-welcome show. I wouldn't discriminate against singing and dancing, but it would be way more cool to have acts we haven't seen a gazillion times before."

"Like what?" Hayley asked.

"I don't know. Paper-airplane folding. Trampoline tricks. Even Kevin telling time in his head."

"You can tell time in your head?" Ros asked.

Kevin shrugged. "Freaky, huh?"

"You've already seen my parking skills," Quentin reminded her slyly.

"What would *you* do, Ros?" I asked, to change the subject again. "In a talent show, I mean."

"Oh, I could never be in a talent show. I'm completely talentless."

"That's not true!" Quentin protested.

"You must have some talent," I told her. "Everybody does."

"I don't," Ros insisted. "Definitely none."

"You have to understand Cassie's theory of talent," Hayley explained. "It doesn't have to be something obvious."

"No," Fitz agreed sadly. "It can be pretty darn obscure."

Ros shook her head. "Sorry. No talent, hidden, odd, or otherwise."

"You just haven't discovered it yet," I said, warming to the challenge.

"I know what it is." Quentin threw his arms around her and pulled her tight to his chest. "It must be having the world's cutest liddle nose. Wook at dat cute widdle ting!"

"Quentin!" She giggled as he kissed its tip. "You siwwy!"

"Yeah, not admissible," I ruled, afraid I'd lose my Cocoa Critters right there in the hall. "But we'll have to figure this out later. I need to get to my locker before class."

Everyone else suddenly realized they needed to take off too.

"See you at lunch," Hayley said, bailing with Fitz. Quentin and Ros tagged along behind them, still giggling to each other.

"Is it me, or are those two sickening?" I asked Kevin.

"What's the matter? Jealous?"

My heart took a sick, sideways beat. "No!"

"You'd better say that." Tossing an arm across my shoulders, he steered me down the hall. "I wouldn't want you thinking you'd picked the wrong guy."

"I don't."

That wasn't the problem at all. It was just . . . I really had no idea how much Quentin's being with Ros would bother me. I know it's stupid, but seeing him that blissed-out kind of hurt my feelings. All those months I spent chasing him, totally in love, and he never even noticed . . . Then one accidental date with Ros and *wham!* Head over heels.

It's annoying. That's all.

"I just wish they wouldn't talk baby talk in front of me," I said.

"Why?" Kevin pulled me closer. "You don't wike Wos's widdle nosey?"

"Stop it before someone hears you," I begged.

"Stop what?" he persisted, tickling my ribs with his free hand. "I'm not embawassing you, am I?"

"Only every time someone looks our way. I'm *trying* to be cool this year."

Kevin stopped abruptly. "What does that mean? I'm not allowed to use baby talk in the hallways?"

"Or pretty much anywhere else."

"What about tickling you?"

"Not in public."

He rolled his eyes. "I thought being cool meant doing what you want and not caring what other people think."

"Don't talk crazy—that would be *ultra*cool. I'll be satisfied if I can just stay out of Dweebsville."

"Dweebsville, huh? If that's the goal, you'd better fill me in. All these new rules . . . I don't even know if I'm still allowed to do this."

Ignoring hallway traffic, he gave me a kiss that left me holding myself up by two handfuls of his sweatshirt. "Is that still okay?" he asked.

"Yes," I said, when I could speak again. "Yes, that's *very* cool."

Show Business

"A few announcements," Mrs. Conway said after roll. "First off, if you didn't hand me your haiku as you walked in, they'd better be on their way to my desk right now."

A brief commotion followed as a handful of procrastinators passed their papers up the rows.

"Next, Principal Ito has asked the teachers to crack down on tardies this semester. There will be no more leniency when it comes to assigning detention to consistently late students." She smiled ironically. "Perhaps leniency is a problem some of your other teachers have."

Having already done one stint in detention with Conway, I didn't find her little joke nearly as amusing as she did.

"And finally," she said, "the school is hosting a student talent showcase to raise money for cancer research. Obviously, that's a very good cause and I hope you'll all consider participating."

Her expression gave away nothing, but the hairs rose on the back of my neck as I put two and two together.

"I'm the faculty advisor," she added, confirming my hunch. "I'll pass a sign-up sheet around."

Picking up a clipboard with a dangling pencil attached, she handed it to Darlene Walters, who barely glanced at it before passing it to the girl behind her.

"Now let's take a look at these haiku," Conway said. Choosing a poem from our stack, she wrote it on the board.

> *I arrived in fall*
> *And slumbered through our winter.*
> *You woke me like spring.*

"Hey!" Kevin whispered. "That's mine!"

I caught my breath, barely able to believe he'd written something so romantic about me.

"Any comments?" Conway asked the class.

Cyn Martin's hand went up. "It's not spring yet."

"*Like* spring!" I blurted out.

Heads swiveled my way.

"It's a metaphor!" I said defensively. "Or a simile, anyway. He—I mean, the author—is obviously doing that seasonal thing Mrs. Conway told us about."

"I think it's about a bear," someone offered.

"Yeah, a hibernating bear," Mike Peters chimed in. "I can totally see that."

I gave Kevin an outraged look, but he just shrugged, amused.

The class sucked the life out of four or five more defenseless poems before Staci Garcia turned around and handed me a clipboard with a pencil. I stared blankly a moment before I remembered what it was.

Mrs. Conway's talent show sign-up sheet.

Without a single signature.

"There aren't any names on this!" I hissed to Kevin, tilting the clipboard his way.

"You're the one who called the whole idea cheesy."

"Shhh!" I hushed him frantically. "That was before!"

"Before what?"

"Before I knew Mrs. Conway was in charge."

Kevin looked stupefied. "Right. Because that is a huge selling point."

"No, but . . . it's going to hurt her feelings."

"She'll get over it."

"It's for *charity*!"

"Be my guest," he dared me, nodding toward the sheet.

I hesitated, my visions of potential coolness slipping away. Then I snatched up the pencil and wrote down my name.

"I can't believe you just did that."

Smiling, I added his name under mine.

"No way," he said, grabbing. "Erase that right now!"

"Calm down," I whispered, holding the clipboard out of his reach. "Once more people sign up, you can drop out."

"Who else is going to be that crazy?"

"It's a big school, full of crazy people."

Kevin didn't look convinced.

"We need a few more names here," I said, "just to get the ball rolling."

"I don't know whose. That sheet's already been through the whole room."

"Yeah."

Looking back, I probably should have let it go. Okay, I *definitely* should have let it go. But I'd promised myself I'd keep an eye on Mrs. Conway and help her out if I could.

The way I saw it, that sign-up sheet was a cry for help.

Taking a deep breath, I started filling up lines:

Hayley Johnson
Quentin Zane
Marc Fitzgerald
Rosalind Pierce

"There," I breathed, satisfied. "That looks better."

"Are you insane?" Kevin whispered, reading from across the aisle.

"It's for charity. They'll understand."

"You'll regret this," he warned.

If only I'd known how much.

Secondhand News

"You did *what?*" Hayley leaned across our lunch table and peered into my eyes, trying to see if I was kidding.

Kevin smirked. "I told you."

Everyone else in our group stared at me in disbelief.

"It's for *charity*," I explained, squirming. "Cancer research."

No one even blinked.

"We can always show up and then drop out, but you have to admit it's a worthy cause. Besides, it could be fun to all do something together."

"Yeah, like take a drive to the beach," Hayley said. "Weren't you listening this morning when we said we'd never be in that show? In fact, didn't you say that yourself?"

"Yes, but—"

"I would do a magic act," Fitz announced. Five amazed faces turned his way. "If we were participating, I mean," he added, embarrassed.

"Magic?" Quentin razzed him. "How dorky is that?"

"Right. Because the biggest acts in Vegas aren't magic," Hayley retorted defensively.

"You don't even know magic, Fitz," Quentin persisted. "Unless you're practicing it alone at night in your bedroom. Dude! Tell me you're not practicing alone in your bedroom."

"I have a book," Fitz said. "I got it for Christmas."

Personally, I was in complete agreement with Quentin on magic's geek factor, but nobody needed to know that. Especially not when encouraging Fitz helped my case.

"See?" I said eagerly. "Fitz can do magic. And Hayley, you could just whistle some song. That's not even hard for you."

She rolled her eyes because she couldn't say I was wrong.

"What are you going to do, Cassie?" Ros asked.

"Well, um . . . maybe I could work backstage. There have to be people helping who aren't actually in the show."

Ros perked up. "I could help backstage. I wouldn't mind."

"See?" I challenged Quentin. "If your *girlfriend* is willing to help . . ."

"I can't," he said. "I have to work."

"Can't you get time off?"

"I need the money."

I would have loved to argue with that, but the reason he thought he needed the money was seated directly across from me. "Just come to the first meeting," I cajoled, "to make sure enough people show up. And after that, you never know. Maybe they won't even need us."

"That's good, since I don't have an act."

"Could you please be a little less negative?" I asked, exasperated. "It's not like I signed you up to dance in *The Nutcracker*. Nobody has to wear tights."

Quentin grinned. "I'm pretty sure magicians wear tights. Especially when they practice alone in their bedrooms."

"That's it!" Fitz said, losing his temper. "At least I'm not chicken."

"I know you're not calling me chicken."

"Bawk! Bawk, bawk, bawk!" Fitz flapped his elbows like wings.

"Oh, it's on!" Quentin said. "I'll be there now, and I'm taking you and your top hat down."

"It's a show, not a contest," I put in, but they continued glaring at each other. Quentin can be so childish sometimes.

"What will you do, Kevin?" Ros asked.

"In the show?" Kevin shook his head. "As little as possible. This wasn't my idea."

On the other hand, at least Quentin supports *his* girlfriend.

"Excuse me for trying to help cancer patients!" I snapped. "I thought maybe you'd all care about sick people, but obviously I was wrong."

Everyone looked sheepish. A guilty twinge reminded me that I wasn't being completely honest about my motives . . . but I wasn't lying, either. I *did* want to help a cancer patient. And his wife.

"We didn't say we *wouldn't* help," Hayley objected. "It just would have been nice to make that call ourselves."

"You guys do what you want. I have to finish my psych homework before fifth period." I stood up, abandoning two big cookies. "Eat those, if you want. I'm not hungry anymore."

"Call me tonight," Kevin said as I stalked off.

"See you in badminton," Hayley added.

I waved without turning around, determined to make my escape while I still held the high moral ground.

"You're in badminton?" I heard Ros ask. "With Sterling and Tiffany Hughes?"

"You know her?" Hayley replied.

"Tiffi?" Ros laughed. "Oh, yeah. I know her."

I ached to turn around and reclaim my seat, but somehow I forced myself to keep moving. I'd get the dirt on Tiffi later.

Alone in the hallway, I took my homework out of my locker and sat down on the floor. I'd already read the chapter, but I'd left the discussion questions blank. Now I flipped through the textbook, hoping the answers might jump out at me.

What caught my eye instead was a hulk in a letterman's jacket. Tate the Great had just rounded the corner at the far end of the hall. I heard the rumble of his voice as he spoke to someone still out of sight, and the giggle he got in reply.

Perfect, I thought, scooting lower and using my book for cover. *He's with Sterling.*

But the girl who cleared the corner behind him, slapping coyly at his broad back, had long, swingy black hair.

Angie Yee.

"Oh, Bryce!" Her voice carried to my ears. "You're so funny!"

A girl is generally flirting whenever she tells a guy he's funny, but in Tate's case there had to be some other explanation. Bryce may have the most built body at school, but he also has the sense of humor of a cauliflower. No, wait—a drunken, piggish cauliflower. If that weren't such an insult to cauliflowers. And pigs.

Why would a popular girl like Angie want him?

For that matter, why does Sterling? I wondered.

Not that I cared. Whatever kept her away from Kevin worked for me.

Tate turned and caught Angie's hands. Angie giggled again and moved a little closer. They were practically chest to chest, staring into each other's eyes. . . .

I pulled my book over my face, afraid to watch. What was going on? Was it possible Sterling and Bryce had broken up and I just didn't know it yet?

No. Not possible. That news would have traveled the school in sixty seconds flat.

So what was he doing with Angie?

Curiosity forced me to take one last peek.

Bryce and Angie were gone.

"This shuttle smells funny," Hayley said in the gym that afternoon. "They all do."

"Why are you . . . ?" I shook my head. "Never mind. I don't want to know."

"No, smell it," she insisted, shoving her hand under my nose.

"Hayley!"

I slapped the plastic shuttlecock away and started hunting for a racquet that didn't have missing strings.

"Why are you so touchy today?" Glancing around, she lowered her voice. "If you hadn't been on your high horse at lunch, you could have heard about Tiffi Hughes."

"Heard what?"

"Oh, not much," Hayley said with a grin. "Just that she got kicked out of the all-girl Catholic high school her parents sent her to."

"Saint Stephen's?" I gasped, naming the only Catholic school I could think of.

Hayley nodded. "Apparently, Tiffi was a little too interested in boys in eighth grade, if you catch my meaning."

I'd have had to be dead not to catch her meaning.

"Why did they kick her out?" I asked wide-eyed.

Hayley deflated a little. "Ros doesn't know. Or maybe

she just won't say. I guess she and Tiffi and Sterling all hung out in eighth grade."

"There's a shocker."

Hayley shook her head. "I get the feeling Tiffi was more of an outside friend, not really part of their group."

"Not cool enough?"

"I don't know. They look pretty tight right now."

Across the gym, Sterling and Tiffi were gossiping on the sidelines, Tiffi soaking up Sterling's every word. Her new sleeveless T-shirt was exactly like Sterling's, and identical blue ribbons graced their perfect ponytails.

"Okay! Listen up!" Coach Crawford bellowed, walking in. "We're going to start rallying some birds without the nets, to loosen up your arms and get a feel for the sweet spot. Do any of you girls already have doubles partners?"

The first four arms up were mine, Hayley's, Sterling's, and Tiffi's.

"Okay, good. You two against you two," he said. "Take that court over there."

"Tell me you don't believe in karma now," I grumbled as Hayley and I shuffled across the gym.

"I don't think you understand karma."

"I understand that the universe is out to get me."

We took places across from Tiffi and Sterling, off to one side of the net.

"Should I serve?" Sterling asked. Before we could answer, she aimed a lob at Hayley.

The first thing I noticed was, shuttles (or birds, as our cute coach calls them) move a lot slower than tennis balls. They basically just float along, giving you all day to line up for your shot. Hayley batted our shuttle back to Tiffi. Tiffi hit it to me. I aimed for Sterling's midsection and smacked the bird hard, just to see if it went any faster.

It did. Sterling had to leap to one side, practically dislocating her elbow to get behind it, but she returned the shuttle to Hayley. One thing about socs: racquet sports are in their blood. Tennis whites and country clubs—it's absolutely genetic.

"This is supposed to be a *rally*," Tiffi complained as Hayley returned the bird to her. "You're not supposed to hit it hard."

"Please!" Sterling scoffed. "They couldn't hit it hard if they wanted to."

Tiffi sent the shuttle my way, too high to be returned underhanded. It registered on me that she'd probably intended to hit it over my head as I called up my tennis overhand and smashed that thing for all I was worth. My toes lifted off the floor. I nearly smacked myself in the shin with my followthrough. And that baby streaked toward Sterling's head like a fluffy plastic bullet. If she hadn't covered her face with her racquet, she'd have been eating plastic feathers. Instead, the bird bounced off her strings and landed harmlessly on the floor.

"Ha!" I said triumphantly. "I guess I can hit hard after all."

Sterling picked up the shuttle. "That *must* have been hard," she said, "to turn your face so red. If you could move some of that color into your legs, you might be on to something."

Tiffi laughed mockingly. "You're like a cherry snow cone—red on top and white on the bottom."

Which was a flagrant rip-off of Sterling's Creamsicle jab, but Tiffi didn't seem to notice. Or, judging by the way she looked for Sterling's approval, maybe she did.

"You don't know how lucky you are," I muttered, glancing enviously at Hayley's brown legs.

She rolled her eyes. "Just hit it harder next time."

I readied my racquet as Sterling served the shuttle again. The thing sped toward me with just enough spin to make it hard to track. Taking a wild swing, I connected with the outside edge of my racquet. The bird stayed on my strings, hooking toward Tiffi on release. I didn't get nearly the power I'd had on my previous shot to Sterling, but I did hit Tiffi in the knee.

"Ow," she complained, backing up.

When my turn to serve finally came, I drilled my first one right at Sterling. She returned it way too low. The shuttle bounced off the ground, rolling to Hayley's feet just as Coach Crawford walked over.

"You girls are ready to play at the net," he said. "Go ahead and start a game."

Tiffi and Sterling gave him smarmy smiles. "Thanks, Coach," they said in unison.

But as soon as he'd moved on, the smiles died on their faces. We took our positions on opposite sides of the court like we were about to play in the Olympics. Hayley started to hand me the shuttle.

"No, we'll serve," Sterling announced.

"I don't think so," I said. "I was serving."

"Right. You *were*," Tiffi retorted. "Give me the shuttle."

We glared at each other through the net. I wouldn't have thought it possible, but she was almost more annoying than Sterling. At least Sterling was the real deal—an actual Queen Bee. Tiffi was just a wanna-bee suck-up.

"Go ahead, Hayley," I said at last. "Flip Tiffi the bird."

Hayley snorted with laughter. Even Sterling cracked a smile. But Tiffi never lost her haughty expression as she picked up the shuttle and stepped behind the line.

"Service! Love all," she called, giving the bird a good smack.

It came directly at me. I aimed my hardest swing at Sterling. Sterling rallied easily. Hayley smashed. Tiffi picked up Hayley's shot with a long, arcing lob that sent me running for the back line. I hit with my back to the net, barely making the shot. Sterling took advantage, racing forward for the kill. Hayley blocked her. Tiffi popped it up again.

"All right!" Coach called approvingly. "Now we have a game!"

One to Love

By Wednesday all the new-semester novelty had worn off and classes had settled into their usual grind.

"Let's do something after school today," I begged, pulling Kevin away from the others in the lunch line. "Do you want to come over?"

"To your house?"

"Trevor's a pain. But your mom hovers the whole time."

"Plus she made me promise to mow the lawn today. I pretty much have to go straight home if I'm going to make her happy."

What about making me happy? I thought. We'd barely had a moment alone since our vacation ended.

Or hadn't he noticed?

I glanced enviously at Quentin and Ros, who were baby-talking like fools.

"How about the basketball game Friday night?" Kevin asked. "Want to go?"

"We'd have to ride with someone."

Kevin doesn't have his license yet, and the way my mom is holding on to her grudge about that whole driving-Dad's-car-without-supervision thing, I'll be eighteen before I see mine. It's been over two months since I got busted for my "joyride" with Trevor and I'm still not even allowed to practice for my license.

"We'll have to catch a ride," he acknowledged. "But once we're at school, we don't have to stay in the gym." He smiled and my heart melted. "We didn't last time."

"True," I said, wrapping my arms around him. At the Snow Ball we'd left the gym to dance alone outside. "Okay, let's go."

"I can't wait," he said, bending to kiss me.

Honestly, neither could I. Kevin and I alone together, outside under those same stars . . .

It would be the perfect time and place for him to say he loved me.

Skater Boy?

Trevor practically pounced on me when I walked in the door, a black skirt in his hands.

"Can you try this on for Mom?" he begged. "I want to make sure the hem is pinned straight before I sew it."

My little brother sews like a genius, but this isn't something he's proud of—at least, not publicly. In fact, he's sworn me to silence on the subject, so don't tell him I brought it up.

It all started last semester in home economics, a class Trev and his friends only took to meet girls. Or so Trevor claimed. That story holds less water all the time, especially since he can barely stop fiddling with the sewing machine Mom gave him for Christmas.

"I don't know why you dropped home ec," I said, grabbing the skirt and heading for my room. "It was obviously your favorite class."

"One semester was okay, but who needs the rep for two? Bill and I are moving on. We're buying skateboards to ride at that bowl in the park."

That stopped me dead. "Does Mom know?"

"Why should she care? I'm using my Christmas money from Grandma."

"Yeah, but who's going to pay for the hospital bills?"

"Funny, Cassie."

"It will be, unless you've suddenly become coordinated. Hey, maybe you can sew yourself a sling!"

Trevor snatched back Mom's skirt, stormed into his room, and slammed the door.

"Oh, Trev, don't be such a baby," I yelled through the wood. "You have to admit that was funny."

The lock on his doorknob clicked.

For someone too macho to stick with home ec, my brother can be a real diva.

Three Longish Letters

Friday morning Conway announced a new unit on epistolary novels. I spent most of the period gazing at Kevin, fantasizing about our date later that night, but I paid enough attention to catch the gist.

"In epistolary novels, the entire story is told in the form of letters written by one or more characters," Mrs. Conway informed us. "There is no other narration, no point where the author breaks away and fills us in. Everything the reader needs to know is contained within the letters."

Apparently this style was big in the 1700s, which sounds about right, since they didn't have phones. Or instant messaging. Or electricity.

"For the next couple of weeks, we'll be reading selections from Richardson's *Pamela*, one of the earliest and most famous examples of the form, as well as writing epistles of our own."

Which, translated into English, meant we'd be reading a book written in 1740 about a fifteen-year-old serving girl whose boss keeps hitting on her. They obviously didn't know about sexual harassment back then. As far as our own epistles went, our assignment was to write three separate letters (totaling six to eight pages) that collectively told a story.

"I already like haiku better," I whispered to Kevin.

"I'm going to write as my future self and send a letter back through time warning me not to take this class," he said.

I choked down my laughter too late and ended up snorting so loudly that half the class turned around. Mrs. Conway gave me a glare that curled my toes. Luckily, the bell rang.

"Just a reminder," she told us. "There's still time to sign up for the talent show. Our first meeting is Monday after school." She placed the sign-up clipboard on the corner of her desk, where we could see it as we filed past.

Out in the hallway, I grabbed Kevin's arm. "There's only one name on that sheet I didn't write myself!"

"And you find that surprising?"

"Kevin!"

"There have to be other sheets around school. Conway isn't signing up everyone single-handed."

"You're right," I said, calming down. "Of course there are other sheets."

"So I'll see you at lunch?" he asked.

"And then at the game tonight."

"We're riding with Quentin, all right? Everyone's going in his van."

Not ideal, but better than being driven by our parents. "Is Ros coming?" I asked.

He gave me an odd look. "Why wouldn't she be?"

"She does have other friends. At least, she used to, before she started dogging us."

"Quentin's her boyfriend now."

"I know, but don't you think it's wrong, the way she's always with him instead of with Sterling? I can't take a breath anymore without gagging on her perfume."

Kevin gave me an incredulous look.

"Not that I care. Whatever."

"I have to go," he said. "I'm going to be late for third period."

"Okay. See you at lunch."

I was halfway to geometry before I realized we'd forgotten to kiss good-bye. It scared me to think we were already taking each other for granted.

We'll make up that kiss tonight, I reassured myself. *When I get Kevin alone, he'll know I don't take him for granted.*

I decided to give him an extra kiss at lunchtime anyway. Just to be sure.

My shuttle streaks past.
Swinging, she clobbers the blonde.
It makes me laugh. Hard.

Game Boys

"Where do you want to sit?" Hayley asked as the six of us crowded into the gym.

Students milled about shouting, their echoes combining with the thud of bouncing balls and the squeaks from the basketball players' shoes to create an indescribable din.

"I don't see many empty spots," Fitz said, scanning the packed bleachers. "We should have gotten here earlier."

"I'm so sorry we were late!" Ros's umpteenth apology grated on my nerves. "Quentin was on time, but I never know what to wear to these things."

"Clothes. Thank God she figured it out," I muttered under my breath.

Quentin and Ros were walking ahead of us. There was no chance of Ros overhearing, but Kevin gave me an annoyed look.

"Well, it's true," I insisted.

If I'd just wanted to be rude, I could have pointed out that the outfit she'd finally chosen was totally over the top. While the rest of us had dressed in jeans and sweatshirts, Ros was wearing strappy heels, white pants, and a candy-pink Izod polo. A lime green sweater rested on her back, its sleeves knotted over her shoulders like a preppy membership flag.

"I see a place we'll all fit," Quentin said, weaving his way up the bleachers.

Grabbing Kevin's hand, I pulled him back. "Let's sneak out of here now, just us."

"Now?" He didn't seem too eager.

"Why not? Those guys will save our seats."

"Don't you want to see the game?"

"Of course not. Not unless . . . do you?"

He shrugged. "We're here. And it's cold outside."

"Not that cold. Come on," I coaxed, tugging on his hands. "Just for a little while."

"Okay," he relented.

But out on the patio behind the gym, I quickly discovered how right he'd been. The stars were obscured by ominous clouds, and a piercing wind swirled empty snack bags around our ankles.

"I should have worn my down jacket," I admitted, huddling up inside my hoodie.

"I'd let you have my sweatshirt, but then I'd have to go back in and leave you out here by yourself."

We sat side by side on a concrete planter, our backs turned toward the wind and our hands jammed into our pockets.

"So," Kevin said. "Here we are."

"Here we are," I agreed.

Not exactly the romantic moment I'd hoped for. Then again, it's hard to be romantic when your teeth are chattering.

"Just over a month since we were here last," he said. "Happy anniversary."

A little warmth rose up inside me. "I can't believe it's been a whole month," I said, snuggling closer.

"What do you mean? Why not?"

"Because it went by so fast."

He shrugged.

"You don't think so?" I asked, confused.

"A month isn't long. Especially not when half of it's vacation. This semester will be the real test."

Test of what? I wondered.

But then he kissed me and I pretty much forgot about everything but kissing him back and how good it felt to be in his arms again.

"You're the only person I'd still be out here with," he said after a few minutes. "You know that, right? Anyone else, and I'd have gone back inside when I stopped feeling my feet."

"My rear end's a block of ice," I admitted. "Whose idea was it to sit on this cold concrete?"

"That would be yours."

"Well . . . maybe we should go back in. Those guys are probably wondering where we went, and at least we can thaw out on the bleachers."

Kevin jumped off the planter wall, staggering to catch his balance. "Oh, good. My feet didn't snap off. I guess I don't have frostbite after all."

"Your lips don't, anyway," I said, hopping down behind him.

"Some of my other parts are pretty warm too."

I couldn't help blushing as he took my hand and led me back toward the gym. Despite all our making out, that's as far as we've ever gone, and the truth is, I'm not in a hurry. For one thing, virginity isn't in the box of stuff you get back with your CDs when you break up. For another, it seemed like a lot of other things ought to happen before we even considered going further. For instance—and just for starters—Kevin ought to tell me he loved me. Out loud. With the two key letters right.

"Wait," I said, stopping him outside the gym door. "I just remembered something."

"What?"

I chewed my lip, not sure how to say "I just remembered you were supposed to tell me 'I love you' out there on the patio."

"Spit it out, Cassie," he begged. "I'm freezing."

Obviously, this wasn't the right time.

"Never mind. I, um . . . I forgot again."

We hurried into the gym, the air inside like the blast of a furnace on our cold faces. We were walking to the bleachers when a disgusting sight caught my eye. Next to the drinking fountain, in full view of the crowd, Sterling was pinned to the wall, Tate looming above her as they made out, their hands all over each other.

"Looks like they're still together," I said.

"What? Who?"

"The tonsil twins over there."

Kevin followed my nod, then shook his head. "I swear you track their every move."

"I do not! It's just . . . they're everywhere! Besides, she *wants* people to notice."

He had already begun climbing the bleachers. I followed at his heels, wanting desperately to defend myself, knowing I should drop it. He couldn't have heard me unless I'd shouted anyway. The game was in full swing by then, and an enthusiastic crowd was rocking the bleachers.

"Where were you?" Hayley asked as I wedged in next to her.

"Outside."

"What for?"

I raised an eyebrow at her.

"Oh, please."

Right. Like she didn't wish she'd thought of that herself.

Fitz was on her other side, totally mesmerized by the game. There were two empty places next to him.

"Where are Quentin and Ros?" I asked.

"Popcorn. I think." Hayley shrugged. "Maybe they went outside too."

"They didn't," I said firmly. "I would have seen them."

She gave me a strange look. "Because you canvassed the entire school?"

"No. It's just . . . they're not out there, all right?"

"I'm going to get a soda," Kevin interjected. "Does anyone want anything?"

Hayley and I shook our heads. Fitz was so busy cheering he didn't even notice Kevin leaving.

"Look, there's Quentin," I told Hayley, pointing down the bleachers. "Talking to Ros's soc-y friends in the Spirit Section."

All kinds of people yell in the Spirit Section, which is where the cheerleaders focus the majority of their attention, but the couple Quentin and Ros were talking to wore sweaters over their shoulders in a very familiar way.

"That'll be next," I predicted grimly. "Just wait. She'll have Quentin abusing his sweaters too."

"What have you got against Ros? I mean, besides the fact that it kills you to see her with Quentin after you were in love with him for so long."

"What? No! What are you talking about?"

"I'm just saying . . . she's always nice to you, and you're always on her case. And if it's not because you're jealous—"

"I'm *not* jealous!" I cut in, desperate to shut her up before anyone overheard us. "Quentin's ancient history. I have Kevin now."

"You have Kevin," Hayley agreed. "You never actually had Quentin."

"But I could have. That was my decision."

"Exactly. So what have you got against Ros?"

Next to my mother, Hayley is the best arguer I know. Even when they're wrong, they both twist things around until they sound right. And when they might be on to something . . .

"I'm not jealous, okay?"

"Then stop acting like you are. When Ros gets back here, try being nice for a change."

"I am nice."

"You know what I mean."

I did, too. There are some truly irritating drawbacks to having a smart best friend.

"Did the cheerleaders get different shoes?" I asked.

By the time Kevin got back, Hayley and I had dealt with the shoes, moved through four more topics, and were pretending the whole Ros discussion had never happened. Fitz was screaming about fouls, still oblivious to our every word.

"Hey." Kevin slid back onto the bench beside me. "That line was ridiculous. I bought you some Red Vines," he added, dropping them into my lap. "You like those, right?"

"I love them!" I said, impulsively kissing the side of his face.

"Good, because I don't want to stand in that line again." He drank from an enormous soda, then offered the straw to me. "Thirsty?"

I wasn't, but I took a sip anyway. "I'm glad you're back," I said, putting an arm around him and snuggling in.

He kissed the top of my head.

I snuck a glance at Hayley, who was still being ignored by Fitz, and allowed myself a smug smile.

Hayley might be smart, but she doesn't know everything.

Except . . .

All right, fine. If you have to know, I *was* kind of jealous. But I didn't want to be. I told myself it was just a phase, that if I ignored it long enough it would go away.

It *had* to be a phase, because the first two weeks Kevin and I were together, I never thought of Quentin once. At Christmas, when we exchanged cards and hugs, I might have felt a twinge of something less than completely platonic. But was it any surprise I missed the guy when we used to be so close?

Honestly, I never even *thought* about being jealous until school started back up and I noticed how conjoined he and Ros had become. I mean, Kevin and I are together (I think) and I guarantee you that he doesn't live for me the way Quentin lives for Ros.

You know what? Maybe that was the problem.

All I wanted was a commitment. I wanted *what* Ros had, not who she had.

If Kevin had just stepped up . . .

Not that that's any excuse.

Home Yech

I slept in late the next morning and woke up feeling clobbered. Not only had I lain awake half the night, I'd spent my only hours of sleep debating Hayley in my dreams. Groaning, I kicked my way out of the covers and headed to the kitchen.

Unfortunately, Trevor had beaten me there. And the chaos he had going on every counter made getting to the cereal impossible.

"What's this mess?" I complained. "Trevor!"

"Fruit salad, bacon, and French toast casserole," he said proudly. "Five more minutes and we're ready to eat."

"French toast casserole? Home ec is over, Trev. Let it go."

But the eggshells littering the counter proved my advice had come too late. Besides, his bacon smelled good. I took a seat on a barstool and decided to have Cocoa Critters for lunch.

"Hey, Dad!" Trevor called, rousing my father from behind his newspaper in the den. "Want to help me out here? You can make the orange juice."

I had no idea why Trevor was attempting to coax my dad into the kitchen; I was just happy to stay out of it. I watched from the safety of my barstool as Dad entered Trev's disaster zone and looked around in a daze.

"Where's the can?"

Trevor turned with the bacon tongs in one hand, nearly searing my dad with hot grease. "What can?"

"The orange juice can."

Trev cackled like Emeril's evil twin. "Would I go to all this trouble and then use canned orange juice? You've got to kick it up a notch, Dad." He pointed to a bag of oranges lying on the counter. "The juicer might be under the sink."

I watched, amazed, as Trevor returned to his bacon and Dad rummaged for an appliance he probably hadn't even realized we owned. His normal forays into the kitchen involved grabbing a cup of coffee or putting his dishes in the sink, but now he was opening cupboards that seldom saw daylight.

"Will you look at this!" he exclaimed, retrieving an ancient basket from the cabinet over the refrigerator. Reaching inside, he pulled out a cobwebby plaid cloth. "I didn't know we still had this!"

"What is it?" I asked, shuddering involuntarily.

"My picnic basket," he answered with a faraway look in his eyes. "When your mother and I were poor college students, I'd make us a couple of my trademark sandwiches. Then we'd take this basket and blanket up the hill behind campus and hang out there all day, just watching the world go by."

Honestly, I was kind of stunned by that information. First off, anything that happened before I was born always strikes me as vaguely fictional. But by far the bigger shocker was the idea of my mother spending a whole day lying around doing nothing. That went against everything I'd learned about her through fifteen years of extremely up-close-and-personal observation.

Trevor was amazed too, but for a completely different reason. "You had a trademark sandwich? Cool! What was it?"

Setting his moldy basket on the counter, Dad held his hands a foot apart. "The Howard Hoagie," he said reverently. "I'd get these fresh rolls in Little Italy and load them with cold cuts until they groaned. Three kinds of cheese, mustard, mayonnaise, olives, peperoncini, Italian salad dressing . . . Man, those were the days."

"How come I've never had one?" Trev asked.

"Huh? Oh." My dad snapped out of his trance. "I stopped making those years ago."

"Why?"

He shrugged. "We graduated. Then your mother said they were fattening."

Mom chose that moment to join us, her reading glasses still perched on her nose. "What's fattening?"

"A Howard Hoagie," Trevor said.

"I remember those!" Her voice took on a hint of Dad's nostalgia. "They *were* fattening. I put on ten pounds senior year."

"And you couldn't have been more beautiful," Dad told her.

Mom made a face. "I already married you, Hal—you're off the hook. Tell me what you're doing in the kitchen."

"Looking for the juicer. I'm making orange juice."

"From scratch?" Irritation replaced nostalgia. "It's the twenty-first century. We have ways of avoiding that mess."

"It tastes better fresh," Trevor argued. "Besides, how else are we going to use that many oranges?"

He had her there—and Mom always appreciates a good argument. "All right. But let me do it," she said, shooing Dad out of the kitchen. "Everything gets sticky if you don't know what you're doing."

"It's juice, not rocket science," he grumbled. "I could probably figure it out."

But he retreated anyway. In the interest of drama-free living, our dad always does what Mom says.

At least, he did back then.

So Mom made the juice and we all sat down to eat.

"It's just like regular French toast," Trevor bragged about his casserole, "except that after you dip the bread, you layer it in a dish, pour the extra eggs over, and bake the whole thing."

"It's not bad," I allowed. Actually, it was delicious, but no one likes a show-off. "I thought you were done with home ec, though. What happened to skateboarding?"

"For your information, Mom's taking me and Bill to Skateboard Hut this afternoon."

"Leave your brother alone," Mom added with one of her significant looks.

Have I mentioned how my mom thinks seeing a guy cook is some sort of triumph for the feminist movement? It turns out there's an age limit on that deal, but none of us knew it then.

Oh, I'm sorry. Am I being obtuse?

You're the one who wanted to do this in order.

Waiting to Inhale

"This can't be a good idea," I said the next morning. I was pedaling my bike down a street near our house while Trevor balanced on his new skateboard, catching a tow by gripping the back of my seat. "You can barely stand up."

"Just go slow," he ordered.

"If I go any slower, the bike will tip over. Let go and push with your foot."

"Pushing makes me fall off."

"And yet we're on our way to the skate park. You do realize they won't let me tow you around those ramps with my bike?"

"Pedal," he said bossily.

All that safety gear had obviously made him feel invincible. I started pedaling faster, to remind him who was in charge.

"Okay, okay, slow down," he whined.

I let him sweat another half block before he really started wobbling and it suddenly occurred to me that if he didn't let go of my seat we were both going to crash. I hit my brakes too hard, nearly causing that accident for him. Somehow we both got our feet on the pavement instead of falling there face-first.

"You're dangerous," he griped.

"I warned you." I was about to tell him to skate the rest of the way to the park himself when he suddenly went rigid.

"Don't move, Cass," he hissed. "I'm not kidding."

"Why?" I whipped my head around, trying to spot whatever was making his eyes bug out.

"You're moving!"

"Trevor. What's—?"

One of his hands grabbed my forearm, squeezing with surprising strength. "It's Julie. Just act natural!"

"You might want to try that yourself," I said, struggling to break free. "Where is she?"

His eyes rolled toward the corner up ahead, where a dark-haired girl in sweats had just jogged into sight at the intersecting street. Miniature headphones filled her ears, their cords trailing down to the iPod clipped to her waistband.

"Go talk to her, Trevor," I urged.

"I can't. She's running."

"Sort of."

Julie's knees lifted extra high as she crossed the street, but her steps didn't cover much ground. She was keeping time to her music, more interested in hitting the beat than in speed.

"Go on," I said. "You can catch her."

"What would I say?"

His voice sounded strangled. I gave him a second look.

"Breathe, Trev! Geez! You're going to pass out."

He opened his mouth and inhaled raggedly as Julie disappeared. "There she goes," he said with a sigh. "Do you think she likes me?"

"I don't think she even noticed you."

Trevor looked devastated.

"She seemed pretty into her music," I said, taking pity on him.

"She did, didn't she?" he asked hopefully.

"You could still catch her. Take my bike, if you want. I'll wait here."

For a second I thought he might actually try it. Then he shook his head. "I still don't know what I'd say. And what if she doesn't know who I am? What would I do then?"

"Gee, I don't know. Introduce yourself?"

"Funny, Cassie. It's not that easy. Besides," he said, taking an attitude, "you're supposed to introduce us. That was the deal, remember?"

That *was* the deal. Unfortunately.

And then I had a great idea.

"Hey, do you want me to go after her?" I asked, seeing a

brilliant way out of that whole mutual-party nonsense. "I could introduce you two right now."

"You'd better not! I want to meet her and hang out. Get something started. What good will it do me to see her for two minutes on the street?"

What good will it do you to see her at a party? I wondered. The odds of an eighth-grade boy starting something with a high school girl . . . Even Einstein couldn't do that math.

"Do you think she likes me at all?" Trevor moaned. "I mean, do you think I have any chance?"

I was about to tell him the truth—that he had no chance whatsoever—when I looked into his pleading eyes and knew I could never say that. My brother was in agony, unraveling as I watched.

The poor guy couldn't breathe.

And I knew exactly how he felt.

Bag Lady

"Where are you going?" my mother asked as I dragged my bike back out of the garage late Sunday afternoon.

"I *told* you," I said impatiently. "I'm out of notebook paper and Trevor drank all the milk."

"So you're going to the grocery store?"

"They don't sell milk at Staples."

Mom's eyebrows did that dangerous, don't-mess-with-me climb.

"I'm in a hurry!" I whined. "It's going to be dark soon, and I want to finish riding while I can still see the pavement."

"And I need a few things for dinner. It won't kill you to save me the trip."

All the way to the store, I replayed that exchange in my head. If she needed groceries anyway, why couldn't she have just driven to the store and bought the paper for me? My legs pumped extra-hard as I took out my frustration on my pedals. It's not only that I want to start driving—and believe me, I'm desperate to drive—but also that the older I get, the more I hate riding my bike anywhere. There's the pounding heart, the sweat-soaked bra, the way my face turns crimson . . . and the helmet, of course. That's a fashion statement all by itself. And to add insult to injury, my mother had given me such a long list I had to strap my grade-school basket back onto my handlebars. I locked up to a post on the fringes of MegaFood-Mart's giant parking lot, hoping no one would notice my transportation.

Luckily, the store was pretty empty. I rushed through the aisles with one of those plastic store baskets dangling from my arm as I filled my mother's list: milk, bread, two onions, fresh broccoli, sour cream, hamburger, and noodles. That took the mystery out of dinner—Stroganoff Surprise. Grabbing my notebook paper last, I checked out through the express lane and headed for the exit.

"Do you need help out with that, Miss?" a familiar voice asked behind me.

I turned to find Quentin grinning, his blue MegaFoodMart

apron tied sloppily around his waist. "Love the helmet. Very sexy."

My hands went straight to my head despite my dangling shopping bags. The helmet I'd meant to leave with my bike was still strapped to my noggin.

"How embarrassing," I groaned. "I'll probably end up on one of those surveillance-camera specials: *When Idiots Shop*—I can see it now."

"I'll walk you out," he offered, still grinning. "Time to corral some carts anyway. I'm very important here, you know. They count on me for *all* the hard stuff."

One of my favorite things about Quentin is how he never makes me feel stupid, even when I am. The silly way he puffed out his chest made me completely forget my helmet lapse.

"I didn't think you worked Sundays," I told him as we crossed the parking lot, Quentin snagging empty carts on the way. The outdoor security lights were just coming on, but the storefront was already lit up like Las Vegas. "How many shifts are you working now?"

"As many as I can get. It's not cheap having a girlfriend, you know."

I was about to reply that it wasn't bankrupting Kevin when I noticed Quentin's eyes. They were crinkled up at the corners, the way they get when he's happy, and for reasons I didn't care to examine, that made me all hot and awkward.

Luckily we reached my bike just then. I used the excuse to drop to my knees and took my time with the lock. When

I finally stood back up, Quentin had removed my grocⁱ
from their bags and neatly repacked them in my basket.

"Thanks," I said uncomfortably. "Is the service always
this good at MegaFoodMart?"

Quentin laughed and pointed to my basket. "Hey, if
you're going to spend that kind of coin, it's the least we can
do. See you tomorrow, right?"

"See you."

He waved and headed back toward the front of the
store, gathering more carts into a clattering train as he
went. His long apron flapped open in back, a slice of dark
T-shirt and the worn seat of his jeans reassuring me that he
was still the old Quentin underneath. I felt my heart pull after him exactly the way it used to.

He didn't have to walk me out and pack my bike basket.

Did that mean he still felt something too?

Stop it! I thought, remembering Kevin. *Quentin is your
friend. You have to stop thinking about him this way. Do you
want to break up with Kevin?*

No. That definitely wasn't what I wanted.

I just wanted . . .

I didn't know what I wanted.

> Boy. Friend. It's easy.
> At least, it ought to be. Could
> Someone tell my heart?

Threat Level: Orange

That night I was washing my gym clothes for the up-coming week of school when I had a not-so-brilliant idea. Not that I realized my sad lack of genius at the time. On the contrary, when I snagged that old bottle of SpeedTan out of the clutter beneath Mom's bathroom sink, I thought I'd struck gold.

As I believe I've already mentioned, true redheads never tan. They fry. Then they peel. Then they fry. Then they peel. Last summer I kept that up until I had some pretty impressive tan lines, but even then my "dark" parts weren't much browner than cream. Unfortunately, I'd faded since then. No wonder I was the (blinding white) butt of Sterling's jokes.

But that state of affairs was about to be over. At least, that was what I told myself as I shook that old bottle of SpeedTan and slathered a coat on my legs. So what if my tan was fake, as long as my legs looked better? And honestly, when I got done they looked pretty good.

That was when I decided a second coat would look even better.

Except that somehow the second coat grabbed the first one and pulled the color into streaks. And the more I rubbed, the worse things got. I had to use a bunch more goop just to even things out.

Did you know you have pores on your knees?

Mine started filling up like giant tan blackheads. I got so busy trying to scrape them out that I forgot about the lotion on my ankles I hadn't rubbed in yet. When I finally remembered, the places it had been sitting looked like splotchy tan birthmarks. Not to mention the blobs on top of my feet, where I'd touched myself by accident. So then I had to coat my feet. And my toes.

Did you know you have pores on your toes?

When I finally got all that color evened out, I was way past any shade that could be mistaken for natural. Still, it was a tan, and I was pleased with it overall.

Until a few hours later, when I went to take a shower and discovered things had changed.

"Is that *orange?*" I gasped, flipping on the overhead light to get a better look.

The thing they don't tell you about SpeedTan—unless you read the stupid bottle—is that the color you put on is not the one you ultimately get. No, the actual, final color takes hours to "develop."

And mine had developed like a bad Polaroid.

"Water!" I cried, panicking. "*Hot* water. And a loofah!"

Half an hour later, the mirror was steamed opaque, my loofah was in tatters, and my legs were pink *and* orange. If anything, scrubbing the top layer of bronzer off had only made things worse.

"I had to mess with nature," I moaned. You'd think I'd remember the tragic results of a summer of Sun-In abuse, but no. I never learn.

"Cassie!" Mom called, pounding on the bathroom door. "What's going on in there? Are you okay?"

"I'm fine," I said, not wanting her or anyone else to see what a moron I was.

Which made me think of PE the next day. Which made me groan out loud.

"Cassie?"

"It's nothing!"

If I asked very, very nicely—and got very, very lucky—maybe Coach Crawford would let me wear sweats.

Sophomore Honors English
Mrs. Conway
Sunday, January 11

Dear Grandma,

Thank you so much for the Christmas money! I haven't decided what to spend it on yet, but don't worry—I'll save it for something good. Trevor spent his on a skateboard. That might seem like a waste, but when you consider that constantly landing on his butt is both exercise for him and entertainment for the entire neighborhood, it looks like a much better buy.

I wish you could have come to our house this Christmas. It's been so long since we've seen you! But Mom says it's easier for you to spend Christmas with Aunt Catie than to fly out to California. Maybe next Christmas we can visit you in Ohio. Except that Mom says it snows and sleets and is completely miserable there in December. So I'm guessing we probably won't.

How are Aunt Catie and Uncle Roy? It seems like such a long time since you all came out with Cousin Matt for that trip to Disneyland. He must be getting big now. Does he remember me? I wish Aunt Catie had put his school picture in her Christmas card this year.

My school picture is hideous! Not that they're ever great, but ever since the Sun-In/hair-chopping incident, they've been even worse than usual. I know Mom sent you one, but if you love me, you won't show it around. That picture of me at the Snow Ball is a million times better. I would have sent you one of me with my new boyfriend, but Mom said you'd rather have one of just me. Honestly, you're missing out.

Things at home are as boring as ever. We took down the Christmas tree this weekend, so now everything's back to normal. Mom would have packed up the decorations a week ago, but Dad said she was rushing him. He said when he was a boy the tree went up on Thanksgiving and hung around until Easter. I wish I'd met Grandma and Grandpa Howard when I was old enough to know them.

Anyway, happy new year! I hope you had fun at Aunt Catie's and that everyone liked their presents.

Love,
Cassie

Am I a Genius or What?

Since Grandma's always asking me to write and I pretty much never do, Mrs. Conway's epistle-writing assignment was the perfect way to kill two birds. All I had to do was finish all three letters, make copies for my grandma, and cut off the part that mentioned Conway's class. Grandma would never even know. Because it's not like I don't *want* to write her—it's just that I never know what to say.

It might help if we saw each other more often. Every Christmas it's the same discussion: are we flying to Grandma's or is she coming here? And just about every year we end up staying home and Grandma goes to Aunt Catie's. She sends me and Trevor checks, though, and she always writes the same thing in her cards: *No matter how you grow, this gift always fits!*

I have a huge soft spot for my grandma. But unfortunately, Grandma and my mother don't get along too well.

I guess they used to, when Mom was a girl. As far as I can tell, things didn't start getting tense until Mom decided to go to law school. Grandma didn't understand why Mom wanted to be a lawyer when she could stay home and raise a family. Mom said homemaking was a waste of her talents. And Grandma took that personally—which makes more sense if you understand that my grandma's an *awesome* homemaker. Honestly. I'd fly to her house in a sleety snowstorm anytime if we were staying for dinner.

Anyway, Mom's younger sister, Catie, picked up the Martha Stewart torch, and that must make Grandma happy because it drives Mom completely nuts.

"I just settled a case for two million dollars, but Catie made new curtains," I once heard her snipe to my dad. "How will I ever compete?"

Not that Mom doesn't like Aunt Catie. But you get the idea.

We have the same name, by the way. Me and Aunt Catie, I mean. If we both went by Catherine, things could get kind of confusing, but she's always been Catie and I've always been Cassie. Which is weird, when you think about it. Why do people bother with family names if they don't intend to use them?

Anyway, I walked into English Monday morning fully prepared for another boring discussion about epistles and filled with the following fresh resolutions:

1. I would be a perfect girlfriend and think only of Kevin. I would make my affection for him so obvious he would *have* to say he loved me.
2. I would ignore Quentin completely.
3. I would treat Ros with such total angelicness that no one would suspect I didn't always like her.
4. I would do my best to like her.

Kevin and I whispered back and forth while Conway droned on about *Pamela*.

"I missed you this weekend," I said. "We should have done something together."

"We went to the game Friday night."

"Yeah, but . . ."

Did he think that was enough?

"Let's do something this Saturday," he suggested.

That's more like it, I thought, nodding happily. "Do you have something in mind?"

"Not yet," he whispered, "but—"

"Excuse me, Mr. Matthews," Conway interrupted in a tone that made the whole class cringe. "I hate to cut into your social life with all this education."

"Um." He gave me a desperate look. "That's okay."

She scowled before resuming her lecture. Ten minutes went by before Kevin dared to pass me a note:

You were some kind of genius to sign us up for that talent show. Now we have to spend all afternoon with her too!

Sweating the Small Stuff

"You'll never get away with it," Hayley told me that afternoon in the girls' locker room.

Our school, in its not-so-infinite wisdom, has decided that allowing sweats in PE violates its antigang dress code banning excessively baggy clothing. Like we're all going to wait for PE to break out our deadly weapons.

On the other hand, PE is as good a place as any.

Especially lately.

"It's an emergency," I said grimly, struggling to pull my sweatpants on over my sneakers. "Can you imagine how much crap I'll take if Sterling thinks I care what she says about my legs?"

"Except that apparently you do." Hayley gazed at my orange skin in amazement. "How many coats did you say that was?"

"I had to make it even!"

A massive tug freed my sweats and I pulled them up over my shorts. At least no one but Hayley had seen me change clothes. Now all I had to do was convince Coach Crawford to bend one stupid rule.

Hayley shook her head. "If I were you, I'd be bracing for Sterling's worst."

"Way to think positive," I told her.

I led the walk to the gym with what I hoped was a confident air. Coach Crawford seemed like a reasonable guy. Reasonably young, anyway. A carefully worded explanation, just the right amount of wheedling . . .

"Howard!" Coach's voice rang out before I was five feet onto the floor. I froze as he bore down on me and Hayley slipped away. "Where are your gym shorts?"

"Underneath." I peeled my waistband back far enough to let him glimpse blue. "I'm totally wearing them, it's just—"

"Good. Ditch the sweats." He started walking away.

"Coach, you don't understand!" I argued to his back. "I *have* to wear sweatpants today. I . . . I may have to wear them all week."

He turned to stare in confusion. Then this horrifyingly

understanding expression broke across his face. "Oh. All right, Howard. Got it."

Oh. Dear. God. My cheeks flamed crimson. Not only *didn't* he get it, the truth would have been a lot less embarrassing.

"No," I said, mortified. "It's just—"

"Wear the sweatpants, Howard. It's fine."

He lifted the whistle around his neck and walked off blowing it loudly, even more anxious to end the conversation than I was.

"I can't believe he let you!" Hayley exclaimed, sidling up and handing me a racquet. "What did you tell him?"

"Not nearly enough."

"Now everyone's going to want to wear sweats."

"Yeah, well. I know how they can," I muttered, still blushing.

The whistle blew again and Coach began rattling off that day's court assignments. Hayley and I got paired against China Watson and Kristy Grant. I heaved a sigh of relief at not playing Sterling again, but soon I was so involved in the game that I forgot everything else. China and Kristy were good, but we took the first game. We were tied midway through the second when Coach dismissed the class.

"Already?" I protested. "Hey, if you guys want, we can stay and finish this."

"No, we can't," Hayley told me. "What about rehearsal?"

"Oh. Right. Sorry." But China and Kristy had already joined the groupies following Coach to his office.

"Come on," Hayley said. "We'd better hit the showers fast if we're going to get there on time."

The showers?

The showers! How could I have failed to realize that signing us up for the talent show would mean finally showering at school?

At least our school has individual shower stalls—not like the horror stories my mother tells about the communal showers at her high school. But still. No one could call those flimsy white shower curtains private, especially not with everything above the shoulders and below the knees exposed.

Below the knees.

I was dead.

But I had no choice. I'd be sitting with Kevin for the next hour and not only was I sweaty, I could smell fake tanning goo rising out of my pores. Wrapping myself in upper and lower towels, for maximum coverage, I bolted for the nearest stall.

Military style, I encouraged myself, closing the curtain and turning on the water. *If soldiers can do this in three minutes, so can I.*

With one last peek outside to make sure no one was watching, I stripped off my towels, hung them over the shower rod, and rinsed down in a hurry. I was reaching for the soap when a soc-y drawl assaulted my ears:

"Here's a riddle, Tiffi. What's red and white and orange all over?"

Tiffi Hughes giggled. "It's a bird, it's a plane . . . it's Captain Carrots!"

"Captain Carrots!" Sterling hooted, delighted. "Good one!"

They walked off braying like a couple of hyenas, leaving me without a comeback—as usual.

Or wait, maybe only donkeys bray.

Jackasses.

Okay, actually, that works for me.

Showing Up

By the time Hayley and I arrived at the school auditorium, everyone else was already there.

And I do mean everyone.

"Don't look now. It's Captain Carrots!" Tiffi mocked as I walked down the sloping center aisle.

I spotted her and Sterling yukking it up in a couple of back-row seats by themselves, but before I could respond, Hayley grabbed my arm, pulling me to where Fitz, Quentin, and Kevin had saved us seats down by the stage. Not that they'd had to fight for them. Aside from us and the Soc Sisters, there were only maybe twenty people in the theater. Ros could have sat with Sterling and her old buddy Tiffi, but as usual she was glued to Quentin. Not that I cared. I flashed her a superbig smile as I took the seat next to Kevin's.

"Why don't we get started?" Mrs. Conway said, walking past the stairs at one end of the stage to lean against its center, where the platform rose to her shoulders. "But before we launch into a roll call and our vision for the show, I want to thank you all for coming. It speaks volumes about what kind of people you are. Working for charity isn't work—it's a labor of love. In the coming weeks, when this show *feels* like work, let's all remember that."

Was she getting choked up? I couldn't tell. She glanced down at her clipboard, and when she looked up again, her expression was as inscrutable as ever.

"All right, then!" she continued. "We're not going to rehearse today. The purpose of this first meeting is to find out who's here and what types of acts we have so we can start putting together a program. Obviously we want to arrange things so all the singers don't bunch up together, we don't have two jugglers back to back, et cetera."

I nodded—that made sense. Conway noticed and actually smiled at me before she went on.

"Let's start at the back of the room. Why doesn't everyone tell the group their name and their talent?"

Conway pointed to Sterling.

"Sterling Carter," Fourteen-Karat said promptly. "I'm going to sing 'Wind Beneath My Wings.'"

"Have you sung onstage before, Sterling?"

"No, but I take voice lessons and I'm really good. I should be the opening act."

Only F.K. would say something like that in front of a room full of people and feel absolutely no shame.

Conway made a note. "And you?" she asked Tiffi.

"I'm just here to keep Sterling company," Tiffi replied in a bored voice. "I don't care about the show."

"I see," Conway said coolly. "Let me know if you change your mind."

She went through the room that way, turning up all the usual suspects: singers, dancers, a baton twirler, a juggler, a string quartet from band, a thespian wannabe with a Shakespeare monologue, and—I'm not even kidding—a unicycle rider.

Finally, she got to us.

"I'm not exactly sure," Hayley told her, with a significant glance at me. "I'm a decent whistler, but I'd rather do something else."

"Such as?" Conway prompted.

I could guess what Hayley was thinking: *Such as nothing*.

"Can I tell you next week?" she asked.

"Certainly. Cassie, what about you?"

"I'm not sure either. I want to help out, but there's nothing I can do onstage. Maybe I can sell tickets?"

"We're all going to sell tickets. Give it more thought and see if you don't come up with something."

Fitz said he'd do a magic act, which went over well. But then Ros, Kevin, and Quentin all asked to work backstage.

"Well," Mrs. Conway said, thoughtfully. "We will need someone on lights and sound."

"That's me," Kevin put in quickly.

"I could do publicity," Ros offered. "Make posters for around school, flyers to put up in stores. My dad knows a couple of DJs who might plug us on the radio."

"Excellent!" Mrs. Conway said, beaming. "That would be fantastic, Ros."

Ros squeezed Quentin's hand, smiling happily.

"Our show date is February thirteenth, which gives us only

five weeks to pull this together," Mrs. Conway said. "Start practicing your acts at home. Beginning next week, we'll meet for rehearsal every Monday, Wednesday, and Friday."

Sterling's hand went up. "Next Monday is Martin Luther King Day."

"Oh, right. Well, practice on your own and we'll start rehearsals next Wednesday."

Everyone got up to leave. Quentin hurried forward to catch Mrs. Conway.

"I have a job after school and I can't miss that much work—not three days a week," he said. "I had to get my shift pushed back just to come today."

"I understand completely," she said with a surprising lack of sarcasm. "People have to work."

"Maybe I can still be an usher or something."

"We'll need ushers. Thank you, Quentin."

She swept out of the room with her clipboard.

"You guys said she was so intimidating!" Quentin scoffed at me and Kevin. "She's not scary at all."

"Cheat on an assignment and then see how you like her," Kevin suggested darkly.

We were all following Quentin to the exit when Sterling stepped into our path.

"Hey, Ros," she said, completely ignoring the rest of us. "Is Tess picking you up? Because Tiffi and I need a ride."

Ros shook her head. "Quentin's dropping me off on his way to work."

"Perfect," Sterling said shamelessly. "We'll ride home with you. You can make Tess drive us later."

I could barely believe her nerve. And then I noticed something a lot more dangerous: Tiffi Hughes was gazing at Kevin like he was the last piece of cheesecake.

"Hello!" she said, pursing her full lips. Her curls formed a perfect cascade around her heart-shaped face. Three-inch platforms brought her up to his chin, and as she took another step closer, I noticed that even her toes were cute.

"I'm Tiffany," she told Kevin. "You can call me Tiffi."

"Hey. I'm Kevin."

"Now I see what all the fuss was about," she purred, glancing from him to me to Sterling.

I about died. Sterling didn't look much happier.

Tiffi treated Kevin to a conspiratorial grin. "It's not easy, is it? Being beautiful, I mean."

"I'll take your word for it," he said, smiling back.

My hand clamped down on his elbow. "I just remembered! We need to go this way, Kevin. See you guys tomorrow!" I called, dragging him back down the aisle and out the side door.

"This way?" he protested as I pulled him along. "Why?"

"I'll tell you outside," I said, stalling, as I led him away from Tiffi with all possible speed. Because let's be real: Kevin's choosing me was a fluke. True, I threw myself at him with everything I had, but that's never gotten me anywhere before. Not to mention how many other sad and embarrassing things had to take place before he finally realized that I was the girl he wanted. If someone like Tiffi tried to take him away, was there any actual chance I could come out on top again?

Frankly, that wasn't something I wanted to test.

I know I'm insecure and I should like myself better and blah, blah, blah. But please. That's just the way it is.

I don't have to front for you.

Socializing

By Tuesday I'd decided that not only wasn't I jealous of Ros, but it couldn't hurt to have her on my side if Tiffi tried any more moves on Kevin. I made sure I sat beside her at lunch.

"Did you and Sterling have fun yesterday?" I asked. "Or is it weird having Tiffi tagging along again?"

Ros shrugged. "We had fun. And once Tiffi makes friends with more people, she won't be so glued to Sterling."

"I wouldn't count on that. You should see those two in PE—Sterling is Tiffi's idol."

Hayley shot me a scowl, but I could tell she was kind of fascinated to see where I was going.

"Plenty of people worship Sterling," Ros said.

"It has to be annoying, though. You finally get some time with your best friend . . ."

"I'm not worried. Hey!" Ros's face lit up. "I almost forgot. Are you guys going to Bonfire this weekend?"

Once a year, Harrison Park, a few heavily wooded acres between Hilltop and the adjacent foothills, becomes the site of a major unofficial school event. For one day only, the otherwise lonely park positively crawls with socs, jocks, and other members of our school's cultural elite. Bonfire is one of those things most people know about but only the privileged few dare attend.

"You're kidding, right?" Fitz asked. "Why would we go to that?"

"Because it's fun!" Ros put her hand over Quentin's on the table. "Quentin and I are going, aren't we, Q?"

I nearly choked on my soda to hear her call him my personal private nickname, but I recovered quickly.

"We should go," I told Kevin. "We said we were going to do something this weekend."

"What's Bonfire?" he asked.

I smiled encouragingly as Ros filled him in. Bonfire would be a big step up for me, socially speaking. But between being Snow Queen runner-up and snagging a hot new boyfriend, it was exactly the type of thing I *ought* to be doing.

I'd totally earned it.

"Okay," Kevin said when Ros had finished. "We can go if Quentin will give us a ride."

"Sure." Quentin looked relieved to have male backup. "Come on, Fitz. You have to go now, man."

"You want to, right, Hayley?" I coaxed.

I was prepared to plead if necessary, but Hayley was already nodding. "Sure. Why not?"

"Yeah, why not?" Fitz echoed sarcastically. "Jocks don't stuff girls into trash cans."

"Don't be ridiculous, dude," Quentin scoffed. "Half those people were at my Halloween party and nothing bad happened there. Besides, it's not like anyone owns the park."

"Right!" I exclaimed eagerly. "This is going to be fun!"

And I totally believed that. My first megapopular event, with my best friend, my boyfriend, and a bona fide soc at my side . . .

What could possibly go wrong?

Of Popcorn and Pep Talks

Tuesday evening my father was complaining again. His boss had made him work late for the second night in a row. Meanwhile, Dad was still ticked off about "missing" the holidays.

"Other people get an entire week off. With pay," he griped over the movie we were watching in the den. "Some companies actually *close* between Christmas and New Year's, so their employees can spend that week with their families."

Mom gave him a skeptical look. "I've never worked for a company like that."

"Neither have I. That's the problem."

"You guys," Trevor whined, twisting to face the couch from his pillow on the floor. "I'm trying to hear this."

"Sorry, Trev." Dad reached over the coffee table. "How about giving up that popcorn you've been hogging?"

Trevor handed it over, and maybe he could hear the movie after that. All I could hear was Dad chewing, grinding each kernel to pulp.

"You know what the problem is?" he finally burst out,

smacking the empty bowl down on the table. "I'm too easy to take advantage of. I didn't say squat when they down-graded our health insurance to that lousy HMO crap. I attend so many useless meetings I end up working through lunch every day just to get something done. And now I'm working unpaid overtime because they're too cheap to hire enough people. I let Percy walk all over me."

"Then stand up for yourself," Mom said, her eyes still on the screen. "Tell Percy what you want."

"He's such a jerk. Anything I say, he'll turn it into an argument."

"Arguments can be won. You just have to pick your battles."

Dad sighed. "I guess some things are worth fighting for."

"Of course they are," Mom said absently, patting his knee.

Later, when she looked back on that night, I bet she wished she'd paid a lot less attention to the movie and a lot more to my dad.

Put Your Lips Together and Blow

"It has to be some sort of joint act with you," Hayley insisted Thursday afternoon in my room. "I'm not going on-stage by myself. That auditorium is huge!"

"But I can't do anything." We'd been arguing this point for an hour. "Besides, you know how I freeze on a stage. If you're afraid, imagine how much worse it would be for me."

"This whole thing was your idea! Why did you sign us up if you don't want to participate?"

"I want to help out. Just not onstage."

Hayley sighed. "I guess I could be Fitz's magic assistant."

"That would be such a waste. Try to believe me, Hayley—your whistling is the best thing Conway has going."

"But what if I get nervous and lose my breath? I won't be able to whistle."

"I've got it!" I cried, sitting up on my bed. "You can whistle-synch! We'll tape you beforehand. Then all you have to do for the show is purse along to the playback."

"You're insane."

"It would work! Why not?"

Hayley spun circles in my desk chair, obviously trying to choose from a truckload of reasons. "Hey!" she said suddenly. "If we used your idea, we could perform a duet!"

"You know I can't whistle. I'd blow."

She rolled her eyes at my accidental pun. "The whole thing's on tape anyway. I'll just record two parts. Then we can *both* purse along to the playback."

My brilliant plan abruptly lost its luster. It's one thing to fake to your own whistling, but to fake to someone else's . . . I'd never live that down. Unfortunately, now I had to convince her that whistle-synching was lame if I did it but perfectly fine for her—a delicate situation, considering how easily Hayley gets angry.

"Well," I started slowly, "there might be—"

"Hey, what are you guys doing?" Trevor asked, poking his head into my room.

Normally I would have been furious at such a rude interruption, but that day his timing was perfect. "Just talking about school," I said. "What are *you* doing?"

"Nothing."

"Come on in," I offered.

He shot me an amazed look, then cautiously entered my room and leaned against my closet door. "Hi, Hayley."

"Why aren't you skating?" I asked.

He shrugged. "I ate it yesterday. I don't think I'm ready for bowls."

I could have told him that. Wait—I *did* tell him that.

"You just need more practice," Hayley said.

"You think?" he asked, encouraged. "I did do one cool thing yesterday. There's this coping at the top of Psycho Bowl and I was trying to turn, but my front wheels hooked it and I actually ground sideways. Before I fell backwards, I mean. But if I could do that on purpose . . . and skip the part where I fall . . ."

"You'll get it eventually. Okay, see you later." I figured we'd wandered far enough off the subject of whistling to make it safe to dismiss him.

But Trev was just settling in. "So what's going on this weekend? Any parties?" he asked.

"Trevor!" I groaned. "I told you I'd tell you if—"

"Just Bonfire," Hayley said.

I nearly croaked on the spot. There was no way to even contemplate bringing my eighth-grade brother to Bonfire.

"What's that?" Trevor asked, perking up. "Is Julie going?"

"Not likely," I said quickly. "It's not the crowd she hangs with."

"It's not the crowd *we* hang with," Hayley pointed out. "We could always invite her to come."

Hayley knew Julie even less well than I did, but she knew about my promise to Trevor and she obviously thought she was helping.

She obviously wasn't.

"I don't think—" I began.

"Is it on Saturday?" Trev asked. "Is there dancing?"

"It's on Sunday, and it's not that kind of party," Hayley explained. "Everyone just gets together and hangs out in the park. The guys might play football. And there's a bonfire."

"How do they play football in the dark?"

"It starts in the afternoon," I said impatiently.

But I was slowly warming to the idea. If I *could* make up some reason to ask Julie, and if we *did* take Trevor with us, those two could go lose themselves in the woods until we were ready to leave. Or, more likely, when Julie shot him down, Trevor could go get lost on his own. After all, Harrison Park was a public place, where nobody had to be introduced, or even seen together. There were some huge advantages to taking him there instead of to someone's house.

"You know what?" I said. "This might work after all. I'll ask Julie tomorrow, and if she wants to come you guys can ride with us in Quentin's van."

"There are only seven seats," Hayley reminded me.

"So we'll squeeze—it was your idea. What do you say, Trevor?" I asked, feeling incredibly noble. "Want to come to Bonfire?"

He thought about it a second. Then, to my total amazement, he shook his head.

"It's too fishy if you invite Julie—she needs to come on her own. Besides, the whole thing sounds pretty lame. I'll wait for a real party. With a band."

He pushed off of my closet and headed for the door.

"Are you crazy?" I gasped. "*Lame?* Do you have any idea what you just turned down?"

"I'll wait," he repeated, walking out.

"This could be the best chance you'll ever get!" I yelled down the hall after him. "No, the *only* chance. Why should I keep trying if you're going to act this way?"

"Because you promised me a party."

"I never promised you a band!"

Oh, man. I have to change the subject. My head aches again just thinking about it.

> Brain melting like snow.
> Hayley couldn't understand
> Lucky only child!

Social Climbing

Friday morning I found this card in my locker:

You are invited to
Rosalind Pierce's Sweet 16 Party
Where: Edgemont Manor

(see attached map)
When: Saturday, January 24,
8 p.m. to ?
Celebrate Ros's 16th in style
with food, drink, and dancing to
The Answer
RSVP to Ros or Tess at 555-2398

"Whoa!" I said, barely able to believe my eyes.

I don't know about you, but personally, I don't hang out at a lot of houses that have names instead of addresses. Not only that, but The Answer is a big-time band in Hilltop. Their faces are plastered on clubs all over downtown. And finally, I knew from talking to Quentin that Tess is the Pierces' personal assistant.

What type of birthday party involves a manor, a band you've actually heard of, and a personal assistant? Let me answer that for you: a top-tier, A-list, megasoc party.

When it rains, it pours, I thought happily, tucking the invitation into my notebook. *Bonfire this weekend and Ros's birthday next . . . I'm really moving up!*

I was on my way to class before the should-have-been-obvious horrifying thought finally hit me. I stopped dead in my tracks, frozen by a dilemma so epic and so ugly I almost forgot to breathe.

Did I have to bring Trevor?

Because unlike most school parties, this one involved written invitations, which gave me a solid out.

On the other hand, did the promise I'd made my brother mean I had to at least ask Ros?

There was no question Trevor would leap at an invite. This party was such an airtight fit with all his absurd requirements it almost made me wonder if the little creep was psychic. Not only that, but something told me that if I explained the situation—how Trevor had sewed my Snow Ball dress, extracting this foolish promise in return—Ros might help me out.

But did I really want my immature brother at the most important party of my life? Did I need him hovering when Kevin and I got romantic? Did I care to have even one of Ros's uberpopular friends know I was related to Trevor in any way?

In short, did I want to jeopardize my growing chance of moving from B to Bee?

No. I did not.

And if I simply kept my mouth shut, none of that had to happen.

20/20 Vision

Mom was pretty upset about the takeout going cold on the counter by the time Dad finally got home Friday night.

"Good evening, family!" he boomed, throwing his arms open wide and grinning like a maniac. "What a lovely night!"

First off, it was pitch-dark and fifty degrees outside—freezing by SoCal standards. Second, my dad hadn't been coming home in such a stellar mood the past couple of weeks. But it was the twinkle-toes twirl he did while taking off his suit coat that had me and Mom and Trevor dropping our jaws.

"Hal?" Mom said uncertainly. "Honey? Have you been drinking?"

"Not yet! What's for dinner?"

"Chinese. I just have to heat it back up."

"Delicious!" he exclaimed. "Perfect! What a perfect day!"

Waltzing over to the breakfast bar, he dropped a hand on Trevor's head, mussing his hair. He pinched my cheek, then danced into the kitchen and grabbed Mom by the waist.

"It's nice to see you in a better mood," she said, obviously still confused. "Did you have a talk with Percy?"

"I did!" he confirmed, with obvious satisfaction. "I walked into his office and I said, 'Percy, I'm looking at this year's new schedule of holidays and I see we don't have Martin Luther King Day off on Monday. Or Presidents' Day or Veterans Day—as usual. Fourth of July is on a Sunday. Christmas and New Year's fall on Saturdays, so you could have given us those Fridays off—but you didn't. There's such a thing as the final straw, Percy. I've worked myself into the ground here for seven years, and every year I give you more and get less for it. The late nights, the lousy benefits, the constant nickel-and-diming . . . it all comes down to this: I resign, effective today.' "

My mother gasped. "You quit? Hal!"

"Oh, it was sweet, Andrea. I wish you'd been there to see his face."

"I wish I'd at least been there for the part where we discussed it!"

Trevor and I gaped at each other, stunned.

"You're the one who told me to stand up to him," Dad reminded her, dipping his finger into a carton of orange chicken and sucking off the sauce. "Yum!"

"There are *ways* of taking a stand, Hal. Degrees of escalation. I never suggested you march into his office and quit."

"But boy, am I ever glad I did! I feel like I just lost a thousand pounds. Honestly, I might be giddy. Is this what giddy feels like? Let's eat!"

Mom stared in disbelief. "Let's go over this *rationally*," she suggested. "Look at it from Percy's perspective. Why would a person stick it out through Christmas and New Year's, then suddenly quit over Martin Luther King Day? I don't know a single adult who gets that holiday off."

Dad giggled and smacked Mom's rump. "You do now!"

"Hal!" The forced calmness was deserting her voice. "Will you please be serious?"

"Fine." He stopped skipping around the kitchen and took a couple of deep breaths, becoming very grave. "I *had* to quit, Andrea. There's something wrong with my eyes."

"With your eyes?" she repeated, concerned.

"Yes. I can't see myself at that job anymore."

Trevor and I started laughing so hard we nearly fell off our stools. Mom was a lot less amused.

"You kids heat up that food if you want to eat. Hal, can I see you in our bedroom a minute?"

"Only a minute, baby? You can see me all night!" Grabbing her by the hand, he dragged her off down the hall.

"Oh, yuck. Scarred for life," I complained as Trevor put our orange chicken in the nuke.

"At least Dad's happy again."

"Judging by Mom's face, I doubt that's going to last."

I honestly believed that he'd be back at work on Monday.

Bonfire of the Minivanities

I should have realized the instant Quentin picked us up that I was in over my head. One second Kevin and I were waiting happily in my driveway, me proud of my vintage gauze top and the fact that I'd finally been able to comb my shortest layers of hair into an actual ponytail. The next we were crammed into a minivan with Quentin, Ros, Fitz, Hayley, and—here's where things get ugly—Sterling and Tate the Great.

"What's *she* doing here?" I hissed to Hayley as Kevin and I tried unsuccessfully to wedge ourselves into the only remaining seat, a captain's chair.

Hayley cast a disgusted glance toward the back bench, where Sterling and Bryce were sucking face like the rest of us weren't even there. "Mostly making out."

Kevin gave up and sat on the floor.

"Great," I muttered, turning to give Ros my best dirty look. "Not at all nauseating."

Ros was crammed into the six inches of bench on Sterling's other side, trying to act like everything was normal. "So! Is everyone psyched about Bonfire?" she asked.

"I *was*," I said pointedly.

"This ought to be great!" Quentin replied from the driver's seat.

I shot him a dirty look too. Fitz half turned in the passenger seat, caught my expression, and decided to keep quiet.

"We're going to have fun," Ros persisted. "Right, Ster?"

"Huh?" Sterling came up for air long enough to make eye contact with me over the back of my seat. "Oh, hello, Cassie," she said. "All by yourself? Kevin dump you already?"

"He's sitting on the floor," I gritted out.

"Just kidding." She smirked, then resumed her lip-lock with Tate.

For the next twenty minutes I clenched my jaw while Quentin drove obliviously onward. Off the freeway and onto a two-lane highway. Off the highway and onto a winding rural road. And finally, off the road and onto a wide expanse of packed dirt and parked cars. I was on my last good nerve when he hit the brakes and stopped in a cloud of dust.

The instant we were out of the van, I grabbed him by the arm and pulled him off to one side. "How could you bring Sterling?" I demanded. "Did you ever stop to think that that might be a bad idea?"

Quentin shrugged. "She was going to be here anyway."

"That's not the point!"

"You know how I feel about her, but she's Ros's best friend. Just try to be nice."

"Tell her that!"

He sighed. "New plan: ignore her."

"What's going on?" Kevin asked, walking around the van to join us.

I noticed his eyes on my hand and realized it still held

Quentin's elbow. "Nothing," I said, guiltily breaking off contact. "Come on, let's go."

"Don't you want to wait for the group?" Kevin asked as I led him across the dirt lot and up the nearest brushy path.

"Nope." Hayley would find us eventually, and I was mad at everyone else.

"Cassie! Hey, Cassie, wait up!" Ros called. My heart contracted at the unwelcome sound of her footsteps running up the path behind us. "You're going the wrong way," she huffed, closing the distance.

Her ensemble that day looked like some warped fashion-magazine idea of socialite hiking attire, complete with tweed and elbow patches. Interlocking gold Cs flashed from the sides of her dark glasses.

"Hey, Kevin," she said. "Can I talk to Cassie a second?"

"Sure. You girls walk ahead and I'll wait here for everyone else."

"You'll be waiting a long time." Ros pointed back the way we'd just come. "The fire ring is over there."

Kevin gave me an irritated look and took off the way Ros had pointed.

"We should go too," I said, in no mood to be alone with Ros. "We don't want to get lost."

"*I'm* not lost," she teased.

I started to walk around her.

"No, Cassie, wait. If I'd realized you'd be this upset, I wouldn't have offered Sterling a ride. But she spent the night last night, and I thought . . . I mean, hasn't enough time passed? I just want all of my friends to be friends with each other."

I stared in disbelief. "Does she tell you *anything* about PE?"

"A little," Ros admitted. "But can't we put the past behind us and all just get along?"

The incredible part was, she was serious.

"*You* don't even like her all the time. Remember all that trash she talked about Quentin?"

Ros nodded. "But she wasn't trying to keep Quentin from me. She didn't want to lose me to him."

Sterling's had tons of boyfriends—literally, if you count Tate. Could she really begrudge Ros one?

"Well, that backfired on her, didn't it?" I said. "If she hadn't been so nasty to Quentin, maybe you wouldn't always have to choose between them."

"Exactly. And I don't want to do that anymore. Quentin's willing to forgive and forget. If the rest of you would just give her a chance, you'd find out she's not like you think."

I grimaced skeptically.

"All right, sometimes she is," Ros allowed. "But you have to get to know her."

"Why would I want to? That girl's been tormenting me from the day we met."

"She's jealous of your hair."

I blinked a few times. "My hair?"

"It makes her completely crazy. Why did you think she was always harassing you?"

"Well—but—"

"Your hair makes you stand out in any crowd. As far as Sterling's concerned, that's like a red flag to a bull."

It's a red flag, all right. And comparing Fourteen-Karat to a raging horned animal didn't strike me as wrong either.

"So it's not actually my *hair* she's jealous of," I said, digesting this new information. "It's the attention it attracts."

Ros smiled. "You catch on fast."

"Not that fast," I muttered.

She glanced down the trail at the parking lot. Everyone else had vanished. "We ought to catch up. There's just one more thing it might help to know: Sterling's parents split up two years ago. Her dad wants a divorce, but her mom keeps putting him off."

"Because she still loves him?"

"Please!" The way Ros laughed made her sound much older. "She wants more money. And to drive him crazy. This year they're playing dueling significant others: he gets a hot young girlfriend—she finds an even younger boy toy. They just keep jerking each other around and Sterling's caught in the middle."

"That sounds . . . bad."

"Classic passive-aggressive. And while those two are working out their issues, they're giving Sterling a whole new batch. She'll make some lucky shrink rich one day."

I could have already guessed that, but for totally different reasons.

"So when is it going to end?" I asked.

"Never, according to Sterling." Ros touched my hand. "But you have to keep this between us. She'd kill me for telling you. I only thought . . . if you knew . . . You and I, we have an understanding, right?"

I flashed back to the winter formal, to the moment I'd grabbed Ros in the gym and made her listen about Quentin. A bond had formed between us then, and though I'd ignored it ever since, I felt it tighten now.

"I won't repeat what you've told me."

Ros smiled with relief. "You're about to see Sterling in a whole new light."

She Must Have Meant Firelight

Because, honestly, when Ros and I joined the party, Sterling looked as annoying as ever. She had already abandoned our group and wormed her way into the thick of things around the fire ring. People were milling about there, talking and laughing, while Tate and some other guys unloaded wood from a pickup truck they'd backed over the grass. The crowd was full of the social elite, making me unexpectedly nervous.

"I'm back," I said, slipping my hand into Kevin's.

"What did Ros want?"

"Nothing. She's sorry you had to ride on the floor."

"I'll bet Sterling's broken up about it too," he said, rolling his eyes. "Hey, do you want to walk around? It's going to be a while before they light this fire."

I have to admit, Harrison Park wasn't as thrilling as I'd imagined. The fire ring was centered in a clearing of packed dirt and patchy grass about the size of a soccer field. Two weathered tables, a trash can, and a barbeque grill on a pole were the only other amenities in sight. Kevin and I walked slowly around the clearing, taking in the growing crowd at its center and peering into the trees, boulders, and bushes blanketing the slopes surrounding it.

"Not exactly impressive," I said, when we'd completed our loop.

"It's not bad."

"For hiking, maybe. Not for a big crowd like this. There aren't even any bathrooms."

Kevin pointed. "What about those lovely structures?"

"Tell me they're kidding!" Two green plastic outhouses lurked at the edge of the woods, unisex placards on their doors. "That's just gross."

"What's gross is the honey sucker, the truck they pump those things out with. Have you ever seen one?"

"No, and thanks for putting that picture in my head."

"Slurp, slurp," he said, which was pretty disgusting for such a cute guy.

But that wasn't even my biggest concern.

Maybe this is just me, but as soon as I know there's no chance of using a bathroom, I immediately have to go. I could already feel the urge.

"Let's go back to the fire," I said to take my mind off my bladder.

"You mean the big pile of wood?"

"Whatever. Let's go find Hayley and Fitz."

Someone had turned on the stereo in the pickup and opened both its doors, creating a giant boom box. Coolers of sodas had appeared, and judging by the way a few guys were stumbling, there was beer stashed somewhere too. There was maybe an hour left before dark and the crowd was already getting wild.

A gang of girls ran by shrieking, pursued by guys with water balloons. The cheerleaders were working out some sort of line dance—clapping and spinning and just generally acting like cheerleaders—while Tate and his football buddies had started tossing a ball around. I watched Tate go long and nearly bash into a tree.

"Hey, we're just about to start singing 'Kumbaya,'" Hayley joked as Kevin and I walked up. "Anything to get this party started."

"Where are Fitz and Quentin?" I asked.

"Fitz went to the van, and Quentin . . ." Hayley pointed.

Quentin and Ros were sitting side by side on a patch of grass, familiar mushy expressions on their faces. I took a deep, cleansing breath and let it go, turning my eyes instead to the people sitting around them—five or six more couples and a group of girls with Sterling at its center. She was telling some sort of story and her friends were pretending they cared. All right, maybe some of them *did* care, but the only one who cared for sure was Tiffi Hughes. She had appeared at the edge of the crowd and was hanging on Sterling's words like the girl was preaching a new gospel.

"Look at Tiffi," I said scornfully. "How bad does she want to be Sterling?"

"I'm sad for her," Hayley said.

"Tiffi?" Kevin echoed.

"What? Oh." I'd been so busy scanning the crowd

I'd forgotten he was there. "Just some tragic girl in our PE class."

"Wasn't she with Sterling at the talent show meeting?"

I felt the little hairs lift on the back of my neck. If I'd managed to forget that, why did he remember?

"She seemed pretty nice to me," he added.

"She *was* pretty nice. To you." I'd meant to be clever, but that wasn't how I sounded.

Kevin's eyes singled out Tiffi on the grass. "She just wants to fit in. Cut the new girl some slack."

I was still trying to form a suitable reply when Fitz walked up and handed Hayley a Coke.

"Want one?" he asked me and Kevin, raising a dripping six-pack into view. "I just pulled these out of the ice."

"I'll take one," Kevin said.

My bladder spasmed. "Not for me." I was never going to make it through the night without finding a bathroom.

And then I had an idea.

"Hey, Fitz," I said casually. "If I'd known you were going to the van, I'd have asked you to get my coat."

Fitz shrugged. "Sorry."

"Are you cold?" Kevin asked.

"A little. Plus it'll be dark soon and I'd rather get it now. Is the van unlocked?"

Fitz nodded and popped open a soda. "Don't lock it, either, because I don't know where Quentin put the keys."

"I'll go with you," Kevin said.

"No! I mean, I'll be right back." For a second I considered begging Hayley to come, but since I'd just declined

Kevin's company, that wasn't an option. "See you in a minute," I said, jogging off toward the parking lot.

As soon as I was out of sight, I pushed through some bushes at the side of the path and started walking uphill, away from the clearing and the parking lot. My plan was simple: find a nice private spot to pee, then drink as little as possible for the rest of the night.

I'd been hiking maybe five minutes when I found the perfect place: a giant boulder with a thick hedge of bushes in front of it—practically an outdoor stall. I squeezed in and dropped my chinos, relieved in more ways than one.

Now I'll be able to enjoy myself instead of worrying all night, I thought as I zipped my pants.

I was just stepping out of the bushes when a sudden noise made me freeze. Was that a stick snapping? What had snapped it? I held my breath and listened until I heard a horrifying new sound: footsteps crunching dry leaves. Someone was in the woods with me, and they were headed directly my way.

My heart started pounding like crazy. No one could have seen me squatting behind those bushes. Could they? No, definitely not. But maybe someone had heard me crashing around and was coming to investigate. Except that everyone I knew was down below.

And I was so far away they'd never even hear me scream.

"Hello?" My voice came out all quavery, which, based on the slasher films I've seen, is practically an invitation to attacking psychos. I sucked down a breath and tried again. "Quentin? Kevin? Is that you? We're all over here."

Better. Not only had I sounded more confident, I'd given the illusion of strength in numbers.

Tate the Great burst out of the trees, an amused grin on his face. "Oh, yeah? You look all alone to me."

"Well, you scared me! What are you doing way up here?"

"What are *you* doing?"

"None of your business," I retorted, blushing.

"Ooh, you're cute when you get fired up." Reaching around my head, he swatted my short ponytail. "Then again, that goes with the territory, right?"

One of the more annoying myths about redheads is that we have bad tempers. The actual facts—in this case, that people like Bryce Tate are more provoking than pimples—always get overlooked when a redheaded person gets angry.

"For your information," I told him, "I'm cute *all* the time."

Which obviously wasn't even remotely the right thing to say. Believe me, I'm more surprised than anyone by the things that come out of my mouth.

But Bryce didn't seem put off. "I'm starting to think the same thing," he said, and the way he looked me over made my cheeks burst into flames.

"Why are you lurking around in the bushes?" I asked.

"Probably the same reason you are." He smirked. "Do you want the details? Measurements? A photograph, maybe?"

"No!" If any more blood diverted to my cheeks, there was a good chance I'd pass out.

"Anyway, you ought to thank me for coming to your rescue. There are mountain lions up here."

"You think?" The mere possibility made me happier to see him.

"Sure. They're crawling all over places like this, just waiting to snap a tender young neck."

He reached for me again, closing both hands around my throat like mountain lion jaws.

Okay. Not so glad to see him after all.

"Knock it off!" I protested, slapping him away.

Bryce laughed. "All right, take it easy! Ow! You hit like a girl."

"Stop trying to choke me!"

"If I wanted you choked, you'd be choked," he bragged, flexing his huge hands. "I'm just playing with you."

"Yeah . . . well . . . we'd better get back. People will be wondering where we are. Especially Sterling."

I had hoped to make him feel guilty, but Bryce just pointed out the path back to the clearing. "Ladies first," he said, motioning for me to walk in front of him.

I was seriously happy to comply. I'd barely stepped past him, though, when his hand swung down and slapped my rear end.

"What is your deal?" I demanded, spinning around. "Are you making some sort of pass?"

He grinned wickedly. "Do you want me to?"

"I have a boyfriend, you know."

"I do know. He used to date my girlfriend."

"Right." If he was going to make my argument for me, I didn't know what else to say.

"Don't touch me again," I threatened, hurrying down the path.

Busted

The sun was setting behind the hills as Bryce and I crashed out of the woods and into the crowded clearing.

"Hey, Tate!" one of his buddies called, spotting us instantly. "Whatcha doin', man? Having a little fun in the bushes?"

Heads turned. People sniggered. I expected a quick denial, but to my horror, Bryce laughed.

"A guy doesn't say no," he replied, adding more swagger to his step.

That was when I spotted Sterling steaming toward us, Tiffi and Ros bobbing in her wake.

"Bryce!" She was trying to sound casual, but she looked like that female Terminator. "Where have you been?"

"In the woods," he said.

"With her? What were you doing?"

He took too long to answer. I couldn't stand it anymore.

"Nothing!" I blurted out.

"I wasn't talking to *you*," she said.

Hayley, Quentin, Kevin, and Fitz were on their way over by then with a bunch of other people. Behind the gathering crowd, the first flames of the bonfire struggled to get started.

"I just ran into Cassie in the bushes. That's all," Bryce finally admitted.

"Nothing happened," I said loudly.

"Like it would!" Sterling linked her arm through Tate's and pushed her best assets forward. "I'm so worried!"

"You *look* worried," I retorted.

Someday I'm going to learn to think before I speak.

Maybe.

Sterling's eyes narrowed. "You must need glasses."

"Yeah. Or a mirror," Tiffi tittered.

Bryce could have set them straight, but he just kept grinning, enjoying the fuss. Ros was the one who finally stepped in to break things up.

"Can't two people walk on the same trail?" she asked. "Bryce, I thought you were in charge of the fire. Look—they started it without you."

"Hey!" he protested, walking off just as Kevin reached me.

"What's going on?" Kevin asked. "Where's your coat?"

"Huh? Oh!" I'd totally forgotten my alibi. "I, uh, I was on my way to the van, and then I got turned around, and then I ran into Bryce . . ."

I gave Hayley a desperate look, begging her to rescue me.

"The van's that way," she said, pointing. "Do you need a compass?"

Thank you very much, I thought. *Way to leap to my aid.*

Sterling, Ros, and Tiffi had started whispering back and forth. Everyone else was staring at me.

I could have just told the truth.

If I wanted to be the Girl Who Peed in the Bushes for the rest of my high school career.

Someday I'm going to learn to think before I act. Maybe.

"Can we just go stand by the fire?" I begged. "I won't need my coat over there."

Bursted

The fire had begun to roar when Quentin and Ros joined us at the back of the group surrounding its ring. Flames licked the sky, illuminating the curve of Hayley's cheek and the gold tones in Ros's hair. Beyond our circle of light, we could barely make out the silhouettes of people still running around the darkened clearing, screeching and having fun.

"So now what?" Hayley asked Ros.

"What do you mean?" Ros said.

"I mean, do we stand around all night or—"

Wham!

Something slammed into my back so hard I gasped. Or maybe my sudden lack of breath had more to do with the icy blast of water that splashed up my neck into my hair. Reflex twisted me in the direction of the attack just as I got pelted again, the second water balloon bursting across my chest in a way that made the appeal of wet T-shirt contests instantly obvious.

"Cassie!" Hayley cried. "Hey!" she shouted into the gloom. "Who did that?"

People around the fire started laughing and pointing.

"Are you okay?" Kevin asked. "Are you hurt?"

I could only cross my arms over my chest and hyperventilate. I was cold, I was humiliated—again—and I was seriously not amused.

"It was probably an accident," Ros said. "People have been throwing those things since we got here."

True. But they'd been throwing them at each other, not at random dry people minding their own business.

"Come on, Cassie," said Hayley. "Let's go get your coat."

I let her lead me away from the fire, still mute with indignation.

"I'll find out who did it," Kevin promised as we left.

"I have an extra T-shirt in the van," Quentin called after us. "Wear it, if you want."

My teeth chattered as we picked our way down the dark path.

"It probably *was* an accident," Hayley said at last. "Those balloons could have been aimed at anyone. Or no one."

I nodded, but we were thinking the same thing: Sterling. Part of me couldn't *not* believe that she was the one behind this. After all, if hitting me was an accident, a simple "sorry" called out of the darkness would have made everything better.

Everything except the shivering.

Inside Quentin's van, I stripped off my soaked top and, after a moment's hesitation, my equally soaked bra. Hayley found Quentin's spare T-shirt in back. It smelled like it had already been worn, but it smelled like Quentin and, therefore, good. I pulled the elastic off my bedraggled ponytail and ran a brush through my hair. With my coat on, I looked almost normal.

"If you don't want to go back there, I can run and ask Quentin to take us home," Hayley offered. "Or we could go someplace else. Who cares about Bonfire?"

The second she said that, I knew I had to go back. Not because I was having such a great time, but because it was Bonfire. If I wanted to be somebody, didn't I have to at least pretend to like it?

"No, that's okay," I said, huddling up inside my coat. "I'm already getting warmer, and my hair will dry by the fire."

"Are you sure?"

"You can't tell I'm not wearing a bra, can you?"

Hayley laughed. "Under all that down? I think you're safe, Chesty."

We headed back to the clearing.

"There's Fitz," Hayley said, spotting him on the other side of the ring. We were working our way over when I heard a burst of laughter from the outer gloom.

Kevin was on the edge of the crowd, talking to Tiffi Hughes.

My stomach started churning like an off-balance washing machine. Not because they were talking, but because Tiffi so obviously wanted it to be more. She hung on Kevin's every word, her eyes lit up like a kid's on Christmas. I watched in horror as she practiced Sterling's not-so-subtle lean forward, the one intended to put her cleavage directly in Kevin's line of sight.

"What does she think she's doing?" I gasped.

"She'll strike out," Hayley said. "Wait and see."

"Would you wait if she was hitting on *your* boyfriend?"

"They're just talking."

"*He's* just talking. She's pure evil."

You might suppose I'd learned the pitfalls of rushing in first and thinking later. I've had some fairly brutal experience in that area. But when Tiffi put her hand on Kevin's shoulder and gave a tinkling little laugh, something inside me snapped.

I think it was my common sense.

Marching over to Kevin, I fastened my arms around him and gave Tiffi a poisonous look.

"Whoa!" Tiffi mocked. "That's subtle."

"How would you know?" I shot back.

"Cassie, what are you doing?" Kevin asked, attempting to loosen my death grip.

"I just feel like hugging my *boyfriend.*"

"Okay, but I still have to breathe."

I let him go reluctantly. It would have been better if he'd hugged me back, but it would have been worse if I'd made him escape.

Tiffi smirked at me. "If you love something, set it free. Right, Cassie?"

Wrong. What kind of moron would take that chance? I planted my feet, took a deep breath, and opened my mouth to tell her off just as Ros came rushing up.

"Hey, Cassie!" she blurted out. "Did you leave the van unlocked? I need to get something."

"It's open," I said tersely.

"Can you come with me? It's dark."

"Get Quentin."

"He's in the outhouse." Ros latched on to one of my arms. Before I could shake her off, she pulled me away from Kevin, back toward the parking lot.

"What are you doing?" I asked angrily. "Don't you see what's going on?"

"I see exactly what's going on. Do you?"

"Tiffi's hitting on Kevin right in front of me!"

"You're almost right. Tiffi's hitting on Kevin and hoping you'll wade in and try to stop her."

"What? Why?"

"Because nothing's going on—at least not as far as Kevin's concerned. Start a fight with Tiffi and you'll just look jealous and paranoid. She'll act all innocent and wronged, and Kevin will feel sorry for her. Believe me, that's what she wants."

In the first place, I *was* jealous and paranoid. I also wasn't a bit convinced Ros knew what she was talking about.

"So I'm supposed to let her just run wild?"

"You're supposed to trust your boyfriend. If you don't, you'll make this a lot worse."

"I *hate* that girl!" I exclaimed, glancing back over my shoulder while Ros continued towing. Tiffi was giggling with Kevin again as if I had never been there. "And it's not just Kevin, in case you haven't noticed—she's trying to steal your best friend too."

"Sterling could never drop me. I know too much," Ros said with an ironic smile. "For that matter, I could do some damage on Tiffi, too."

"I'll bet it was Tiffi who threw those water balloons!" I cried in a moment of sudden clarity. "She wanted to get me away from Kevin."

Ros considered. "Do you really think she has the arm?"

"I don't know." Based on what I'd seen in PE, Tiffi wasn't very strong. Plus, she was awfully tiny. . . .

Then I realized what Ros *hadn't* said.

"Hey! Shouldn't you be telling me she's not capable of something so mean?"

Rosalind shook her head. "I think Tiffany Hughes is capable of pretty much anything."

(Finally) Silent Night

I guess all that psychotherapy has taught Ros a trick or two about human nature, because a couple of hours later Tiffi drove off with Sterling, Tate, and some guy from the basketball team, leaving me and Kevin unmolested by the fire.

I leaned back into his chest, sighing happily as he folded his arms around me. "This is nice."

"You're nice," he said.

"No, you."

"You."

Fine. I admit it. We were perilously close to Quentin-and-Ros-style baby talk. But when Kevin leaned over and kissed me, I didn't care one bit.

"I—" I blurted out, coming to my senses just in time to shut up.

"You what?" he asked.

I had nearly just said that I loved him. Worse, everything inside me was still aching to do it.

"Nothing," I said, shaking my head.

"No, what were you going to say?"

Pulling his lips back down to mine, I murmured up against them. "Just that I wish you would kiss me again."

Sophomore Honors English
Mrs. Conway
Monday, January 19

Dear Grandma,

Happy Martin Luther King Jr. Day! Trevor and I had a holiday today. The weird part was, so did Dad.

Did Mom call to tell you Dad quit his job Friday? Probably not, because she's not too happy about it. She wanted him to go back to work today and tell Percy he temporarily lost his mind but that he feels much better now. Dad says all he lost is a seven-year migraine and he *is* much better now.

The truth is, he's acting a little weird. Like this morning, when I got up, Mom was at work and Dad was making pancakes in the shape of Martin Luther King's profile. Trying to make them, I should say, because when they came out looking like blobs, he switched to letters spelling *DREAM*.

"Dr. King was a great man and this is a great day!" he declared, plopping down plates in front of me and Trevor. "Free at last, free at last. Thank God Almighty, I am free at last!"

What's a person supposed to say to

that? I'm pretty sure Dad quitting his job isn't what Dr. King had in mind. But he just kept smiling at us, all happy. I think I asked for the syrup.

Then tonight, when Mom got home, she asked Dad if he'd been working on his résumé. He said he'd do it "*mañana*." But as soon as she left the room, he told us, "*Mañana*'s a beautiful word. It doesn't mean 'tomorrow,' it just means 'not today.'"

I feel like I'm living with a stranger. I want to shake him and yell, "Where is my father and what have you done with him?" Except that those pancakes were pretty good. And he's been in a killer great mood for three straight days. Honestly, I'd be enjoying this if Mom weren't so stressed-out.

I heard them arguing last night. Dad said, "Andrea, you're a *lawyer*. It's not like we're going to starve." But she still wants him back at a job right away. She says any gap in employment history looks deadly on a résumé. You didn't hear it from me, but Mom might be a little obsessed with résumés.

Anyway, Dad will start looking for a new job this week and everything will go back to normal—normal being a relative term in a family that includes Trevor. He wasted this entire three-day weekend inventing a row of training wheels to put on the back of his skateboard. He calls it a wheelie bar.

Right. Sure it is.

I hope you're doing fine, and that it's not too cold in Ohio. When it's all snowy on the ground, how do people drive?

Love,
Cassie

Random Acts of Charity

Wednesday's first talent show rehearsal couldn't have been what Conway was hoping for, but she did a pretty good job of hiding her disappointment.

"That was . . . forceful," she declared after our aspiring thespian finished shouting his monologue. "It's good to carry to the back of the room. But remember, we will have a microphone."

The juggler dropped his balls and nearly knocked himself out with a wild bowling pin. Conway decided he just needed more practice.

The string quartet from band was actually good, but their long piece of classical music left everybody snoozing.

"Very soothing," Mrs. Conway said, frantically reworking her program. "That will make a nice break somewhere."

A bunch of people, like Hayley and Fitz, hadn't expected to perform so soon and didn't have anything ready.

But the biggest joke of all had to be Sterling. The little diva had been given the opening act, exactly as requested, but she flat-out refused to sing, claiming to have some sort of nodule on her vocal cords.

"My coach says I shouldn't stress my voice by singing outside of lessons," she announced, handing Conway a CD. "Here's my music. If you want, we can work on the staging."

"Staging" turned out to mean that we were all subjected to a karaoke version of "Wind Beneath My Wings" (did anyone *ever* like that song?) while Sterling strutted around silently mouthing the words into a pretend microphone.

The worst moment for me personally was when Mrs. Conway asked what my act would be.

"Well," I said. "Hayley and I talked about doing something together, but—"

"A duo with Hayley?" Conway got busy with her pencil again. "That would be great. I'm putting you girls behind Sterling."

"The second act?" I protested.

But between the triumphant look Hayley shot me and the way Mrs. Conway forged ahead, I couldn't argue. Not right then, anyway.

Fitz's magic routine was given the next-to-last spot in the show. Kevin got put in charge of lights and sound. And Ros stayed on publicity, which didn't require being anywhere near the stage.

"That's all we have time for today," Conway finally announced. "We'll meet again on Friday, and I should have our tickets by then. With five hundred seats in here, we'll need to sell about twenty each."

She was walking out the auditorium's side door when I bolted after her.

"Mrs. Conway?" I called. "Can I talk to you a minute?"

She stopped outside in the hall. "What is it, Cassie?"

"About the show . . . I really want to help backstage."

"Oh. There's not much glory in that, you know."

"That's fine. I mean, it's not about me, right?"

"Well, okay. Why don't you be our stage manager? You can make sure all the props and people get where they're supposed to be."

"Great!" I said enthusiastically.

"And since you and Hayley are the second act, you'll be free nice and early to work for the rest of the show."

"What? No!"

Conway lifted one brow in that heart-stopping way of hers.

"I mean, I want to work backstage the *whole* time," I explained politely.

"And not be onstage at all?"

"Exactly."

"Oh, no, Cassie," she said. "What fun would that be?"

Not-So-Model Behavior

I was walking back into the auditorium, still trying to figure out whether Mrs. Conway was serious about making me stay in the second act, when I realized I had bigger fish to fry: Tiffi Hughes was all over Kevin.

Not that she was actually touching him. Not yet. But she'd switched into my old seat and was pressing against its flimsy armrest like she couldn't wait to get closer. Even Kevin had to realize what she wanted. I mean, guys can be slow, but she was practically drawing him a map to her bedroom.

I hustled up the side aisle, my heart pounding double time as I edged down the row behind them. I heard Tiffi babbling as I got closer.

"You could!" she was insisting. "I get lots of magazines, and you're as cute as any guy in them. Have you ever had head shots or anything?"

I won't deny it. The first time I saw Kevin, I thought he should model too. But I never actually told him that. And now that he was my boyfriend, having girls drooling over his picture was obviously a truly bad idea.

"My hands were in an ad once." Tiffi stretched out her slender fingers, rings sparkling on every one. "Do you think I have nice hands?"

"Yeah. They're pretty," he said.

I shoved my chipped nails into my pockets as I continued to close the distance.

"You should let me introduce you to my agent," Tiffi said. "We can go there tomorrow if you want."

"Tomorrow?" Kevin *should* have looked like that was the worst idea he'd ever heard. Unfortunately, he didn't. "I'd have to—"

"Hi!" I blurted out, afraid to let him finish. "I'm back!"

"There you are!" Tiffi said, all fake sugar. "We were afraid you'd gotten lost."

You wish, I thought, steaming. But I took a deep breath. And I took Ros's advice.

"Hello, Tiffi!" I said, with enough fake syrup of my own to open a House of Pancakes. "Thanks for keeping Kevin company for me. Are you ready to go, Kevin?"

"Well, yeah. I just—"

"Perfect!" Grabbing his hand, I hauled him to his feet. "Do you mind if we stop by my locker? We can go to yours too."

"I guess that's—"

"Great. See you later, Tiffi!"

She didn't say a word as we walked away, and Kevin didn't either. I kept up a steady commentary—the talent show, our English homework, Ros's party on Saturday—to make sure he didn't get the chance.

"So what are we doing tomorrow?" I wrapped up as we reached my locker. "After school, I mean."

"I didn't know we were doing anything."

I got this hollow feeling in my gut. "You, uh . . . you don't have other plans, do you?"

"No."

"Then don't make any," I said. "I'll come up with something."

"Oh, yeah? Like what?"

Like keeping you far, far away from Tiffi Hughes and her evil modeling empire, I thought. *Like spending all afternoon thinking only of each other. Like making you say you love me.*

But I just smiled mysteriously, needing time to come up with something I could actually say.

Tate the Snake

That night, after dinner, my dad dropped me and Hayley off at the mall.

"Do you know what you're wearing to the party?" I asked her as we headed for Visions, our favorite store.

"No, and I'm still broke from Christmas. I'm going to check out the mannequins. Maybe I can make a new outfit from something I already have."

We were just outside Visions's front door when Hayley stopped abruptly. "Isn't that Bryce Tate?" she asked, pointing across the courtyard. "Who's that girl he's with?"

Sure enough, Tate and some girl were hogging a bench in the shadows. He had one arm around her shoulders and his free hand under her jacket. Their faces touched at the forehead as they gazed into each other's eyes.

"His sister?" I guessed.

"Eew. Don't be gross."

"*He's* gross. At Bonfire he slapped my butt."

"You said nothing happened!"

"Nothing did. But . . . he might have asked if I wanted it to."

Hayley stared in disbelief.

"Maybe. I'm not sure."

Hayley turned her gaze back to the bench. "*That* looks pretty sure. Do you think he's cheating on Sterling?"

A vision of Tate and Angie flitted into my mind, but whatever that hallway encounter had been, it obviously hadn't gone anywhere.

"I think he just likes to play around. Like take it as far as he can without actually doing anything."

"Cassie!" she squealed. "They're kissing!"

For a second, we both stared. Then Hayley grabbed my arm and pulled me into Visions.

"What do we tell her?" she asked, peering out the window through a sweater display.

"Tell who? Sterling? Nothing!"

"Girls ought to look out for each other," Hayley argued.

"She'd never believe us anyway."

"She'd believe Ros."

"Maybe. But what if we're wrong? Shouldn't we just mind our own business?"

Hayley gave me an incredulous look.

"It's one kiss! Besides, what do I owe Sterling?"

"Nothing," she admitted grudgingly.

"Believe me, Sterling Carter can take care of herself. Tate is the one who had better watch out."

Home Alone? I Wish!

Thursday I had a horrifying realization: it didn't matter how much I bribed Trevor to leave me and Kevin alone after school, because my dad was going to be home. We could still hang out, but we wouldn't have two seconds of privacy.

"It doesn't matter," Kevin said at his locker after lunch. "I've got a ton of homework anyway."

"Then let's go to the library. We'll get one of those tables in back. If we're lucky, no one else will be around."

Anything to keep him away from Tiffi and her stupid modeling agency.

But Kevin shook his head. "We never accomplish anything in there. I'd better just go home."

"Are you sure?"

"Yeah. I'll miss you, but I'll see you tomorrow."

No, are you sure you're going home? The words were right on my tongue, but somehow I choked them back.

"We have rehearsal tomorrow," I reminded him.

"I know."

"And Ros's party Saturday."

"Which is why I need to get these assignments finished today."

By the time I got home from school, I was in a rotten mood.

"You have to see this!" Trevor greeted me at the door. "Dad is baking cookies!"

"Are they edible?"

"If you don't eat the burnt parts."

"Great. I'll be in my room."

Trevor followed me down the hall. "Wait. How about this weekend? There's a party, right?"

I froze. "Why? What did you hear?"

"Ha!" he shouted. "I knew you were hiding something! What time should I be ready?"

"I'm not hiding anything," I told him, annoyed. "This party's by invitation only. And since you don't have an invitation, why bother mentioning it?"

"Does Julie have an invitation?"

"I doubt it."

"Then you have to get them for us."

"Forget it. The deal was that I'd sneak you into some open party, not score you two written invitations."

"I'm telling Mom," Trevor threatened.

"Nothing would amuse me more."

We faced off in the hallway, staring each other down.

"Cassie! Trevor!" Dad bellowed from the kitchen. "Come try these cookies. I melted chocolate on top!"

I blinked at the mention of chocolate. "Be reasonable, Trevor. Let's just go eat Dad's cookies."

"Go without me," he said sullenly, heading into his room.

"Oh, what? Now you're going to sulk?"

"I'm not hungry."

"No, because you're pining away with love and I'm ruining your life, right?" I asked sarcastically from his doorway.

"Okay."

His bedsprings squeaked as he flopped melodramatically onto his mattress, heaving a broken sigh.

"Fine. Stay here and mope," I said.

"I will."

"Good."

I left him staring at his ceiling, refusing to feel guilty about something I couldn't help.

Probably.

"Cassie!" Dad said excitedly as I walked into the kitchen. "You have to try these. They're my own recipe."

Dad's cookies were lumpy, lopsided blobs, but they *were* covered with chocolate. Picking one up, I took a big bite.

"Good, right?" he asked as it crumbled into saliva-stopping dust on my tongue. "Biscuit mix and apple juice."

"Mmm," I said, trying to smile and starting to cough. Puffs of powdery crumbs blew out the corners of my mouth.

"How about a glass of milk with that?"

"Mmm!" I said, nodding frantically.

Dad opened the fridge and slapped his forehead. "Oops, we're out. Hey, you know what? With all this free time I have now, I can run to the grocery store before your mother gets home. Do me a favor, Cassie: wash up these dishes for me."

I would have loved to argue, but I was choking at the time. As soon as he left, I stuck my head under the sink and drank about a gallon of water. Then I spent the next half hour scrubbing burnt cookie sheets, mixing bowls, and utensils.

And the whole time I ached for Kevin.

He was probably at home, doing his homework, like he said.

But what if he wasn't? Even thinking about where he might be instead made me sick to my stomach. Sicker, I should say, since Dad's cookie was churning around in all that water like a rock in a washing machine.

If Kevin really loved me, I didn't have to worry.

But what if he didn't? What if he was tired of me, or he'd finally opened his eyes and realized he could do better?

Tiffi pried them open, more like, I thought.

Finishing the dishes, I holed up in my room and joined Trevor in his sulkfest.

If there's anything more depressing than thinking your boyfriend might not love you, it's imagining him loving someone else.

Party Politics

At lunch on Friday, the whole school was buzzing about Ros's party. The six of us had a table, but we could barely carry on a conversation with all the people walking up to ask about Saturday night.

"Nearly everyone I invited is coming," Ros reported as the third or fourth group walked away. "I've lost track of how many people that is."

Fitz stripped the paper off his straw. "Give us a ballpark figure."

"Around two hundred, I guess."

"Two hundred!" Kevin exclaimed.

Ros allowed herself a small, pleased smile. "If you're going to have a band, you want people to hear it."

"Imagine how many would come if it were an open party," I said.

"That would be a *disaster*!" Ros proclaimed, reverting to

her old soc-y tone. "I'd never hear the end of it when my parents get home from Europe."

"Wait—huh?" Hayley said. "Your parents are in Europe?"

Ros's eyes widened as she realized her slip. "They're skiing, but keep that to yourselves, okay? It'll only encourage crashers."

"But it's your sixteenth birthday!" Hayley protested.

"Which is why they're paying for this major party." Ros took on a cynical air. "I'm pretty sure I'll get a car out of this deal too, so don't feel sorry for me."

I didn't. But Hayley was already brimming with unwanted sympathy. "You won't be lonely without them?"

"I'm used to it," Ros said.

Quentin put his arm around his girlfriend's shoulders.

"Yes, but—"

"Hayley! It doesn't bother her." I was actually starting to suspect it might, but that seemed like all the more reason for us to stay out of it.

"Hey, Ros!" Brian Nickerson and a couple of his friends walked up to interrupt us. "We heard you're having a party Saturday night."

"Yes, and I wish I could invite more people, but my parents set a limit."

"Oh, yeah. That's cool," Brian said, like he hadn't just been angling for an invitation.

"Happy birthday," one of the guys added as they walked off.

"I feel bad turning people away," Ros told us. "But no matter how hard you try to keep these things quiet, news always leaks out."

"It's not easy keeping a live band quiet," Fitz said.

"He's right," I said. "You should have seen my brother yesterday, throwing a fit because he wanted to come. And he's only in eighth grade! You'd have chaos if you opened this thing up."

"Without a doubt. But I could make an exception for your brother."

"Excuse me?" Blood whooshed in my ears, explaining why I must have misheard her.

"Sure. That's totally different, Cassie. If you want to bring Trevor, it's okay with me."

But what about the limit? What about your parents? I thought, speechless.

Why had I even mentioned Trevor?

And that was when I realized that everyone at the table was waiting for my answer. My cheeks turned hot. My brain hit a wall. So much sudden pressure . . .

I never should have let Trevor make me feel guilty.

"Well, see . . . the thing is . . . ," I stammered. "It's more complicated than I made it sound."

Ros looked intrigued. Except how could I explain without breaking Trevor's rules of silence? *If he really wants to go to this thing, he has to compromise,* I decided.

"Trevor has a desperate crush on this freshman, Julie Evans. He's convinced himself that if they end up at some party together she'll fall madly in love with him."

"How cute!" Ros cooed.

"How deluded, you mean. I don't think Julie even knows who he is."

"I know who she is," Ros said. "She's in my French class."

"Really?"

"*Mais oui*. I could ask why she hasn't RSVPed, pretend her invitation got lost . . . I mean, if you want me to."

Did I want her to? I'd opened this Pandora's box, but it wasn't too late to slam on the lid.

"You should do it," Hayley urged. "A promise is a promise."

"Besides, it's sweet," Ros said. "I'll feel just like Cupid."

"Well . . . if you're positive you don't mind," I finally said. "But you guys all have to pretend you don't know what's going on. Plus, Julie can't guess it's a setup or Trevor will kill me."

"You take care of your brother and leave Julie to me," Ros replied with a wink.

She seemed so pleased about the whole thing that I couldn't help feeling guilty. Not about Trevor anymore— after all those weeks of stressing, I was actually kind of relieved to be getting out of his debt. No, I felt guilty about Ros.

Considering how nice she was to me, I really should have liked her more.

Dog Day Afternoon

Whenever things start going right for me, I ought to lock myself in a cage, because as long as I'm out walking around, it's only a matter of time.

And not a lot of time, in this case.

It all started in badminton.

I was wearing shorts again by then, my hideous fake tan a distant memory, and Coach Crawford had teamed us up against Abby Anderson and Kari Buchanon. So far, so good. But Sterling and Tiffi took the court next to ours, and they wouldn't give it a rest.

"I just don't get it," Tiffi said between shots, pitching her voice for me to hear. "It's like pairing Best in Show with a shelter mutt."

"He's not *that* great," Sterling said. "I was plenty sick of him."

"Yeah, but he was lucky to get you. That's an entirely different deal."

Sterling beamed and served the bird, temporarily suspending gossip.

"Cassie!" Hayley exclaimed, crossing to my side of the court. "Are you paying attention?"

"I sure am. Did she just call me a shelter mutt?"

"What? It's your serve."

Hayley held out a shuttle while across the net Abby and Kari stared impatiently.

"Didn't you hear that?" I insisted. "Are they talking about me?"

"I wasn't listening—I'm paying attention. To the game. Which we're losing, by the way, if you'd like to help me out."

I tried to concentrate after that and I hit a few good shots. Then I saw Tiffi and Sterling giggling and clearly heard the words *Captain Carrots*.

"Okay, they're definitely talking about me," I insisted.

"Pretend they aren't there," Hayley advised. "That'll get them back."

"For calling me a *shelter mutt*? Oh, yeah, ignoring them makes us totally even."

We lost the game, which drove Hayley crazy. The whole time we were in the locker room, showering and changing for rehearsal, she badgered me about how lousy I'd played.

"It's only badminton!" I finally burst out on our way to the auditorium. "I have more important things on my mind."

"It just sucks to lose when we should have won."

"Welcome to my world," I muttered.

In the hallway outside the main entrance, we ran into Sterling and Tiffi.

"Look who's here," Tiffi said. "Oh, goody."

All right. In hindsight, perhaps *oh, goody* aren't really fighting words. But when you factor in *mutt* and *Captain Carrots*, is it any wonder I finally snapped?

"What is your problem?" I asked. "Do you have any idea how pathetic you are, following Sterling around like a lost little puppy? You're not even in this show, so why don't you go find a life of your own?"

I braced myself for a scathing reply. But to my surprise, Tiffi's eyes went all big and helpless. "I didn't know I was bothering anyone."

"How could it *not* bother people, the way your lips are attached to Sterling's butt? You're never going to be her, you know. You'll never be more than her pale, sad shadow."

An amazed grin spread across Sterling's face. I should

have realized right then that something was up, but I figured she just liked the compliment.

"Why are you so mean?" Tiffi whimpered. "I've never done *any*thing to you."

"Are you serious? You're more irritating than a permanent diaper rash."

Sterling burst out laughing. And that was when I finally noticed that neither she nor Tiffi was looking directly at me. Instead, their gazes were aimed at something right behind my shoulder. Turning my head, I found Kevin glaring.

"Hey!" I exclaimed nervously. "How long have you been back there?"

"Long enough," he said.

The merest hint of a smirk played at the corners of Tiffi's mouth.

"For what? That? That wasn't what it sounded like," I said urgently.

"Really? Because it sounded pretty rude."

"Yes, but—"

"You know what? I'm not going to be at rehearsal today."

"But we need you!"

"Suddenly, I'm not in the mood." He turned and started walking.

"Kevin!"

I tossed Hayley a desperate glance and caught Tiffi grinning, loving the mess she'd created. That whole shrinking violet act . . . She'd seen Kevin coming!

And I'd played right into her hands.

"Kevin, wait!" I cried, running after him.

I caught up partway down the hall. "Listen, you're not mad at me, are you? Because Tiffi—"

"I thought you were nice, Cassie."

"What? I am nice!"

"Nicer, then."

I stopped, stunned, watching as he walked off without me. He'd gotten the whole thing wrong.

So why didn't I feel more right?

Second-guessing

Rehearsal was a nightmare, what with Kevin AWOL and Tiffi gloating and me wanting to cry the whole time. I could barely believe what had just happened.

I had no idea what it meant.

Were Kevin and I still together? Or was our first fight as a couple our last? And how could he be so angry when he didn't even know what had happened? The way he'd just stalked off . . . Should I be mad at him?

Only one thing seemed crystal clear: we wouldn't be going to Ros's party. Nothing short of a miracle could patch us up in twenty-four hours.

When I finally got home, the last thing I wanted to hear was my parents arguing about résumés, official holidays, and whether or not we needed one of those "cool" new vacuums with the gravity cyclones, but those were the topics at dinner. For a man who used to run miles to avoid a conflict, my dad has turned over a whole new leaf.

I left the table at the first opportunity. I didn't even tell Trevor about his miraculous last-minute party invitation. Now that we weren't going, it seemed cruel to torture him. Besides, if I even mentioned the party I knew I would burst into tears.

Shutting my bedroom door, I flopped back on my bed and stared at the ceiling with stinging eyes. I was too depressed to watch TV, so I was obviously way too depressed to do my homework. Or call Hayley. Or pretty much anything else. I had just decided to lie there until I turned eighteen and Mom made me move out, when a noise outside my window jolted me upright.

The best thing about ranch houses is that there aren't any stairs. The worst thing is that all the windows are at ground level. When I was little, I used to have nightmares about a monster climbing in through my bedroom window, but the scariest thing Dad ever chased out of those bushes was a couple of cats in heat. Whatever was flattening my flowers now, though, was tons bigger than a cat.

I crept to my feet and stood paralyzed, eyes glued to my closed blinds, ready to sprint for my father. . . .

Something clunked into the glass. I gathered myself for a bloodcurdling scream.

"Cassie!" Kevin hissed. "Cassie, are you in there or what?"

Forcing my feet into motion, I hurried to the window and fumbled the sash open. "What are you doing? Why didn't you come to the door?"

"Shhh! I wanted to surprise you."

He'd surprised me, all right. My heart was pounding

halfway out of my chest. But that racing heartbeat wasn't all fear. He looked so adorable standing there in my bushes, his face lit by the glow from my room. . . .

Did he want to make up?

"So, are you coming in?" I whispered.

"Yeah. Here, this is for you." Producing a small potted plant from behind his back, he handed it to me through the window and climbed in over the sill.

"For me?" No one had ever given me a plant before and I wasn't quite sure what to make of it. Flowers are clearly romantic. But a houseplant? "It's cute."

"Not as cute as you are."

Taking the plant from my hands, he put it on my dresser. Then he wrapped his arms around me and lowered his face close to mine. "I wish today had never happened."

"Kevin—" I began.

He pressed a finger to my lips. "Because the more I thought about it, the more I realized you would never be that mean without a reason. I should have stayed to listen. I'm sorry."

"No, *I'm* sorry. I should have kept my big mouth shut. It's just . . . Tiffi's not nearly as sweet as you think she is. Anytime I see her near you, I just go nuts inside."

"Don't you trust me?"

His question took me by surprise. "Well . . . but . . . you don't see what she's up to."

"I'd have to be blind not to see it. That doesn't mean I'm interested."

"Then why don't you tell her to knock it off?"

"Because she's not hurting anything. She's just talking."

"But—"

"Listen, Cassie, do you trust me?"

"Yes, but—"

"No buts. Do you trust me or not?"

"It's not about you!"

"See, that's where you're wrong. It's all about me. All about me and you."

My knees went wobbly even before he kissed me. Then our mouths came together and the rest of the world disappeared. I forgot that we were in the middle of my embarrassingly messy room, forgot that my parents and Trevor could have their ears pressed to my door. For one blissfully perfect moment, I even forgot about Tiffi. That kiss said everything—the way we felt about each other, the way we'd always feel. . . .

His body pressed more insistently to mine. His hands wandered lower and the spell was broken.

"Wait," I said, pulling away. "I would seriously hate to explain to my mother why you didn't come through the front door. Especially tonight."

Kevin's grin was full of mischief. If he guessed a potential busting by my mother wasn't the only reason I'd stopped things, he didn't let on. "I have to get home anyway."

"How did you get here?"

"My bike." He dropped one last kiss on my lips, then climbed out over my sill. "See you tomorrow," he said, dissolving into the darkness.

"I'll miss you!" I whispered.

"Miss you back" carried to me from the sidewalk.

Pedals squeaked. His wheels bumped over the curb.

And then I realized something.

"Wait!" I cried, totally forgetting to be quiet. "Does this mean we're going to Ros's party?"

> His eyes follow her,
> But only his heart matters.
> I'm a fool. Again.

Driving It Home

Trevor nearly had a fainting spell when I told him about his invitation to Edgemont Manor. My mom was a little less thrilled, but she eventually relented—after imposing a ridiculously early curfew.

"You're both too young to be out past midnight," she said. "Besides, that's as late as I want to come get you."

Quentin was driving us to the party, but since he was staying late with Ros, we had to find our own ride home.

"Let Dad pick us up," I suggested. "He likes doing errands now that he's not working."

My mother squinted irritably over her mug of tea. Dark circles ringed her eyes, like maybe she hadn't been sleeping much. "Are you certain you want to open that topic?"

"Fine. But my birthday's only a month away. You guys could give yourselves a break in the driving department."

She gestured to her haggard face. "You're standing right in front of me. . . . Does this *look* like a good time to mention your license?"

"It's never a good time," I grumbled. "At this rate I'll forget how to drive before you let me do it again."

"And I'll bet you wish you'd thought of that before you took your father's car."

If anyone knows how to make a point, it's my mother.

High Society

Edgemont Manor was even more deluxe than I'd imagined. I'd been prepared for a fancy house (*manor* pretty much covers that), but the yard—excuse me, the *grounds* were like a set from a Disney movie. A golf course–sized lawn sprawled in front of a turreted castle, thousands of white twinkle lights illuminating every manicured tree and shrub.

"This place is crazy!" Fitz told Quentin as we rolled up the long, winding drive. "How come you never mentioned that?"

"Well, you know," Quentin said uncomfortably. "To Ros, it's just her house."

"More like her palace," said Kevin.

"We knew she was rich, but this is *rich*," said Hayley.

"Please don't act impressed," Quentin begged. "This stuff is normal to her."

"I could get used to it," Trevor declared from the passenger seat. He was wearing new jeans, sneakers, a preppy blue blazer, and, despite my repeated threats to shove his head under a faucet, about a pound of hair gel. Oh, yeah—and Dad's cologne. He smelled like a collision between a coconut tree and a perfume truck.

"You won't have a chance to get used to it," I told him. "Just try not to embarrass me."

"Hey!" he said, offended. "When it comes to embarrassing yourself, *I'm* not the one you need to worry about."

I would have loved to throttle him, but Quentin had just pulled up to the front of the mansion, where a valet in a red vest ran out to meet us. We all piled out of the van and stood staring, awed by the splashing marble fountain in the driveway and the open, ten-foot-tall front doors. I slipped my hand into Kevin's and tried to comprehend the massive, *Phantom of the Opera*–style chandelier in the vaulted entryway.

"We're not in Kansas anymore," I breathed, prompting nervous chuckles. Even Trevor had the sense to look a little less cocky. Then a Land Rover pulled up and we hurried inside before we got caught gawking like a busload of tourists.

"I'm going to find Ros—catch you guys later," Quentin said, taking off.

"Mmm," I said, distracted.

The thing about a valet whisking away all the cars is, you don't know how many people are inside until you walk in and see them. Ros's enormous living room was packed with a standing-room-only crowd that pressed close to the roaring fireplace and spilled through the large arched doorways into the other rooms. Most of the guys wore jeans or khakis, but rhinestones and glitter glimmered on girls who had come dressed to dance. There was plenty of bare skin too, defying the January weather and making the guys' heads swivel. I felt a pang of regret that I'd opted for such a tame long skirt and top, but at least I'd worn my sparkly eye shadow.

"Look at that buffet!" Fitz said reverentially, heading through the entryway toward a staggering display of snacks visible in the adjacent room. Fruit, cheese, and hors d'oeuvres in silver dishes loaded one long line of tables, while a triple-tiered silver and white iced birthday cake towered on its own special stand.

"It figures Fitz is thinking of food," I told Kevin, squeezing his hand appreciatively as Hayley took off after him.

"He is kind of skinny."

"It's not that. It's just . . ." How did I explain it, the way Hayley and Fitz always found the least romantic course of action? "Wouldn't you rather walk around? See stuff?"

"Okay."

We started crossing the room. Trevor stuck right to our heels.

"Aren't you supposed to be looking for someone?" I asked.

"I'm looking. And when I find her, you're supposed to introduce us, so don't think you're ditching me now. I don't care how much you guys want to play tonsil hockey."

Charming. If you haven't experienced the joys of a little brother, you can't begin to imagine.

"Listen, Trevor," I said, turning red. "Back up a few paces, all right? Do you want Julie to think you're afraid to make a move without your big sis?"

That got through to him. He trailed us from a distance after that as we wandered through the manor.

The property behind Ros's house was even more of a soc fantasy than the front. Twinkle lights blanketed the backyard, too, whole masses of them strung in lines over-head like the starry roof of an open pavilion. A real wooden dance floor occupied the center of a huge stone patio, and on the patio's other side was an actual concert stage draped in black fabric and more twinkle lights.

"Wow," said Kevin.

"You're not kidding," I agreed, squeezing his hand again.

"Hey! There you guys are," Quentin said, walking up with his arm around Ros's shoulders. She was wearing something out of Paris Hilton's closet—pink, short, and in serious danger of a wardrobe malfunction. "Cool stage, huh?"

"When's the band going on?" I asked.

"Pretty soon," Ros promised. "We want everyone to get here first, so right now the guys are hanging out in the pool house."

"The Answer is in your pool house?" I didn't even try to hide how impressed I was.

"If you have a pool house, where's your pool?" a voice piped up behind me. Trevor had resumed the hover position.

"Under the dance floor," Ros said. "That floor's just portable sections. The grounds crew set it up yesterday."

"Wow," Kevin said again.

Quentin gave him a pleading look—apparently we weren't supposed to notice everyday things like live bands, grounds crews, and portable dance floors.

"Where are Fitz and Hayley?" Ros asked.

"Eating. I think," I replied.

"Oh, yeah. You've got to check out the spread," Quentin

told us. "They've got these crab-stuffed mushrooms I could eat by the tray load."

"Let's go get some," Trevor said.

"Good idea," I told him. "Why don't *you* do that?"

He gave me a huffy look before he stalked off toward the house.

"So that's your little brother?" Ros asked.

Too late I realized I should have introduced them. She was already in on the whole deal, so my cover was blown with her anyway.

"Yeah, sorry," I said.

"He's cute."

"You don't have to lie."

Ros shook her head. "Why do girls always think their brothers are ugly? If I were lucky enough to have a brother, I'd appreciate him."

"Why do only children never realize how good they have it?" I asked with a sigh.

"I'm not an only child," Ros protested. "I have an older sister. She lives in France."

"You never told me that!" Quentin said.

"I must have. Are you sure?"

"I think I'd remember," he told her, pouting.

"Uh-oh, here comes the lip," she said in a little girl voice. "I'm gonna get it!"

"No," he said childishly.

Ros made pincers with her fingers. "Yes, I am," she persisted. "I'm gonna get that lip."

Her fingers pinched closer, her mouth right behind them.

"You couldn't get it," Quentin dared her in a sulky tone. It was so clear he wanted her to.

"Yes, I can. Here I come!"

Before I could look away, Ros launched herself at him and planted one on his kisser. I turned a pained face to Kevin, expecting him to share my disgust, but he just stared back at me like I was the one with the problem.

I am *the one with the problem*, I realized. I'd been so worried about Tiffi stealing Kevin that I'd barely thought of Quentin for days. But now all of a sudden . . .

A hand landed on my shoulder.

"Hey there, Red," said Tate the Great.

Have we discussed the utter lack of imagination that results in nicknames like Red?

"Hey," I returned sullenly, shrugging away from him and glaring at Sterling. She was attached to his hip like a bad case of cellulite, but Bryce didn't seem to notice.

"Kevin, my man!" he brayed, slapping Kevin on the back. "Long time, no see!"

Kevin and I exchanged bewildered looks before the truth sank in. Tate was drunk. Again.

"How's it going?" Kevin said, moving out of range.

"Ros!" Sterling cooed. "Happy birthday!"

They traded air kisses, which has to be the sociest thing ever. They probably learn it along with ballroom dancing, how to speak to the help, and the way to pronounce *petits fours*.

"What did Quentin give you?" Sterling asked.

Ros pointed proudly to a chain around her neck, from

which a gold star dangled. Envy stabbed so hard it made me wince—until I remembered my own birthday was coming and Kevin would have to give me something. Hopefully jewelry. The kind that would prove we were serious too.

Tate whistled. "That's a lot of *dinero*," he said, cuffing Quentin's shoulder.

"I earned it," Quentin replied.

"I can't believe you work at a grocery store now," Sterling said in her most condescending voice. "What exactly do you do there? Mop up spills on aisle five?"

Quentin tensed and for a moment I thought he was finally going to tell her off. But one look at Ros and he exhaled.

"Aisle five, aisle six," he said. "No one mops up a spill like I do."

"Dude!" Bryce jumped in. "This one time, me and some guys from the team were buying eggs, and we had like ten dozen or something, and Baker insisted on carrying them all himself. So Rodriguez *tripped* him. Right in the middle of the store. First Baker's like, 'Aaahhh,' trying to juggle everything, and the cartons are opening and eggs are flying out. And then he falls right on them. I've never seen a mess like that in my life! Eggs splattered everywhere, loose eggs rolling down the aisle . . . *Hilarious*, dude."

"Did you have to pay for them?" Quentin asked.

"The eggs? How would I know?" Tate looked like he'd never heard a lamer question. "I hightailed it out with the rest of the team and let Baker deal with it."

"What a lovely story," Hayley said, appearing at my side. "You must be so proud," she told Sterling.

Which was pretty catty for Hayley, but that's how she gets when people are rude to her friends. She'd obviously been behind me long enough to hear the whole thing.

"You know what?" Ros said nervously. "We'd better go check on the band." She pulled Quentin away before things could get uglier.

"Whoo-hoo! The Answer!" Tate bellowed, pumping his fist in the air. People on the patio started cheering, thinking the band was coming on. Sterling grabbed his arm and practically crawled up to his ear, whispering urgently.

"Listen," Hayley told me during the distraction. "I don't know if you care, but Trevor is camped at the buffet table, eating his weight in shrimp. People are starting to notice."

"Great," I moaned. "I knew he'd embarrass me."

"I'll go get him," Kevin offered.

"No, I'll go. If this is how he's going to act, I—"

There's no telling how I might have finished that sentence, because I never got the chance. I had barely stepped toward the house when my brain was completely derailed by the sight of Tiffi Hughes. She was wearing this disco-bikini-halter-top thing consisting mostly of bare midriff and blue feathers. Her black leather pants were cut so low her hip bones jutted into space. Gold dust gleamed in her long, tousled curls and highlighted her red lips, which were pursed to make sure we'd notice.

"Hello, Kevin," she purred, walking right past me. "I didn't know if you'd be here tonight."

"Why wouldn't I be?" he asked.

"No reason. Just . . . things come up." She was obviously

talking about our fight on Friday, but, as usual, Kevin seemed lost in the dark.

"I try to plan ahead," he said.

"That's smart," she murmured, moving in closer. "I try to plan ahead too, but something keeps getting in my way."

Must . . . kill . . . her . . . now, I thought, breathing in ragged gasps. I felt Hayley's hand on my elbow, ready to clamp down if I moved.

"Tonight, for example," Tiffi continued, "the guy I wanted to bring me here was already bringing someone else."

Sterling sniggered. My blood pressure rose until I had cartoon steam coming out my ears.

"You'll have fun on your own," Kevin said. "There are plenty of guys here to dance with."

"I never said I came alone. And I *always* have a good time." She gave him one last, lingering smile before slinking away, her hips vibrating like a paint shaker.

"She's doing it again," I told Kevin through clenched teeth.

"I'm a big boy," he reminded me. "Your brother, on the other hand . . ."

"Oh, that's right!" I cried, hurrying off to remove my shrimp from the shrimp.

Cupidity

The Answer was halfway through its first set when I spotted Julie Evans. To be more accurate, Trevor spotted her and came shoving through the crowd to interrupt me and Kevin in the middle of the dance floor.

"She's here!" he said, all flustered. "I just saw her walk in."

"All right," I told him over the music. "When this song is over I'll—"

"*Now,* Cassie!"

It will be a long cold day someplace very, very hot before I let myself owe Trevor again.

I danced closer to Kevin. "I have to go take care of this thing for Trevor," I yelled. "I'll be back in a few minutes."

"No problem. I'll hang out and listen to the band." He pointed to the dark far edge of the patio, to show me where he'd be waiting. Sighing, I left with Trev.

Inside the house, the rooms were more crowded than ever. I'd assumed everyone would come outside once the music started, but the place was packed with people eating and fooling around. And it wasn't like you couldn't hear the band. With everyone shouting to be heard, it was as loud inside as out.

"There she is! By the fireplace," Trevor yelled in my ear.

"You go talk to her, and I'll cruise by in a minute, like I'm just passing through. Then you can stop me and introduce us."

"Are you sure that's stealthy enough for you? Maybe we should have code names. Or secret decoder rings!" I made a sound like radio static. "Red Dog One to Red Dog Two—"

"Cassie!"

"Fine. I'm going."

It wasn't easy working my way through the crowd to Julie—even less so making my progress look casual—but eventually I stopped beside her. She was tucked in close to the roaring flames, her hands rubbing up and down her bare arms.

"Hey, Julie," I said, rubbing my own arms and pretending I needed to warm up too. "Pretty cold outside, huh?"

Mercifully, she recognized me. "Hi, Cassie."

"You heat up once you start dancing, though."

"Have you been dancing?"

"Yeah. The band is great!"

"But you're still cold."

"What? No, I'm n— Oh," I said, dropping the arm-rubbing act. "That's because I *stopped* dancing. I'll be fine once I get back out there."

She gave me a strange look. Let's face it—I'm used to that.

"So . . . cute outfit," I said, praying Trevor would hurry.

"Do you think so?" she asked eagerly. "I could barely believe Ros invited me—I had no idea what to wear."

"Yeah, I didn't know either."

"But you were Snow Queen runner-up!"

"If that title comes with fashion superpowers, someone forgot to fill me in."

Julie gave me a courtesy laugh. "Now must be a lot different for you than middle school."

"It's different for everyone," I said, not sure whether I'd just been complimented or insulted.

"Not as different as I'd hoped."

I was still trying to figure out what she meant by that when Trevor finally walked by.

"Hey!" I said, grabbing his arm. "Julie, do you know my brother, Trevor? Trevor, this is Julie Evans."

"Hey." I couldn't tell by her nod if she remembered him or not.

Trevor, on the other hand, was practically twitching with excitement.

"Jool-lee Evans," he drawled, as if he were searching back through his extensive recollection of hot chicks he might have hooked up with. "I think I remember seeing you around, back at old HMS."

Which, I have to admit, was a clever way of letting her think he wasn't there anymore. At least, it might have been clever if he hadn't been acting so weird. And to make things worse, all of a sudden he seemed freakishly short.

"Maybe," she said, smiling vaguely at a spot over Trevor's head.

"You probably remember me, too," he persisted. "Me and my buds, we hung out behind the cafeteria."

Julie looked surprised, but not as surprised as I was. The

patch of asphalt behind Hilltop Middle School's cafeteria is the exclusive domain of stoners, slackers, and . . .

Skaters! I groaned silently. *He can't be serious.*

"I've done some rad tricks back there," Trev lied shamelessly.

Getting in and out of there without being pantsed—that *would be a trick,* I thought.

"You don't look like a skater," Julie told him. "I never would have guessed."

"Oh, totally!" Trevor bragged, oblivious to the look of distaste on her face.

"Well, not *totally,*" I put in, trying to help him out. "Trevor likes lots of different things."

But there was no way he was going to admit to cooking or sewing or playing video games in front of his big crush— his cooler, *older* crush. Instead, he shot me a dirty look and stuck to his lame story.

"I mean, computers are all right, but aside from that I'm down at the skate park pretty much all the time," he said, forcing his voice deeper.

"Oh."

"You ought to come down sometime. I could show you my moves."

I could not believe my ears. What would he do if she said yes? Not that I found that likely.

"Maybe," Julie said. "Sometime."

A guy with any experience would have recognized that for the brush-off it was. Trevor, sadly, has no experience at all.

"All right!" he cried. Then, realizing he'd lost that

fake macho thing in his voice, he tried to play it cool. "I mean, there are usually a lot of chicks around, but I'll remember you."

"Okay." Julie's expression was turning desperate. "You know what? I see someone I need to talk to. Nice meeting you, Trevor. Cassie."

"Yeah, but—" Trevor began as she walked off.

I grabbed his arm to stop him from following. "Give it a rest before you make things worse."

"What are you talking about? She likes me! She's going to come to the park."

"Not a chance. She was trying to let you down easy."

"You're high."

"Then why is she over there, talking to Mr. Football, when she could still be here with you?"

"What?" Trevor whipped his head around, recoiling as he spotted Julie with a guy in a letterman's jacket. "Why does she need to talk to *him*?"

"To get away from you, I'm pretty sure."

"She said she would come to the park!"

If he didn't see it, how could I make him? "I don't think she's into whoever that guy is you were pretending to be. Maybe if you tried being *yourself* . . ."

"I was cool!"

"You were weird! Why do you want her to think you're some skateboard-obsessed loser?"

"Hey, skaters are cool. They're as cool as any football jock."

"And cooler than a guy who sews?"

"Cassie!" The way his face went all pasty, I honestly thought he'd pass out. "You promised not to mention that!"

"All I'm saying is, be yourself. Or at least not someone else. And try talking about a subject she might actually be interested in." I remembered seeing Julie jogging with her iPod. "Music. Try mentioning music."

"Good! And then I'll ask her to dance. It'll all flow together."

"Just let it rest until she finishes talking to that guy," I advised. But I was too late. Trevor was a love-struck geek on a mission, and nothing was going to get in his way.

"Julie! Yo, Julie!" he shouted, loud enough to turn heads. She cringed as he hurried over. "Hey, I just thought of something!"

"Yes?"

"Cool band, huh?"

The letterman laughed. "You just thought of that?"

Trevor drew himself up. He was still a foot shorter than the other guy. "Yeah. And I'm talking to Julie, so how about shutting up?"

My mouth fell open. Trev wasn't normally rude—or stupid—enough to speak that way to someone who could pound him into library paste.

"No problem," said the jock. "I'll shut up when you make me."

I squeezed my eyes closed. This encounter was headed to an extremely ugly place.

"Maybe I will," Trevor bluffed, pumped up on love and adrenaline. "Or maybe you'll get smart and walk away."

"Nah, I'd rather see you take a swing."

I opened my eyes a crack, mostly out of a sense of duty. Someone was going to have to describe Trevor's horrible death to my parents.

"Just stop," Julie told the other guy. "That wouldn't be a fair fight."

Which was completely true and obviously only mentioned out of regard for Trevor's safety, but he still looked as if she'd just slapped him.

"Hurry up, Trevor. What do you want?" she asked.

Her question seemed to hurt him even worse. "I just . . . I was wondering . . . would you like to dance?"

She shook her head. "I'm talking to Rex now."

"Right. I mean, okay. But, like . . . after that?"

"She said no, pipsqueak," Rex taunted. "So how about moving along?"

"How about getting bent?" Trevor retorted. "I'll move when I'm good and ready."

He braced his legs apart, practically daring Rex to do something about it.

My feet started moving on their own. "Trevor!" I called, hurrying to reach him before he could do something stupid. Something stupider, I mean.

"Let's go outside," Julie told Rex.

"Aw, come on," he said. "This guy is begging for it."

"He's so little. He's just a kid."

Trevor's back went rigid. I could only imagine the look on his face.

Rex took a breath and reluctantly let it go. "You're

right. Why bother?" Grabbing Julie's hand, he started leading her away.

I stopped to breathe a sigh of relief.

And that was when Trevor lunged, pushing Rex in the back. "Chicken!"

Rex spun around, fist cocked.

"Trevor!" I screamed.

"Rex!" Julie begged.

Maybe Rex took pity on us, maybe he figured it would hurt his manly rep to clobber someone as weak as Trevor, or maybe he was just a decent guy. In any event, he pulled his punch, planting his hand on Trevor's chest and pushing hard instead. My brother hurtled backward.

And there I stood with open arms.

Trevor slammed into me like a cue ball. Laughter drowned out the band as we both went down in a heap, struggling to untangle ourselves on the Pierces' Persian rug. Which is to say, Trevor struggled while I held on.

"Let go, Cassie!" he grunted, twisting frantically.

"Stop it, Trevor. You're making us both look stupid."

"I'm gonna kick that guy's—"

"You're going to wind up in the hospital. And Julie's not going to visit you."

"Let go!"

Trev burst from my arms like the Incredible Hulk, sprang to his feet, and glanced around for Julie. What he found was a roomful of strangers. Staring. And pointing. And laughing.

I scrambled up beside him. "Let's get out of here," I said, blushing purple.

"Huh?" He seemed suddenly dazed. "Where?"

I started towing him toward the backyard, then changed my mind and headed for the front. We stumbled through the crowd beneath the glittering chandelier, out Ros's front doors to her private drive. Fresh air slapped our cheeks as we hurried away from the entry, dodged the valet, and lost ourselves in the darkness.

"Brilliant!" I exploded. "I'm so glad I brought you."

"He started it," Trev muttered.

"Julie didn't want to talk to you!"

"Because that jerk got in the way."

"No, because you acted like a demented skateboarding butthole! And now I have to find someone to drive you home and spend the rest of my night doing damage control. I *knew* I shouldn't bring you!" I was getting madder by the second. "Everyone's going to find out you're my brother. This story will dog me for life!"

Trevor mumbled under his breath.

"If you have something to tell me, by all means, spit it out. I'm dying to hear your excuse."

"I said I'm sorry!" he barked.

And then he started to cry, big blubbery sobs complete with hiccups and ropes of mucus streaming from his nose. So not macho.

I could totally relate.

"Listen, Trevor . . . ," I said, laying a hand on his shoulder.

"Don't touch me!" Shrugging away, he ran a few more steps down the drive.

"Where do you think you're going?"

"Home."

"You can't walk home by yourself. I'll go get Quentin."

"I'm calling Dad," he said, producing my father's cell phone from his jacket. "I'll wait for him at the gate."

"Oh."

I knew I should stick by him and make sure he was okay. But phoning Dad was safe, and Trevor didn't want me around anyway. Besides, he'd brought the whole thing on himself.

"Tell Dad I'm staying," I instructed. "And ask him if I can stay later, now that you're going home."

Trevor muttered something I didn't catch and probably couldn't repeat anyway. I heard him snuffling loudly as he hurried into the darkness, a miserable bent silhouette against a million twinkle lights.

Somebody Call Jerry Springer

The trip back through the Pierces' living room was even more humiliating than I'd feared. The story had already spread and was dropping from the lips of the rich and popular like a plotline from a cheesy soap. You could have fried eggs on my cheeks by the time I skirted the dance floor, wove through the backyard crowd, and began looking for Kevin, desperately hoping to break the bad news myself.

Except that I couldn't find him.

Ros and Quentin were dancing in front of the stage, really cutting loose. Hayley and Fitz were toward the back of the crowd. But not only wasn't Kevin where he'd said he'd be, I couldn't spot him on the dance floor either.

I was getting frantic when I bumped into Angie Yee and Tamara Owens. Not that I expected any help from them. They never even acknowledged me, despite the fact that we had all competed for Snow Queen. But now all of a sudden they wanted to be friendly.

"Hey, Cassie," Tamara called. "Looking for your boyfriend?"

"Yeah!" I said, surprised. "Do you know where he is?"

"He went that way." Angie pointed. "Try the pool house."

"Thanks," I said, all grateful. "Hey, thanks a lot."

"Thank us later," Angie said.

I heard them laughing as I walked off, and that was when I realized they already knew about Trevor's shoving match.

They only helped me out of pity, I thought, cringing.

Here's an acknowledged fact: Queen Bees don't inspire pity. They inspire envy. And admiration. On occasion, perhaps, a touch of fear. But never, ever pity.

Trevor's stupid behavior was blowing my chance at a whole new rep.

The darkened pool house loomed into view, surrounded by a lavish koi pond. I breathed a sigh of relief as I hurried over its ornate bridge. Kevin would be inside. I'd tell him what had just happened, he'd assure me it was no big deal, and we'd hit the dance floor together. Having conspicuous fun with my hot boyfriend would be the ultimate damage control.

The pool house door stood open. I rushed inside, blinking

to adjust my eyes. The band had left the place in chaos—full ashtrays and empty bottles everywhere. A chair was overturned. Sofa cushions littered the floor. A single dim lamp in one corner barely lifted the shadows, but that didn't stop me from seeing the only two people in the room.

"Kevin!" His name ripped out of my throat before my brain could catch up. He looked my way and my legs buckled.

My boyfriend was alone with Tiffi Hughes, his hands on her bare shoulders and his lips an inch from her neck.

"What are you doing?" I shrieked.

"Cassie. It's not—" he began.

But the only thing that got through to me was the satisfied smirk on Tiffi's face.

"You get away from him!" I cried, running forward.

Kevin and Tiffi stepped back together, his hands never leaving her shoulders.

"How *could* you?" I screamed. Blood roared in my ears. I couldn't have heard him even if he'd tried to explain. " 'You have to trust me,' " I ranted. "What a crock! Do you think I'm stupid?"

Tiffi smiled. "You've just proven that."

My hands clenched at my sides. I fought to catch my breath.

And still Kevin stood there, not saying a word.

I waited another endless second. Then I picked up a sofa cushion, flung it at them, and ran out of the room.

Anger Mismanagement

Outside, the band had turned up their amplifiers. Their music crashed against the blood pounding in my ears. The twinkle lights blurred and ran together as I staggered over the pool house bridge, only dimly aware of the people gathered to stare. I stumbled into Angie as I reached the grass.

"Hey," she said, grinning. "You're welcome."

She set me up, I realized. I had no idea what I'd done to her, but she'd obviously been dying to take me down a peg. Still, that didn't change what I'd just seen. I kept going, pushing my way through the dancers with tears streaming down my face.

By the time I hit the house, I was a dripping, snotty mess. Heads turned as I rushed past the buffet. I heard someone call my name, but that only made me move faster. Dashing across the open threshold, I ran out into the driveway and just kept going.

He didn't even come after me, I thought, breaking into sobs. My feet pounded down the drive, along Trevor's earlier walk of shame. *He'd rather stay back there with her!*

The gate finally came into view. Trevor was sitting beside one stone post, his head down in his hands. He looked up when he heard me coming, the sight of my tear-streaked face snapping him out of his stupor.

"What happened?" he asked.

I shook my head. "Where's Dad?"

"Any minute."

I slumped to the ground beside him and curled my arms over my head. I couldn't believe it was over between me and Kevin, let alone over like *that*. All my hopes and dreams for us came crashing down around me. It felt like my heart would have to stop—it couldn't keep beating in that kind of pain. Every pulse, every breath, was pure agony.

I couldn't imagine never being with him again, seeing him at school and pretending we'd never been anything. I just couldn't believe we had reached the end.

He'd never even said he loved me.

Just So You Know

I'm not proud of myself.

There was probably a high road I could have taken.

Or, if I *had* to make a scene, I should have pushed Tiffi into the koi pond.

Homeschooling and Howard Hoagies

You know what the worst thing about school is? No matter how badly you've been humiliated, your parents still expect you to go back there. Granted, I've caused most of that humiliation myself, but that's not the point. The point is that once things reach a certain level, the only answer is homeschooling.

For once Trevor and I were on the same page.

"I can never go to high school now," he moaned over cereal on Sunday. It was noon, and we were both still unwashed, uncombed, and wearing our rattiest pajamas. "I'm already a joke and I haven't even started yet."

"Yeah, you have it rough," I replied, not exactly brimming with sympathy. "At least by the time you start, some of those people will have graduated."

"I can never face Julie again."

"Maybe if you hadn't been such a tool . . ."

"I know!" he groaned, dejected. "Like I was really going to beat that guy up! I'm lucky he didn't hand me my gonads."

Believe me when I tell you I try to avoid thinking about my brother's gonads. But that morning I barely even winced.

"News flash, Trev: even if you *could* have beaten him up, no normal girl likes a fistfight."

"I just thought . . . He made me look like such a kid . . . and I thought if I got in his face . . ."

"That you'd look like more of a man?"

Trevor dropped his spoon. "I'm such a tool."

"I already said that."

But I didn't take any pleasure in reminding him, not when we were both already so depressed.

"So what happened to you last night?" he asked. "You weren't so upset when I—"

"I don't want to talk about it."

If I did I'd start crying again, and I'd already spent so many hours sobbing that my head felt like a block of wood. I hadn't even taken Hayley's calls, afraid to find out what had happened after I'd left the party.

"There's always homeschooling," I said.

Trevor perked up. "You know, with the Internet, that's totally doable. Mom would barely have to supervise."

"Why not Dad? He's around constantly lately."

As if to make my point, Dad hustled into the kitchen, loaded down with groceries.

"Are you sleepyheads just getting up?" he asked, seemingly forgetting he'd picked us both up in tears the night before. "It's a brand-new day! Time to get out and claim it!"

As usual, I had no idea what he was talking about. "Uh-huh. Did you buy more Cocoa Critters?"

"Even better!" he proclaimed, waving a box in the air. "Look at this: Frosted Fruit Nuggets."

I don't know about you, but the last thing I want to see in the morning is fruit. Even if it's frosted. If God had intended us to eat fruit, he wouldn't have invented chocolate.

"Great," I said with a sigh.

"Has your mother come out of the bedroom?" Dad asked.

"We haven't seen her," Trevor said.

"Perfect!" Dad rubbed his hands together. "I'm going to whip up a batch of Howard Hoagies to surprise her."

He started unloading sandwich fixings, beginning with some impossibly huge bakery rolls.

"Didn't she say those hoagies were fattening?" I warned.

"This is a special occasion. It's our 'Bed and Breakfast Weekend at Home.' Yesterday I brought her pancakes in bed and gave her a foot massage while she ate them."

Not that it helped her mood, I thought, remembering how testy she'd been about curfew.

"Deal me in on those sandwiches," Trev said. "I'll take two."

"Not possible, my boy." Dad opened a bag of salami. "No one has ever eaten two Howard Hoagies and lived to tell the tale. It's too much sandwich for one human being."

"Maybe I'll get lucky and my stomach will explode," Trevor said glumly.

Dad hesitated, like he was finally going to ask about our early pick-up the night before. Then he broke open the mustard.

"One sandwich apiece—that's the limit. You're having one, Cassie, right?"

"No thanks. I just ate breakfast."

"You'll be missing a treat," Dad coaxed.

"Yeah." Getting up, I ditched my bowl in the sink. "I think I'll miss it from my room."

Unfortunately, there was nothing I wanted to do in there. I just sat on my bed, running those gut-wrenching moments in the pool house back and forth through my mind.

I had obviously jumped to conclusions. I might even have overreacted. But if I'd somehow gotten things wrong, shouldn't Kevin have called me by now? Shouldn't there have been an onslaught of frantic attempts to explain?

I flopped back on my bed, my eyes welling over. I just

couldn't shake the image of Kevin and Tiffi alone together, his hands on her bare shoulders. . . .

If I'd had any idea how much love hurt, I might have been happy with luv.

*She said try to be
Momentarily happy.
Moments never last.*

Me and Sympathy

Obviously, in hindsight, I should have called Hayley and moaned to her. But I swear I had no idea where I'd end up when I shucked off my pajamas for thrift-store fatigues and headed out our front door. I just wanted to escape, to think of something besides Kevin and my ruined reputation.

So I walked. All the way down our street and right out of our neighborhood. Miles of Hilltop Boulevard passed unnoticed beneath my Skechers, the loudly whizzing cars no match for the noise in my head. My legs were finally getting tired when I looked up and saw MegaFoodMart's massively patriotic red, white, and blue store sign looming over the sidewalk.

Sunday afternoon.

Quentin would be working.

I should have turned around right there. My brain pulled a U-turn, but my feet kept going, carrying me into the parking lot. Sure enough, Quentin was outside alone, his blue apron flapping in a chilly breeze as he gathered up red carts.

"Cassie!" he called, abandoning his task to jog toward me across the pavement. "Hey, how's it going? Are you all right?"

Here's the problem with sympathy: it always makes me cry. I got one look at his face and the tears began to roll. He didn't even have to say he knew what happened. Everyone knew that.

"I've been better," I said.

"No, listen. It's not that bad," he soothed, pulling me into a hug. "You guys will work it out."

"I don't think so," I sobbed miserably.

"What? Sure you will." Quentin leaned back far enough to look into my face. "What moron would want Tiffi when the other choice was you?"

"Really?" I asked doubtfully.

"Duh! Of course. I'd choose you in a second."

I didn't believe him, but it was nice to hear him say. "You would?"

"Cassie, you're such a great girl. I look back on last year now and can't believe how stupid I was not to see what was right in front of me."

"I wish you would have."

"Me too."

I'm not going to sugarcoat this next part too much, because, basically, I can't.

I leaned in and kissed him.

Right on the lips, no hesitation, nothing friendly about it. For a second Quentin froze completely. Then he dropped his arms and jumped backward, his lips rebounding off mine like a missed free throw.

"What are you *doing?*" he cried.

My heart started pumping wildly. Had I really just done that? What kind of short circuit had hijacked my brain? I could only stare at him in wordless disbelief.

"I'm with Ros now!" he exclaimed, all the sympathy leaving his face.

"I know. I know that," I said frantically. "Quentin, I—"

"I *love* Ros," he told me, making everything worse. "Just because you're fighting with Kevin . . . Are you crazy?"

I started backing up, ashamed. "No, I'm just sad, and you seemed . . . " I trailed off, my gaze on my shoes. "I have to go."

Whipping around, I sprinted toward the sidewalk.

"Cassie!" he called out behind me. "Wait! Come back here and talk!"

But I didn't. How could I?

Of all the stupid things I've ever done, that kiss tops the list.

Few Confessions

I finally called Hayley Sunday night. It was after ten o'clock—risky, considering how her mother freaks when people call after nine—but I knew Hayley would answer.

She snatched it up on the very first ring. "Johnson residence," she said urgently.

I opened my mouth to say hello, but all that came out was a sick little whimper.

"Cassie?" I heard her bedroom door shut. "Cassie, is that you?"

"Yes," I choked out.

"I've been calling you since last night!"

"Sorry."

"Your mom said you went out this afternoon. Did you go see Kevin?"

If only! I closed my eyes against another rush of tears. "No. I was just out walking and . . ."

I wanted desperately to tell her about Quentin. That was the reason I'd called. But I couldn't make those words come out. What would she think of me if she knew? Flinging sofa cushions looked like charming behavior compared to kissing someone else's boyfriend.

I was as bad as Tiffi.

Worse, because Ros trusted me.

I'd never forget the horrorstruck look on Quentin's face. He obviously felt nothing for me anymore. Nothing whatsoever.

". . . and then I came home," I concluded lamely.

"Why didn't you take my calls?" Hayley demanded. "I've been so worried about you! The way you left the party—"

"I stayed long enough."

"Did you? Because I know what you're thinking, but Kevin didn't leave with Tiffi."

"No?"

"No! By the time I heard something had happened, he

was already gone. Meanwhile, Tiffi was on the dance floor with the basketball jock who brought her."

"Kevin probably felt guilty. He ought to."

"Have you talked to him?"

"There's nothing to say."

"Cassie! How can you be so sure?"

"I just am. Besides . . ." Nope. I still couldn't spill it. "I have to hang up now."

"What? No!" Hayley protested. "I've been trying to get you since last night."

"I can't talk about this anymore."

"Well, excuse me for trying to be a friend!"

"It's not—"

"No, you're right. Forgive me for wasting your precious time when I should have been minding my own business."

"Hayley, would you please—?"

"You run along. I'll try to worry about you when you find it more convenient."

"Hayley!"

The line was already dead.

Hair-trigger temper. We've covered that, right?

Apology, Interrupted

Monday morning, I skulked into the main hall praying no one would notice me. I was certain I'd burst into tears if anyone mentioned Ros's party—and that was just for starters. There was no way I could face Quentin. Hayley was mad at me. And it wasn't like I could avoid Kevin, either—not unless I developed an acute case of something life-threatening in the hour before second period.

I was nearly to my locker when a finger poked me in the back.

"So this is how it's going to be?" Kevin accused. "We're not going to talk about this?"

I drew a shaky breath, amazed he would try to put me on the defensive.

"I don't want to talk to you," I said self-righteously.

"That's mature." He started walking off.

Here's the thing: I really *didn't* want to talk to him. But the idea that he would just accept that, then turn around and *leave* me there . . .

"There's nothing to say," I flung at his back. "I saw you!"

"Saw me doing what?" Wheeling around, he closed the gap between us. "What exactly did you see?"

"I saw you two together. I saw you touching her."

"I was fixing her top!" The words exploded out of him like he'd been wanting to yell them for days. "That stupid thing she was wearing blew a strap and I was trying to tie a knot."

"In the dark?"

"In private. We had a light on, but it was lousy. I could barely see my fingers."

I stared at him, at a loss. His explanation was unexpectedly flawless.

But if he was telling the truth, I *really* looked like fool.

"Why couldn't one of her girlfriends help?" I asked.

"Don't you think it's a little weird, her coming to you for that?"

"I was waiting for you, and Tiffi asked me to dance, and we'd barely gotten out there when her strap—"

"Wait. You were dancing with Tiffi?"

"Dancing's not cheating, Cassie. Besides, you're the one who left me there to run off with your brother."

"I *had* to do that!"

"It doesn't matter! The point is you weren't around. And I didn't do anything wrong. You just stormed in and assumed the worst." Kevin shook his head. "You obviously don't trust me. Which is pretty ironic, considering."

"Considering what?"

"Considering you and Quentin."

"What?" I could hear my own ragged breathing as I hugged my backpack tighter.

"Do you think I've forgotten who took you to the Snow Ball? I see the way you look at him. It kills you that he's with Ros."

Wait a minute. Did he know about the parking lot or not?

"Quentin and I are just friends."

"Oh, okay. Should I *trust* you on that?"

"There's nothing between us. I swear," I said, increasingly aware of all the people jostling around us.

"Just tell me this: have you ever kissed him?"

"What? I mean . . . *What?*"

"I just want to know how *friendly* you two are."

"Don't be crazy. He's with Ros."

"Answer the question. It's a simple yes or no."

No, it wasn't. That question wasn't simple at all. If I told the truth, people were going to get hurt for no reason. But if I lied . . .

"If I kissed him before you and I got together, what difference does it make? Have you ever kissed Sterling?"

Kevin gave me a disgusted look. "I have to go to class."

Social Outcast

Conway's class was exactly the nightmare you'd expect. Kevin and I sat two feet apart the entire period and never looked at each other once. At lunch I was so afraid to venture into the quad that I bought some chips from a vending machine and ate them alone on the bleachers, feeling stupid and lowly and judged.

The whole school knew what had happened in that pool house. I could tell just by the looks on people's faces, either pitying, or amused, or—in a few evil cases—thrilled. And the higher up the food chain I looked, the more scornful the glances that came back my way. The elite seemed almost offended, as if I had made *them* look bad by nearly being accepted into their ranks and then proving so unworthy.

But uncomfortable glances in the hallways were nothing compared to being afraid to face my own friends, and they mattered even less against the growing realization that Kevin probably wasn't the one who had screwed up at Ros's party.

I owed him an apology, and sooner rather than later.

I'll do it at rehearsal, I decided. *Assuming I survive PE.*

Hayley and Sterling and—God help me—Tiffi would be in there. And if I somehow made it through badminton, rehearsal could only be worse.

Ros would be at rehearsal.

Did she know that I'd kissed Quentin? Was she going to tell Kevin? Would she bounce my worthless white butt from B right down to Z?

She could do it too. She totally had the power. Ros and Sterling together . . .

I shuddered in my down coat.

Welcome to Dweebsville, I thought.

At Least One of My Friends Will Visit Me

"Hey," Hayley said when I walked into the locker room. I'd waited until the last second, but there she was anyway, dressed out for PE and sitting alone on that long changing bench.

"Hey," I returned nervously. I had no idea why she'd waited, unless she wanted to chew me out in private before we got to the gym. Kicking off my clogs, I got busy with those stupid shorts.

"Listen," she said. "I'm sorry about last night."

Over the course of our friendship, I've apologized to Hayley hundreds of times. For her to say sorry to me is much rarer. My expression must have made this clear.

"I still think if you can't talk to your best friend, who can you talk to?" she added, embarrassed. "But you have a right. I shouldn't have hung up on you."

"Yeah. I mean . . . thanks," I said, amazed.

"We missed you at lunch today. The four of us, that is—Kevin didn't show up either."

I wondered where he had spent his time. I prayed it wasn't with Tiffi.

"I just thought . . . Ros isn't mad at me?"

"For what?" Hayley asked cluelessly.

"Well . . ." I decided to float the less scary reason. "Between Trevor and me, we pretty much trailer-trashed her birthday."

Hayley shrugged. "Stuff like that always happens at parties. I think she was just sorry you guys went home so early. She was worried about you."

"Really?"

"Of course. We all were."

It seemed too good to be true, but if Hayley was telling the truth, then Quentin had kept his mouth shut.

Which actually made total sense. Why risk upsetting Ros when we would clearly never be kissing again?

"You'd better hurry," Hayley told me, pointing to my gym shoes.

I put them on and reluctantly followed her out to the gym, bracing for the taunting I was sure to take when I got there.

But to my surprised delight, PE was one hundred percent Tiffi free. She'd missed school that day, a possibility so beautiful I'd never even considered it. And that wasn't even the best part: no Tiffi at PE meant no Tiffi at rehearsal.

All through badminton, I hit my shots on reflex, busy planning how I'd get Kevin alone in the auditorium and try to patch things up.

As long as Quentin keeps quiet, I've got nothing to worry about, I thought, making China run for three long high shots in a row. *I made a lame mistake, but Kevin never needs to find out about it.*

"Quit fooling around," Hayley griped. "Smash it."

"You're at the net," I reminded her.

Besides, lobs gave me more time to think.

Second Banana

When Hayley and I got to the auditorium, Ros and Sterling were sitting together in back and Kevin was down front with Fitz. Before I could pull him aside, Mrs. Conway walked in.

"I need to talk to you," I whispered to him. "As soon as this is over."

Kevin shrugged. "Okay."

I would have liked more enthusiasm, but at least he'd shown up.

Mrs. Conway approached our row and began passing out papers. "I have show programs here for everyone. I hope you're all prepared to run through your acts."

The pit of my stomach seized. I hadn't spent even one second over the weekend thinking about the act I was supposed to do with Hayley.

"And Cassie Howard has volunteered to be our assistant director," Conway went on. "Come on up, Cassie."

What? The hostile way people looked at me made my

cheeks flush just on reflex. I squeezed the arms of my chair stubbornly, but Conway kept waving me forward until I stumbled to the front of the room.

"We said *stage manager*," I reminded her out the side of my mouth.

"Consider it an upgrade. Assistant director sounds more important, don't you think?"

Yes, and that was the problem. The other students were not going to like the idea of my directing them in any way. Even *I* didn't like that idea.

"I'm still just running props around, right?"

"And sets. And telling people where to stand, and when to go on, and putting out whatever fires come up. Basically just running the show. All right, everyone, listen up!" she called, handing me her clipboard. "Cassie is taking over."

A disgruntled hush fell over the auditorium. Could her timing have been any worse?

"Okay," I mumbled. "Well." Our new show program was right on top of the clipboard, but nervousness made the words swim around until I could barely read them. "Oh! We'll need Kevin in the booth for lights and sound."

He actually got up and went. Encouraged, I risked a peek into the seats. Scattered groups of students regarded me with a mixture of scorn and boredom. "Um, we're ready for Sterling onstage. Hayley, you wait in the wings, so you can come out right behind her."

"You should get up there too," Conway told me from her new spot at the center of the theater. "You can't run things where you're standing. And announce the acts—we need an announcer."

I reluctantly climbed the stage stairs, joining Hayley and Sterling at the edge of the open first curtain. A second curtain behind us stayed closed, providing a plain backdrop.

"I'm going to fake some sort of introduction, to keep Conway happy," I said. "As soon as I'm done, you come out, Sterling."

"Aye, aye, Captain Carrots. Or is it Captain Crybaby now? Humiliate yourself at any good parties lately?"

"Here's an idea: shut up, for once, and do what I say."

Sterling's mouth fell open. I'd just whacked a hornet's nest, but I didn't have time to dwell on the potential paybacks. Instead, I marched to center stage, turned to face the crowd, and froze.

You may recall my dislike of public speaking. Giving my Snow Queen speech was so traumatic I nearly passed out. Granted, that had involved a much larger audience, but there hadn't been a spotlight like the one Kevin shined at me now. The stupid thing was so bright it burned every intelligent thought right out of my brain.

It was déjà vu all over again.

"Say anything!" Hayley hissed from the wings. "It doesn't matter."

"Um, ladies and gentlemen," I finally mumbled, feeling completely foolish. "Thank you for coming to our talent show. Our first act is Sterling Carter."

A smattering of fake applause greeted Sterling's strut to center stage.

"So you'll polish it up as you go along," Hayley consoled me when I rejoined her.

"Actually, I plan to talk Conway out of the whole idea."

Hayley grinned. "Good luck with that."

She must have felt sorry for me though, because when Sterling finished posing to her karaoke song, Hayley went out and whistled without me. Not that she'd prepared anything—she was totally winging it—but she's so good that when she wrapped up people applauded in earnest.

Our talent show finally had some talent.

After that I got crazy busy calling up the acts and making lists of everyone's props. By the time I got to Fitz, I had writer's cramp.

"Let's see," he began. "I'll have two trunks, a dozen eggs, silk handkerchiefs, a wand, my hat, a cape, four doves—"

"Slow down!" I said, scribbling. "Did you say doves? *Live* doves?"

Fitz smiled. "They can't fly if they're fake."

"Right," I said, not nearly as thrilled by that thought as he obviously was. I hate to be a party pooper, but poop is what it comes down to. "Is that everything?"

It wasn't—not by a mile—but the guy onstage had just finished rapping and was holding his last gangsta pose. I pushed Fitz out with the few props he'd brought—a hat, a wand, and some silks—and started taking prop notes for our finale, a modern–ballet–tap dance extravaganza featuring three sisters.

Despite the fact that most people did abbreviated versions of their acts and a few didn't perform at all, rehearsal still ran long. When I finally got Kevin alone in the sound booth, I'd forgotten all the clever things I'd planned to say. I just wanted to apologize and get things back to normal.

"I've been thinking," I opened, trying to ignore the way he kept fiddling with his switches instead of looking at me. "I believe what you said about Tiffi this morning, and, uh . . . I probably overreacted."

"That's what you wanted to tell me?"

"That, and I'm sorry."

"For what?"

"Well, for making such a scene. If I hadn't self-destructed, we could have stayed and had a good time."

"Okay." Kevin finally looked at me, but his expression seemed less than thrilled.

"Okay?" I repeated uncertainly.

"I forgive you for making a scene."

"So, um . . . Are we good now?"

"If you say so."

He turned back to the sound board. I felt stupid just standing there, but I didn't know what else to say. Awkwardness finally overwhelmed me.

"I, uh, guess I'll see you tomorrow, then. Did you finish that assignment for Conway's class?"

"The letter-writing thing?" He shook his head. "I'll be up half the night."

"Yeah. I'm not finished either. I'd better go get on it."

He flipped a few more switches.

"See you tomorrow," I added.

"See ya."

Walking out, I pulled my coat tight around me, not sure what had just happened. Had I just apologized and been forgiven?

That was how it had sounded, but that wasn't how it felt.

Sophomore Honors English
Mrs. Conway
Monday, January 26

Dear Grandma,

You'll never believe what happened tonight. Dad actually just told Mom that he's not going back to work! Pretty much out of nowhere he looks up from his T-bone and says, "I've made a decision, Andrea. I'm happier working at home."

None of us knew what he meant by that until he spelled it out: he's sick of having a job and he wants to be a permanent housedad. I thought Mom would blow a vein. Literally. I could see this thing throbbing in her forehead.

"We'll talk about it later," she said, in that really calm voice she uses when all heck's about to break loose.

"Nothing to talk about," he said. "My mind's made up."

Mom basically told him he was off his rocker, even though Dad kept insisting we can afford it. But Mom said turning him into a hausfrau wasn't her reason for working so hard. Words like *tuition* and *early retirement* got tossed around a lot. Finally she got up and said she needed to take a drive. She still hasn't come back, and it's been a couple of hours.

Dad might have more of a shot if he were better at keeping house. You wouldn't have believed the cookies he made this week, and you definitely wouldn't have eaten them. The T-bones he served tonight? Five nights of steak in a row. He says it's because Mom never cooks steak, but I'm starting to wonder if he knows how to make anything else. Besides pancakes. I have to admit his pancakes are good, but these all-meat dinners are already old. He won't even let us order takeout anymore—he says there's no need now that he's home all day. There is a need, believe me.

And then there's the laundry. I've been doing my own for two years, and Trevor does most of his, but this week Dad decided to do everyone's. He was only trying to be nice, but now all Trev's underwear is pink, and that causes problems for an eighth-grade boy.

Don't get me started on *my* underwear. So far it's all its original color, but I came home this week and found my bras folded in half with the straps stuffed into the cups, making these embarrassing ~~little~~ cones. I can only guess what he did to Mom's clothes, because I distinctly heard the words *dry cleaner's* being shouted in their room. I begged him to let me wash my own stuff from now on, but I'm not sure he listened.

We're having that problem a lot lately.

Like last Tuesday. He rearranged the living room furniture even though Mom specifically asked him not to. She got home late, walked into that antique chest, and practically shattered her kneecap. You ought to see the bruise.

The biggest thing he's not hearing, though, is how Mom feels about him not working. I don't even think it's the money. There's just something about having him home all day that totally freaks her out. She already looks five years older, and that's not counting the extra gray hair she got tonight.

I can only imagine what Dad will get up to now with so much time on his hands. And if Trevor jumps onboard the Home Ec Express, we're all in serious trouble. So far he's been too depressed about a girl to pay Dad much attention, but after Mom left tonight I heard Dad ask him how to make omelettes. Omelettes are Trevor's signature dish—and as long as you don't eat a shrimp one, you'll probably survive. There's no way he'll be able to resist playing the expert and teaching Dad how to make them.

Come to think of it, I should be praying for that. I've never heard of a steak omelette.

I hope you are well. Say hi to Aunt Catie for me.

Love,

Cassie

P.S. Mom just got home. The streets of Hilltop are safe for pedestrians again. Which reminds me—she *still* won't let me drive. Do you think you could say something? Drop a hint?

(But do *not* say I asked you to!)

Pushing the Envelope

You don't have to tell me *now*: I never should have mailed those letters. On the other hand, it seemed like a waste to toss them down the black hole of school assignments when Grandma was always asking me to write. So Tuesday morning I used Mom's fax machine to make copies of all three, stuffed them into an envelope, and dropped it in the mailbox on my way to school. By the time I walked into English and handed Conway my originals, I'd forgotten the whole thing.

"Did you finish the assignment?" I asked Kevin, taking my seat. "Did you have to stay up late?"

"Almost and yes," he replied, scribbling on a half-filled page with more sheets spread around him.

"You'd better hurry and turn it in. The bell's about to ring."

"I know that," he said testily.

"I'm only trying to help."

"If you really want to help, be quiet and let me do this."

He finished just before the bell, running his work up to Conway's desk. But when he returned, smiling with relief, my answering smile was pasted on. I don't care how right he was—it always hurts being told to shut up. I was so wounded that I took his suggestion for the rest of the period, not whispering even a single wisecrack that might have made Conway's return to *Modern English Grammar* more interesting.

"Are we meeting for lunch today?" he asked when she finally dismissed us.

"Why wouldn't we be?" I countered.

He shrugged.

"Don't you want to?"

"If you do."

"Fine."

Geometry involved a chalkboard full of circles, but Mr. Beyerson could have been drawing treasure maps and I wouldn't have paid attention. I just couldn't move past one thought: if you break something and glue it back together, are the cracks always going to show?

Kiss Off

If Kevin and I were going to sit with everyone else at lunchtime, I had to talk to Quentin first. I'd been avoiding him since Sunday—for obvious reasons—but I sucked it up between third and fourth periods and waited outside his classroom.

"I need to see you. Alone," I said the second he hit the hall.

The reluctant way he followed me out the nearest exit would have been more mortifying if I hadn't already hit bottom in the humiliation department. I led him around the corner to the quiet side of the building and stopped beside a trash can.

"Why are we out here?" he asked uneasily, like he expected me to jump him again.

He's a good-looking guy, but please. I got straight to the point.

"Kevin and I are back together."

Quentin's head lolled on his neck. "I *knew* you guys would work it out!" he said, relieved.

"Yeah, well . . . we're still working it out. But it's not going to help if he finds out about Sunday."

"Sunday?" Quentin echoed blankly, flashing me a grin. "Did something happen Sunday?"

"You know I never would have been so stupid if everything else hadn't—"

"Relax," he interrupted. "It was just one of those random things. We never have to mention it again."

"Really?"

"It's not like I want to explain it to Ros. Besides, it didn't mean anything." He gave me a probing look. "Right?"

"Right! Of course not."

"Okay, then. Let's forget it."

I could have melted with relief. "You're the best! It stays between you and me, then. We'll take it to our graves."

"Um . . ." His expression was not reassuring.

"What?" I asked, holding my breath.

"I might have already mentioned it to Fitz."

"Fitz!" I cried. "What for?"

"I was freaked out, Cassie. It kind of slipped. But don't worry—I told him not to tell anyone."

"Like he's not going to tell Hayley!"

"You haven't told Hayley?"

"Not my proudest moment, all right?"

"I'll talk to Fitz. He won't say anything, I promise."

I had no idea what made him so sure, but he knew Fitz better than I did. Besides, it wasn't like I had a choice.

"Tell him it's really important," I begged.

The very last thing I needed was Hayley learning something from Fitz that I hadn't told her myself.

Sew Annoying

Our whole group ate lunch together Tuesday and Wednesday. Kevin and I were a couple again, but things weren't like before and I didn't know how to make them that way.

So I was hardly in the mood to deal with Tiffi's reappearance in PE Wednesday, but reappear she did—tan, dripping silver jewelry, and as full of herself as ever. I heard her talking about Cabo to Sterling, so maybe that explained her absence. Either that or she just got sick and was luckier with SpeedTan than I was. The only good news was that she kept her distance all period, not calling me Captain Carrots once.

She probably thinks I'm a dangerous, cushion-flinging lunatic, I decided. Which was ridiculous, of course. I am so not dangerous. On the other hand, if Tiffi chose to believe I might lose it and kick her petite butt . . .

I can totally live with that.

She kept so far away all hour that I even dared to hope she'd skip our talent show rehearsal. No such luck. She tagged along with Sterling, sitting in back and rolling her eyes every time I opened my mouth. Which was a lot, since Mrs. Conway made me direct again.

When I finally walked in our front door at home, all I wanted was a little peace.

I should have known better.

Trevor was cranking away on his sewing machine, obnoxious music blaring out of his bedroom.

"What are you doing?" I demanded, walking in and adjusting the volume. "Other people live here, you know."

"Dad sucked Mom's curtain into his new vacuum cleaner," Trevor explained without turning around. "Rip!"

I gasped to recognize one of our long living room drapes beneath the plunging needle. "Is it bad? Can you fix it?" I asked nervously.

"She'll never even know."

I heaved a sigh of relief. "You just saved Dad's life."

"Yeah."

He was obviously still depressed about Julie, or he would have been more impressed with himself.

"I still don't understand why you're so determined to keep your sewing a secret. You could probably make money at it." I crossed over to his desk, struck by a brilliant idea. "You could design custom prom dresses!"

Trevor went three shades whiter. "You're out of your mind."

"Everyone loved my Snow Queen dress. You'd probably be really busy."

"I'd probably be beat up daily. I can't get a girlfriend as it is—becoming the school seamstress would seal that deal forever."

"You know what your problem is? You care too much what other people think."

Trev laughed mockingly. "I'm going to let you walk out of here and pretend you didn't just say that."

"Why would I want to pretend?"

"*I* care too much what people think? You're the queen of that!"

"No, I'm not!"

Not technically, anyway. Technically, I already have a queendom that requires my full attention.

But there was another crown, one I'd had my eye on before things had run off into a ditch.

Queen Bee.

I groaned to myself as he resumed sewing.

I hate it when Trevor's right.

It's Only Fun Until Someone Gets Hurt

Thursday I was in the lunch line with Ros when I spotted Sterling and Tiffi at a table in the quad. All their seats were filled with popular people, while more pressed in around them, dying to join the group. Bryce was there with a couple of guy friends, but Sterling's attention was firmly on Tiffi. The two of them were killing each other, whispering back and forth and laughing like maniacs.

"It must feel weird," I said to Ros. "A couple of months ago, that would have been you sitting there."

Ros shrugged. "Sterling is busy with Tiffi, so she doesn't need me right now."

"Or maybe she only needs Tiffi because you're so wrapped up with Quentin."

Ros gave me a look that made me gulp. Had I just given myself away somehow? Had Quentin said something after all?

But Ros just shook her head. "Tiffi's a phase. You'll see."

Two Stupid Little Letters

I invited Hayley over after school, mostly because of that weirdness between Ros and Sterling. It wasn't their problems I cared about so much as the idea that two people could be best friends forever and then just go separate ways. It got me worrying about me and Hayley, and the fact that we might not be as close as we used to be either.

"Maybe we can work on our show act," I said as we entered my house. "I feel bad that you've had to—"

"What is your dad doing?" Hayley interrupted, her eyes wide with amazement.

I backtracked to the entryway and peeked into the kitchen, where Dad and Trevor were standing on the breakfast bar. My father had his new canary yellow vacuum cleaner strapped across his back. Trevor was holding a sponge mop, which he'd managed to hook around the chain of our hanging lamp, pulling the fixture back toward Dad. Oblivious to our presence, Dad flipped on his vacuum and began obliterating cobwebs with the crevice tool.

"Don't ask," I advised, motioning for Hayley to follow me to my room. My father's adventures in housekeeping were the last thing I wanted to talk about.

Shutting my bedroom door, I pushed the clothes off my bed so Hayley could sit down. "If I was busy with Kevin all the time, you'd miss me, right?" I asked.

"You *are* busy with Kevin all the time."

"No, but . . . You're busy with Fitz," I countered, spinning in my desk chair.

Hayley rolled her eyes. "Why are you asking me this?"

"It's just, ever since Ros and Quentin got together, it's like he's come between Ros and Sterling. It made me kind of start worrying you and I aren't as tight as we were. And now I'm wondering if guys always get in the way."

Hayley's brows rose. "You're just figuring this out? I've been worried about that since the day you met Kevin."

"I am *not* always with Kevin!"

"Not this week. Wait until things get good again."

If they ever would. I desperately wanted to confess everything to Hayley and have her tell me none of it mattered. Except that I was afraid she'd say it *did* matter. Plus, I'd made that pact with Quentin.

"That could be a long time," I said at last.

"It's been a rough week," she agreed. "But Kevin will come around. And you and I aren't Ros and Sterling. We'll always be best friends—no guy will ever change that."

"Yeah."

"Look." She held up her right hand, a smile lighting her eyes. "Look what Fitz gave me today."

I spotted the new ring instantly, a plain silver band tucked in behind the garnet solitaire she usually wore. It wasn't very flashy compared to Ros's gold star, but jewelry from a boyfriend is always worth bragging about.

"Nice," I said enviously.

"Read the inside," she said, twisting the rings off her finger and handing the band to me.

The inscription caught the light: *Love you forever, Fitz Love.* With the *o* and the *e*.

"Nice." I tried my best to smile, but I was dying inside. First Ros, then Hayley . . .

Will somebody ever love *me*?

Second Attempt

Friday, I knocked myself out trying to make up with Kevin. Okay, technically we'd already made up, but I wanted it to feel that way.

"Hey, did you do those sentence trees?" I asked him before Conway's class. "Want to compare?"

But for once he had already finished his homework.

"That's okay," he said, passing our papers up the row without even glancing at mine. "I either got them or I didn't—I'm not changing anything now."

I tried again the moment Conway dismissed us. "You

want to go off campus for lunch? Let's ditch the group today and go somewhere on our own."

"Sorry. I'm broke. Besides, I brought a sandwich," he said as we merged into hallway traffic.

"Well, let's at least eat on the bleachers. We're never alone anymore."

"It feels that way, doesn't it?"

Did he sound a little wistful or was that just my own wishful thinking?

"Not to mention that we'll see everyone at rehearsal this afternoon anyway," I added, encouraged.

"Everyone except Quentin."

I was starting to understand why he found my Tiffi fixation so unattractive.

"For the last time, Kevin. I promise you. There is nothing between me and Quentin."

"Yeah, all right. Why don't you buy lunch and meet me on the bleachers?"

Not exactly candlelight and violins, but things were finally looking up.

The instant the lunch bell rang, I ran into the quad to grab some food. I fidgeted in the kiosk line, aware of every second I was losing, but even twenty minutes with Kevin was worth looking forward to. I was psyched when I hit the football field and started across the grass.

I was psyched for exactly as long as it took me to spot him in the bleachers talking to Tiffi Hughes.

My heart and my feet stopped at the same time. What were they doing together? What could they possibly be saying?

Whatever it was, Kevin obviously liked it. His smile stretched wider as Tiffi gabbed on.

Stay calm, I warned myself. *Breathe. This is some sort of sick cosmic test.*

If I made a scene about finding Kevin with Tiffi again, it would prove that I hadn't learned anything. Meanwhile, jealousy, insecurity, and fresh suspicion roiled around in my mind, making it truly hard to think.

Had I learned anything?

Dodging behind the goalpost, I took a few deep breaths. *If I go down this road again, Kevin and I are over.*

It didn't seem fair, but there it was. If we were going to stay together, I had to learn to handle these situations like a mature, trusting adult.

The problem was, I had no idea how to do that. Worse, I didn't trust myself to figure it out. So I lurked behind that post until Tiffi moved on. Then I came out of hiding and joined Kevin as if I hadn't seen a thing.

"Sorry I took so long," I said. "There were big lines at both kiosks."

"No problem. I saved you a seat," he joked, gesturing to the empty bleachers.

"Sorry to leave you stranded out here all by yourself."

I was fishing, but Kevin just shrugged.

"It wasn't *that* long."

And all through lunch, we never mentioned Tiffi once.

The worst thing about finally getting what you want is, second place is always just one screwup away.

Men's Liberation

Mom was at the breakfast bar sipping a cup of milky tea when I got up Saturday. She was still wearing pajamas despite the fact it was almost noon, and the creases between her brows made her look hungover.

"Are you sick?" I asked. "You look terrible."

"Good morning to you too," she said grumpily.

I walked past her and opened the door to our cereal cupboard. "Oh, man! Dad bought that fruit stuff again. I told him five times: Cocoa Critters. He doesn't listen."

Mom shook her head. "Take it to the streets, sister. You're preaching to the choir."

"Where is he, anyway?"

"He and Trevor went out, something about a new attachment for his vacuum."

"I hope it does drapes," I muttered, shifting boxes around in hope of finding more cereal in back.

"What?"

"Huh?" I yanked my head out of the cupboard, Mom's irritable tone snapping me back to my senses. "Nothing! Just . . . he loves that thing, I swear."

"It's the color. And the power. He thinks it's a carpet SUV."

"Then things could be worse, I guess," I said, trying to cheer her up. "He could have bought a sports car."

"At least that's one midlife crisis I'd know how to handle. A Ferrari, hair plugs . . ." My mother forced a smile. "I wish."

"It's not so bad having him home, is it? I mean, aside from the fact that Trev and I have no privacy now, none of our clothes are safe, and don't get me started on steak. But the carpet's real clean. And Dad seems happy."

"He is." Mom sighed. "That's the problem. If he'd been laid off and was miserable, I could totally support him."

Giving up on the cereal, I sat on the stool next to hers. "You'd rather he was miserable?"

"Isn't that awful? I'd *rather* he was at work, but at least if he'd been laid off I could still respect him. Or even if he'd switched to something else that didn't pay as well . . . something *real*, I mean," she said, gesturing around the kitchen. "Not this."

"Can I ask you a question? How come you love it when Trevor cooks and sews, but you don't want Dad doing it?"

"Your father is *sewing* now?" She looked horrified.

"No. But I mean . . . you know."

Mom stared into the dregs of her tea, then tossed it off in one gulp. "I never thought I'd say this, but I'm finding it hard to respect someone who thinks it's fine for his wife to earn all the money. There are a dozen reasons I'd accept if he *couldn't* work. But the fact that he quit, that he's just stopped trying . . . that makes me crazy."

"Maybe he hasn't stopped trying," I said, grasping for a suitably mature thought. "Maybe he's just trying something else."

Mom seemed astonished, but in a good way.

"And maybe," I continued, encouraged, "he'll try this for a while and move on."

"I'm going to pray you're right," she said, "because I don't know how much more of this I can take. I've always prided myself on being a free thinker, but now . . . I don't know. It's like your father's called my bluff. I feel like a bad feminist, a bad wife." She squeezed her temples. "I just feel bad."

The door to the garage slammed, jolting us both off our stools.

"I got the last one!" Dad crowed, rushing in with Trevor and waving a tubular brush in the air.

"Oh, joy," my mother muttered.

"And here, Cassie." His eyes never left his bristled prize as he shoved a grocery bag at me. "I forgot these yesterday."

I stared a moment in disbelief, then snatched out a familiar box. "Cocoa Critters!"

"That's the kind you wanted, right?"

"Thanks, Dad!"

My mother looked betrayed as I made a dash for the milk, but I don't know what she expected.

If I'd eaten that fruit garbage, we'd *both* have been miserable.

The Envelope Pushes Back

When you fight with your boyfriend and then you make up, he ought to call you over the weekend, right? I mean, it's not a rule, but it makes perfect sense. Unfortunately, someone forgot to tell that to Kevin. I waited for him to call all day Saturday, then spent most of that night lying awake, imagining him out with Tiffi. When I shuffled into our kitchen Sunday morning, my mood was even darker than the circles under my eyes.

"Good morning, sleepyhead!" Dad greeted me, waving a wire whisk in the air. "I have a surprise for you."

"I hope it's not that we're out of milk."

Dad stepped in front of the refrigerator before I could even check. "No cereal for you. I'm making brunch!"

I didn't bother to stifle my groan. "I'm not brunch hungry. I just want—"

"Go get dressed," he told me. "And put on something nice. We're having a *family* day."

I won't repeat what I muttered when I got back to my room. You can fill in the blankity-blanks yourself. Fifteen minutes later, I emerged wearing a faded polo and my most trashed jeans, just to make a point. Wetting my rumpled hair, I brushed it straight back and returned to the kitchen still dripping.

Mom and Trevor had beaten me there, Trev looking uncomfortable in his khakis and Mom out of sorts in a velour jogging suit. They'd taken both stools at the breakfast bar, which meant I had to stand while Dad turned sausages at the stove. Breakfast looked like a distant dream.

"Okay, Hal, everyone's here now," Mom said. "And if I don't get some very strong tea in the next ten seconds—"

The doorbell rang. Mom and Trev and I all looked at each other to see if anyone knew who was out there.

"Surprise!" Dad cried, delighted.

"What's going on?" Mom asked suspiciously.

"You'll see."

Trevor and I followed him to the front door, curious. But before we could get there, the door opened wide.

"Is anybody home?"

"Grandma!" I exclaimed.

She was standing on our doorstep surrounded by a mountain of luggage. A taxicab pulled away from the curb behind her.

"Hello, darling!" she said, wrapping me in a crushing hug. Don't imagine my grandmother as some fragile, bent old lady—picture a woman with wrinkles who can still squeeze the breath out of you. "It's so good to see my only granddaughter!"

Before I could ask why she'd come, Dad stepped past me and kissed Grandma on the cheek.

"Arlene!" he greeted her. "What perfect timing! The waffle iron just finished preheating."

"Mother?" my mom gasped, stumbling into the entryway. "What's going on? How did you get here?"

"Hello, dear. I took a plane, of course. And then a taxi from the airport—lovely gentleman, although I'm afraid his English is not good. Still, I think he's very brave, trying to support his family in a strange country."

Mom just stood there, blinking.

"Hey, Grandma!" Trevor said, stepping forward.

Grandma gave him a bear hug too. "Look how big you're getting—big enough to help your father carry all this luggage to my room."

"You're staying here?" my mother asked, confounded. "Are you okay? Is everything all right at home?"

"Fine! Couldn't be better," Grandma said cheerfully. "It's actually the perfect time for a little break in the sunshine. How do you people know it's February, living out here? They were salting the walks back home when I left. Louise Crenshaw slipped on her porch last week and nearly broke a hip."

"Well. That's . . . a shame," my mom got out.

"Come on, Trevor," said Dad. They both took bags in each hand and trundled off down the hall, Grandma following with her enormous purse and a tote bag full of yarn.

"Do you know they made me check my knitting needles?" she complained to Dad and Trev as they all disappeared. "Do I look like some sort of ninja to you? What is this world coming to, when an old lady can't knit on a plane?"

I didn't hear Dad's reply, because Mom grabbed one of my arms and yanked me into the kitchen.

"Did you know your grandmother was coming?" If she didn't exactly look furious, *happy* isn't the first word that comes to mind either.

"I had no idea," I swore truthfully. But I was getting this nervous sort of tingle between my shoulder blades, the kind that grows until it spreads down both arms like a heart attack.

"What in the world could have prompted her to just show up?"

"I don't know."

But the problem was, I was afraid I might. Could it be a complete coincidence that she'd arrived the same week I'd mailed those letters?

"Your father was clearly expecting her."

"Yes! Yes, he was," I agreed, grasping at that straw.

Please, God, I prayed. *Let this be all Dad's doing. Or at the very least, let it have nothing to do with me.*

Personally, I was thrilled to have Grandma visit. But if it turned out she'd come because of anything I'd written . . .

And God? Make sure Mom never finds out about those letters!

I'll Take Weird for One Thousand, Alex

That brunch was the strangest meal I've ever sat down to. Dad put bacon bits in the waffles, and that was the tip of the iceberg.

"Your fruit salad is so interesting, Hal," Grandma said. "What's in the dressing?"

He seemed reluctant to reveal his secret. Then he blurted it out. "Miracle Whip and Kool-Aid powder. That's what turns it blue."

"Interesting," she said again. "I wonder what would happen if you used dry Jell-O instead? You might get more body."

"Jell-O!" he said excitedly. "I'll have to try that."

"We might want to adjust a few other ingredients too," Grandma said. "We'll have plenty of time to tinker with it while I'm here."

Dad beamed while Mom looked silently from him to

Grandma and back again. Ever since she'd found out why her mother had come, she hadn't had much to say.

"Well, I just called to say hello," Grandma had explained while Dad served our brunch. "And Hal picked up the phone and told me about leaving his job, and the next thing I knew, I was on a plane. I think it's so exciting that someone here is taking up homemaking. Not that it's as important as *your* job," she'd told my mother. "But it's going to be great for the kids, having a parent home in the afternoons. Of course I wanted to come lend my support, and maybe a few recipes."

"Your meat loaf," Trev had jumped in. "And those peanut butter jumbles. No, wait—can you teach *me* how to make those?"

I might have made some dessert requests of my own if I hadn't been faint with relief at the way Grandma had just covered my butt.

"I'm not sure how much support staying home to vacuum requires," my mother had said icily. "Especially since we're not sure this state of affairs is permanent . . ."

But Grandma hadn't heard the hidden message there. Or, if she had, she'd ignored it. For the past half hour, ever since we'd started eating, she'd been talking like Dad was the male Martha Stewart.

And Mom had been sitting there steaming. I sincerely hoped I'd be out of the room before she decided to share out loud.

"This is going to be fantastic!" Dad exclaimed. "I can't wait to learn all your tricks, Arlene."

Grandma smiled. "That's why I'm here."

Weirdly Normal

I was walking across Hilltop High's front lawn Monday morning, praying my name wouldn't come up in the discussion Mom and Grandma were having when I left, when I glanced ahead and saw Kevin.

He was actually waiting for me.

For a second, I was paralyzed. And then I started running. "Hey!" I said, jogging up with my book bag bouncing.

"You don't have to run. You're making yourself all pink."

"I thought you liked me pink."

He smiled. "How was your weekend?"

"Awful. Yours?"

"Insanely boring."

"You should have called me!"

"I should have."

We both stood there, grinning ruefully, and suddenly things between us seemed normal again.

Just like that.

"Are you going to your locker?" he asked. "I'll walk you."

He held out his hand and I slipped mine into it, sighing at how right it felt. "You didn't do *anything* fun this weekend?" I probed as we entered the hall.

He shook his head. "Total waste. You could have called me, you know."

"I wish I had."

"Me too."

He walked me to first period. We loitered outside the door.

"I guess I'll see you in English," he said, not leaving.

"Yeah."

"Okay, then."

I couldn't stand it anymore. Rising onto my toes, I planted a tentative kiss on his lips. He hesitated half a second, then grabbed me and kissed me back hard. I can't even describe that feeling—happiness, relief, and something that twisted my gut all rolled into one.

"I'd better take off," he told me. "The bell's going to ring in five seconds."

Four, three, two . . .

Brrrrrriiiiing!

"See you later," he said.

If I'd hustled into class right then, I probably could have skated on the tardy. But I just stood there, watching him go.

If only he'd say he loved me, I thought. *If I only knew for sure.*

He might have already said it if I hadn't been such a moron.

Whistle-stop

That afternoon, at rehearsal, Hayley flat out refused to go onstage unless I whistled with her. We argued in the wings for so long that Mrs. Conway walked up from the audience to see what was going on.

"Can we move this along?" Her tone made the question an order. "If you don't know your part yet, Cassie, mime it. Like Sterling. I've got things to do today."

"But Mrs. Conway—"

"I don't have time to argue," she said, tapping her watch.

Hayley looked way too pleased with herself when the two of us took the stage. There were a million people watching too. Or thirty, anyway.

"I don't even know what I'm supposed to whistle," I whispered through dry lips.

"Just follow my lead," she said.

Right. That's like Beethoven telling a grade-school pianist to jump in anywhere. I pretty much just stood there with my lips puckered while Hayley launched into Christina Aguilera's "Beautiful," packing it so full of trills and runs it was practically a different song.

And then she got to the chorus, stopped, and pointed at me, like she actually expected me to pick up where she'd left off.

I froze like a birdbath in winter. There was a long, completely silent pause while Hayley gazed at me expectantly.

And then she launched in again.

The auditorium roared with laughter. I had just become the straight man in Hayley's new comedy routine.

She tried to pass me the song two more times. Each time I became more futilely puckered and the audience laughed even harder. By the time we left the stage, Hayley was glowing from all the applause and I had a cold sweat trickling down my neck.

"That was great!" she crowed. "I told you it would be better with both of us!"

I was about to fill her in on the many ways it hadn't been better for *me* when Mrs. Conway interrupted.

"We have a new addition to our show," she said, motioning someone forward. "Do you girls know Julie Evans?"

"Um, yeah," I said weakly. "Hi, Julie."

Julie seemed nearly as embarrassed as I was, but whether that was due to events at Ros's party or my recent ridiculousness onstage, I didn't want to guess.

Conway waved on our third act, Gregor King, consulting the director's clipboard as he began his basketball-dribbling routine.

"Let's put Julie here," she said, penciling in a spot between the string quartet and the singer who followed. "We needed to separate these acts anyway—too much music in a row."

"What are you going to do?" I asked Julie.

"Not me, my dog," she said. "He does a ton of tricks."

"Get Julie's prop list," Conway told me. "And we'll have to clear it with Principal Ito, having a dog on campus. Look into that, Cassie, will you?" She handed back the clipboard and walked away without waiting for my answer.

"What are your props?" I asked Julie with a sigh.

"Excuse me?"

"Besides you and your dog, what are you going to have onstage? A leash? Burning hoops of fire?"

She laughed. "No hoops of fire. Really, there isn't much—a couple of dog toys. Can I tell you tomorrow?"

"Tell me Wednesday. That's our next rehearsal."

"Okay." She started to walk away.

"Hey, Julie!" I called impulsively.

She turned around and I realized I had no idea what to say. I needed to apologize for what had happened at Ros's party. But how could I do that without actually mentioning it?

"Um, how have you been?" I faltered.

"Fine." She smiled like she actually understood. "You?"

"Fine," I said, relieved. "Really good."

"See you Wednesday."

I had just lifted my hand to wave when I was pushed from behind by the guy exiting the stage.

"Watch it!" Gregor said. "I can't believe she put you in charge—all you do is get in the way."

I gasped as he blew by me, still bouncing his basketball. "What's his problem?" I asked Hayley.

"He's mad because we showed him up," she said knowingly.

"It's not my fault I have to stand here to call the acts."
My heart dropped. "Uh-oh. Where's the fourth act?"

I couldn't even remember who it was. I was consulting the clipboard in a panic when Sterling walked up.

"I'm changing my prop list," she informed me. "I won't need a microphone stand after all."

"Okay," I said, flipping pages.

"I'm bringing my own microphone—a remote."

"Fine." Shoving the clipboard at Hayley, I stumbled out into the spotlight. "Ladies and gentlemen, please welcome Meg Sawyer on her unicycle."

"She's not here," someone called.

"Oh." I probably should have figured that out on my own. "Then please welcome . . . um . . ."

Honestly, who can think under those lights?

"Mario Zapata," Hayley called to me from the wings.

"Mario Zapata," I repeated gratefully, almost colliding with our Shakespeare buff in my haste to exit the stage.

Sterling was waiting for me. "Did you hear anything I said?"

"About what?"

"The microphone stand!"

"What about it?"

"I'm thinking of new places you can shove it," she said, stalking off. "Assistant director . . . what a joke!"

"It's not my fault!" I called after her. Snickers let me know my voice had carried over Mario's monologue.

"Why me?" I asked Hayley.

"Hey, don't cry to me. This was all your idea."

"Yes, but—"

She handed back the clipboard.

"Karma," she said with a smile.

> Why punish me now
> For acts I can't remember?
> karma isn't fair.

Skatebored

"Julie's in the talent show," I told Trevor when I got home. "She just joined today."

He was playing video games in his room, but he took his eyes off the screen long enough to fix me with a sullen stare. "What are you telling me for? I don't care what she does."

"Sure, you don't. That's why you're sulking alone in your room when you could be down at the skate park."

"Maybe I'm sick of the skate park."

"Fine. Just thought you'd want to know." I made it nearly to my room before I heard his footsteps behind me.

"What's she doing?" he asked from my doorway.

"Who?" I asked innocently, unloading my backpack onto my bed.

"Julie! What's she doing in the show?"

"Some sort of act with her dog. Which sounds kind of lame. Which means she'll fit right in."

Trevor leaned against my doorframe and inspected his fingernails. "Did she ask about me?"

"Not directly."

"What did she say?"

"I asked how she'd been, and she said fine. Then she asked how I'd been, and I said fine too. We both knew what we meant."

Specifically, that the subject of Trevor would never be mentioned between us again. But if he wanted to think she'd somehow been inquiring about his health, that was okay with me.

"At least now you won't whine about coming to the talent show," I said. "Which reminds me, I ought to sell Grandma a ticket. Do you think she'll be here that long?"

"Two more weekends?"

"She said she'd stay as long as it takes to teach Dad all her tricks. If that includes cooking, she could still be here next year."

"Real nice, Cassie. For your information, he's learning to make her meat loaf right now."

"With that red stuff on top?" I asked hopefully.

"If you want to know so bad, why don't you go ask?"

"Because I've got homework, dufus. Meanwhile, you're just holed up in your room, playing with yourself."

His jaw tightened. "By myself," he gritted out.

My little twist on that phrase always drives him up a wall. Oh, well. He started it.

"You might as well go learn to make meat loaf," I told him. "If you're not going to skate anymore, why not embrace your inner geek?"

"You're not funny," he whined, abandoning my doorway. A few seconds later, I heard him in the kitchen, declining Grandma's offer to let him mash the potatoes.

You just can't help some people.

Mind over Mater

The best things that happened at school on Tuesday were a day off from show rehearsals and the way Kevin kissed me at my locker after lunch. For a second, things got kind of hot—although not as hot as they might have if I hadn't been worried about hall traffic and the possibility of having pepperoni stuck in my teeth. Without rehearsal to waste my afternoon, I actually finished my homework before dinner.

My father beamed as he served up lasagna, salad, and home-baked rolls. "Just a little something Arlene and I whipped up," he bragged. "The pasta is from scratch."

"Wow, Dad!" I said, still chewing. "It's good!"

I gave my grandmother a grateful look.

"I should be teaching you to cook too," she told me.

My grin froze on my face. It's not that I have anything against cooking—it's just that I'm a little busy right now. And for the next two and a half years.

"You're plenty old enough to help out with dinner," she went on. "Although it would be easier if you had your driver's license and could run out for groceries and such. When are you taking the test?"

219

My heart missed a beat, then took off double time. This wasn't about cooking! My grandmother was a genius!

Taking a breath for courage, I risked a peek at my mother. Her eyes were firmly on her plate, but the muscle twitching in her jaw proved she was listening.

"I'm not exactly sure," I ventured. "Maybe on my birthday?"

"In your dreams!" Mom snorted, unable to keep quiet any longer. "I might let you start *practicing* again on your birthday. If you're lucky."

"Can I, Mom? Please?" I begged. "Can I please just start practicing again?"

I could tell she was about to say no, but one glance at Grandma and she bit her lip. "I suppose. If you stay out of trouble."

Okay, so it wasn't a license. But it was a whole lot closer to one than I'd been five minutes before.

"Thank you!" I exclaimed, struggling not to look at Grandma. If Mom figured out the two of us were in cahoots, our scheming would be ruined.

"I'm not feeling well," Mom said. "I think I'll go lie down."

She got up from the table, leaving her barely touched dinner behind.

"Are you all right, Andrea?" Grandma called after her.

"She's been getting headaches lately," Dad said, but he couldn't hide his disappointment.

Mom hadn't even complimented his lasagna.

Busy B

It's weird how the busier you get, the more you end up doing the same things over and over, like a rat on one of those exercise wheels. It felt like I'd barely closed my eyes Tuesday night before I was in Wednesday rehearsal.

"All right, people. Attention, please!" Mrs. Conway called from the front of the theater. "Our show is less than two weeks away, so we need to start focusing. I hope you're all selling those tickets."

Judging from the groans I heard around me, I wasn't the only person falling down in that department.

"Also, Principal Ito has informed me that we'll have to clean up the auditorium sometime after our performance, but we'll decide when later. Let's see everyone onstage today, giving their best. Cassie, how about getting us started?"

I pretended not to hear the moaning that accompanied my name, but it was hard to ignore. Slinking up to the stage, I hesitated in the wings, willing the color to fade from my cheeks.

"So are you introducing me or what's the deal?" a soc-y voice demanded behind me. "Some of us have lives, you know, with actual things to do."

"How should I introduce you?" I retorted, turning to face Sterling down. "As a singer? Or are you just posing again today? Like a poser."

"For your information," she said hotly, "you're lucky to have me in this show. As soon as my vocal coach clears me to sing, I'll tear the roof off this place."

"Right."

"It's a medical issue!"

"It's some sort of issue, anyway."

She glared at me and I glared right back.

Sterling's music started. I hadn't introduced her yet, but I didn't care.

"They're playing your song," I taunted. "Time to get out there and pose."

"At least I'm only posing onstage, instead of all over school. You just go ahead and keep believing you're popular now. It gives the rest of us something to laugh at."

At least my boyfriend isn't flirting with other girls! It was right on the tip of my tongue. I wanted to yell it so badly it hurt.

But Sterling had already flounced onto the stage, and I didn't want to shout it in front of the entire assembly.

Which is to say, I did. Desperately. But somehow I restrained myself.

And then Sterling came off, and I had to go on with Hayley. And everybody laughed at me, just like Sterling said.

Because there I was.

Posing.

Social Studies

"You can't let her get to you," Hayley told me as we retrieved our stuff. "If you do, she wins."

"She always wins, so I might as well do what I want."

The guys had already bailed. The auditorium was nearly empty. But Sterling, Tiffi, and Ros were still hanging out, blocking our path to the main exit.

"Look at her! She's so obnoxious!" I complained. "If I walk past her, she'll give me crap. But if I leave by the side exit, she'll say I was scared and give me crap later."

"If you take the side exit, she'll be right," Hayley said.

"Thanks for your support."

Slinging my backpack over one shoulder, I marched up the center aisle. I was nearly to the door when Sterling opened her big mouth:

"Oh, look. Here comes Ms. Bossy."

Tiffi threw me a Nazi salute. "*Heil*, Commandant Carrots!" she cracked, making them both laugh.

I kept walking. That was when a third voice piped up, one that stopped me in my tracks.

"Cassie's just doing her job," Ros said.

Sterling and Tiffi stopped cackling as if someone had flipped a switch.

"Excuse me?" Sterling said.

I knew what she was thinking: Ros's job was to back her up, not to think for herself. Honestly, I was as shocked as she was.

"You shouldn't pick on Cassie for something the teacher's making her do," Ros said.

"Yes! Thank you!" I exclaimed.

I should have kept my mouth shut, though, because the fact that I had opened it only made Sterling madder.

"Oh, I get it," she said, sneering. "Now that you're dating her leftovers, you feel like you have to protect her."

"What?" Ros gasped.

"Precious Quentie might be mad at you if you don't pretend to like her."

"I *do* like her."

Sterling drew herself up and tossed her long hair. "If you like her so much, hang out with *her* from now on. Tiffi and I don't need you."

"Don't be ridiculous," Ros said. "I'm only saying—"

"I heard you, loud and clear. If you'd rather be with these losers than us"—a slight nod of her head included Hayley in the conversation— "then be my guest."

"Hey!" Hayley jumped in. "Who are you calling losers?"

"If the shoe fits," Sterling retorted. "Come on, Tiffi. Let's go." With a final toss of her beauty-queen hair, she marched out the auditorium door, towing Tiffi behind her like a tin can on a bride's bumper.

"I can't believe that just happened," Ros moaned.

Which made at least three of us.

"Come on, Ros," Hayley said, putting an arm around Ros's shoulders. "You don't need Sterling."

"They're best friends!" I protested.

"Not if that's how she's going to treat you," Hayley told Ros.

"I should have known better," Ros said miserably. "Ster doesn't mean anything by her little comments. That's just how she is."

"And you finally stood up to her. Good for you." Hayley squeezed Ros's shoulders and threw me a meaningful look. "Right, Cassie?"

"Um, yeah. Right."

Hayley's eyes demanded more.

"Thank you?" I guessed.

Ros gave me a grateful look and that was when I saw the tears welling in her eyes.

"I mean, that was nice of you," I added, feeling my first-ever pangs of soc sympathy. "You didn't have to do it, though. Sterling's your best friend and I don't want to get between you guys."

Ros shook her head, sniffing bravely. "This has been a long time coming. Besides, you're my friend now too."

"Well . . . yeah."

But Sterling had one thing right. If not for Quentin, Ros and I wouldn't even know each other. His relationship with her was the glue that held us together—and it wasn't super-glue. If she ever found out about that kiss . . .

Guilt overwhelmed me.

Plus, Hayley was giving me that look again.

"You should hang out with us now," I said.

"Really?" Ros blinked back her tears and managed a tentative smile.

"Definitely," I said, adding my arm to Hayley's around Ros's shoulders.

Thursday's Menu at Chez Howard

Chicken cordon bleu
Pommes Anna
French-cut green beans
Homemade éclairs

"Does it really take all day just to cook dinner?" Mom asked irritably.

"I'm learning!" Dad defended himself. "Plus, I *didn't* just cook dinner. I also washed all the windows and power-washed the patio furniture."

"Which reminds me," Grandma told him. "You splashed the back windows with that power washer. You'll have to redo the outsides tomorrow."

"Right," he sighed, looking exhausted.

Crushed

Ros sat with me and Hayley at rehearsal on Friday. We could tell Sterling and Tiffi were whispering about us in back, but we did our best to pretend everything was normal.

Conway rushed in late and went straight to the front of the room. "Sorry. I had to take an important call and I'll be leaving early. I'm going to direct today, to help move things along."

No one was happier to hear that than I was, making the scattered applause and catcalls seem unnecessarily rude.

"Sterling, you're on deck," she said. "Everyone, handle your own props today."

It felt fantastic to lounge in the relative anonymity of the house again. Aside from a few mortifying minutes when Conway made me whistle, no one paid me the least attention. Rehearsal was almost over when I glanced toward the back of the auditorium and blinked in disbelief. I had to be hallucinating—there was no other reasonable explanation for the fact that I'd just spotted my brother lurking behind the last row of chairs.

"Is that . . . Is that *Trevor*?" I asked Hayley, hoping she'd confirm that he was only a mirage.

"Where?" Ros twisted around to see.

Her sudden movement caught Trevor's eye. But instead of fleeing at top speed, like a boy with normal survival instincts, he ducked behind the seats.

"Poor thing!" Ros said. "I'll bet he's here to see Julie."

"Oh, no," I groaned. "You're right." Why had I told him about Julie joining the show?

Because I had no idea he'd be lame enough to come spy on her.

"Does Julie know he's here?" Hayley asked.

We all looked at Julie, a few rows in front of us by herself. As if she sensed our attention, she suddenly turned our way, caught us staring, and gave us a questioning shrug.

I had no intention of filling her in. My brain worked feverishly on plausible excuses while Hayley sat like a statue beside me, trying to solve the same problem. Only Ros moved, and, to my horror, she nodded in Trevor's direction.

Julie shifted her gaze just in time to see Trevor's scruffy head emerge from behind the seats. He locked eyes with her, gulped like a spastic fish, and bolted out of the auditorium.

I squeezed my eyes shut. "My brother, the stalker."

"Poor Trevor," Hayley said. "He's really got it bad."

"Aren't you going to go after him?" Ros asked.

My eyes popped open. "Me? What for?"

"Well, Julie's not going. He must be crushed."

"I'll show him crushed," I muttered.

"Just go," Hayley said. "We'll wait."

With Conway running the show, I really had no excuse. Slipping out of my seat, I tiptoed up the aisle and hurried after Trevor.

I found him at the end of the hall, facing into a corner. His back heaved as I crept closer.

"Trevor?" I said softly, tugging on his T-shirt. "What are you doing here?"

"Being the world's biggest moron," he finally got out, his voice so choky I could barely understand him.

"No, don't say that," I told him. "You just have a crush. I've had a hundred futile crushes. Hurts, doesn't it?"

He turned to face me, his eyes overflowing. "Like a heart attack."

Friday's Menu at Casa Howard

Cheese enchiladas
Beef tacos with guacamole
Chile rellenos
Spanish rice and refried beans
Warm sopaipillas with honey

"Dad, this is your best dinner yet!" I enthused. "Grandma, I didn't know you could cook Mexican."

"A good cook knows the basics of every cuisine," she said with a wink. "Tomorrow, Chinese."

"You know," Dad put in, "there's a really good Chinese takeout over on Laurel. What's that place called, Andrea?"

"I don't remember," Mom said, picking at her enchilada.

"Sure, you do," Dad insisted. "You used to stop there on your way home from work."

"Hmm," she said. "I must have forgotten."

Trevor and I squirmed in our chairs. My mother has a mind like a bank vault—no way had she forgotten. She just didn't want to tell him. Because she was mad at him. And she wanted us all to know it.

"Never mind." Grandma's cheerful voice sailed out over the awkwardness. "We won't need a take-out place, because we'll be cooking from scratch. Is there an Asian market in town?"

"I'm not sure," my father said unhappily.

"Well, that's what the Yellow Pages are for. We'll look at them in the morning. What are everyone else's plans this weekend?" she asked.

"I don't know," Trevor said glumly. "Skating, I guess."

"You're welcome to help your father and me make wontons."

"Maybe."

"Cassie, how about you?"

"I'm hanging out with my boyfriend tomorrow." Kevin didn't know that yet, but I'd call and tell him after dinner.

"Then maybe we girls can do something on Sunday," Grandma suggested. "It's been quite a while since I've taken my granddaughter on a shopping spree."

Shopping spree?

"I'm there," I assured her.

"What do you say, Andrea?" Grandma asked. "We can go someplace nice for lunch. Anywhere you like."

"Can't," Mom said shortly. "Working."

"On Sunday?" Dad protested.

"Might as well. Someone has to. Speaking of which, I have some papers I need to look over." She pushed back from the table and walked out of the dining room.

"Never mind," Grandma said into the silence. "Cassie and I will still go. And Hal, since Andrea's going to be working, you'll have extra time to tackle more chores around here. You know what I always say . . ."

"Home, sweet home equals home, neat home," my father recited reluctantly.

"That's right! There are always a million things to do. I noticed some peeling paint on the garage door today, and the driveway hedge needs trimming. You don't want to let that type of maintenance get ahead of you."

"I guess not," he said with a sigh.

Grandma smiled like it was all settled. "Trevor, how about clearing the table for your father? And Cassie, can you help with the dishes?"

If You Can't Take the Heat . . .

I almost fainted when I walked into the kitchen and saw the mess Dad and Grandma had made. Every pot we owned was either on the counter or already in the sink, the stove was sticky with cooked-on oil, and the blender looked as if it had whirled up a batch of coagulated blood.

"Enchilada sauce," my father said, following my disbelieving gaze. "From scratch."

"And the stove?"

"Taco shells. There's a trick to frying those suckers. You have to get the oil temperature just right—then it still spatters everywhere."

I was tired just thinking about how long it would take to clean up, but Dad looked even more whipped. Dragging himself to the sink, he picked up a dish brush.

"I'd better clear this sink out first, so we'll have someplace to wash the rest. Baked-on cheese is the worst," he said, sighing as he swirled his brush ineffectually around a casserole dish. "Great. Now it's stuck in my bristles too."

"We can run that brush through the dishwasher."

"You'll have to empty it first. The breakfast dishes are still in there."

For the next few minutes I unloaded clean dishes while Trevor walked morosely back and forth, bringing in dirty ones. Dad swished his brush around like he didn't believe he would ever finish. When Trevor brought in the last dirty plate and left us, Dad quit working altogether.

"Nothing against your grandmother, but this has been the longest week of my life. I barely get this kitchen cleaned up before it looks like this again."

"You guys *have* been doing a lot of cooking," I said, trying to wipe down the greasy stove.

"Yeah, cooking. And cleaning. And menu planning. It never ends." He handed me the casserole dish. "Put that in the dishwasher, would you? I'm going to skip prewashing tonight. We'll just use extra soap."

"Grandma says extra soap makes spots."

"I'll roll the dice."

Dropping the sponge, I started stacking, then wedging things into the dishwasher. "We've either got two loads here or we'll have to do some by hand."

"Yeah, okay. I've got the rest. You can run along."

Considering everything still left to do, I was happy to bolt. I was halfway out of the kitchen when Dad stopped me in my tracks.

"Um, Cassie? You wouldn't know anything about your grandmother being here. Would you?"

I made a cautious slow-motion turn, ready to dodge flying frying pans. But Dad was just standing at the sink, a dejected expression on his face.

"What makes you ask that?" I choked out.

"It's just . . . Arlene seems to know a couple of things I don't remember telling her."

"Well, that's what happens when you get old. You forget stuff."

He made a face. "I'm not that old. Did you talk to Grandma about what was going on here before she called me?"

"No!" Technically, that was the truth—and I wasn't about to mention those letters. "I didn't talk to her at all."

Dad shook his head. "This homemaking gig is starting to feel like work. Chores all week, and now all weekend too." Turning back to the sink, he picked up another dish. "The worst part," he told the wall, "is there are *no* official holidays."

Peanut Butter Luv

"You made these yourself?" Kevin asked, taking another bite from one of my grandmother's peanut butter jumbles. "These are awesome!"

"Mostly by myself." Between my grandma and Dad and Trevor, someone had opened the oven or messed with my batter at least once every five minutes. The only person who hadn't interfered was Mom, and that was because she'd gone to work.

I kicked my sneaker heels against the brick wall we sat on, frustrated. The whole point of making peanut butter jumbles that Saturday had been to show Kevin how I felt about him. But the process had been hijacked and now they were just cookies. I hadn't even managed to get him alone—not entirely. We'd met at the park without any of our friends, but once Trevor had learned Dad was driving me, he'd insisted on tagging along to go to the skate bowl.

"I wish we had our licenses," I sighed.

Kevin smiled, his eyes an impossible shade of green in the dappled sunlight. "If we did, where would we go?"

"I don't know." I looked around us at the boringly familiar lawns, trees, and benches. "Somewhere far, far away. With palm trees. And white sand beaches."

"Sounds good to me."

I pushed off the wall, landing on the sidewalk below. "Want to walk around?"

He jumped down beside me. "Sure."

One of the worst things about being fifteen is, there's no place private you can go with your boyfriend. You can't drive and you can't stay home. You can't even complain about it or your parents assume you want to have sex.

"We should have gone to the movies," I said, dodging my third stroller. At least at the movies we could sit in the dark.

Kevin gave me a weird look. "Is something wrong? You seem kind of restless today."

"I am, I guess. Kind of."

"If you'd rather not be here with me—"

"What? No! That's not it at all!"

"Then what?" He pulled me off the path onto the grass beneath a big tree. "Tell me."

"Nothing. It's just . . ." I heaved a sigh. "The park isn't very romantic."

He pulled me closer. "So what? I'm not here to see the park. I'm here to see you."

"I know, but—"

"If I was picky about where I saw you, would I be anywhere near that stupid talent show? Although I have to admit, you're cute in that."

"No, I'm not."

"The cutest thing by a mile."

Then he kissed me. And the next thing I knew we were lying on the grass with our bodies smashed together, making out like Christmas vacation. His mouth tasted of cookies, and something inside me already knew I'd never look at peanut butter the same way again.

Say it, I thought, trying to tease it out with my kisses. *Why can't you just say you love me?*

Angst twisted my heart till I thought it would break. I pulled Kevin closer, kissed him harder, but that didn't stop the ache.

How could I be making out with the love of my life and still be so unhappy?

Remember before, when I said I wasn't crazy?

I might have to take that back.

Pack Animals

Trevor pretended not to see me when I showed up at the skate bowl after Kevin and I parted ways. Bill and Josh were there, the three of them hanging out by the fence with their helmet straps dangling loose, like they were too cool to need protection against concussions. With skulls that thick, they're probably right.

"Hey, Trev," I called through the fence's iron bars. "I'm leaving now, if you want to walk home."

His buddies laughed. Josh pushed him.

Trevor gave me an incredulous look. "I don't need to walk with you. I can walk home by myself."

As if to emphasize Trevor's manliness, Bill let out a belch so disgusting it's a miracle his lunch didn't come up with it. Guys around the bowl applauded with genuine admiration.

"Fine. I'm going," I said before Bill could deliver an encore. It wasn't like I wanted to walk with Trevor, anyway—I just didn't want to get in trouble for ditching him. "Don't tell Dad I didn't ask."

Trevor sneered at me, gulped some air, and delivered his own earth-shattering belch, his mouth open so wide I could see down to his tonsils.

"Lovely," I said, repulsed. "I can't understand why you don't have a girlfriend."

Bill and Josh laughed, proud of their gross-out skills, but the stricken expression on Trevor's face made me regret my low blow. It was too late to take it back, though.

Besides, I wasn't wrong.

My mom has this expression: One dog is a furry person, but two dogs together are dogs.

Substitute *boy* for the first two *dogs* and that saying still works perfectly.

Girl. Friend.

I dove for the ringing phone that night, hoping the caller might be Kevin. The voice on the other end of the line took me by surprise.

"Hi," said Ros. "Whatcha doing?"

"Me?" I glanced around my room as if she might be talking to someone else. "Nothing. Why?"

"I'm bored." She sighed. "Quentin is working late tonight, and Sterling . . ."

"Yeah." No explanation required. "Aren't your parents back from Europe yet?"

"They are, but . . . they're parents. I hate the way Quentin lives at that stupid store. As if his own shifts weren't bad enough, now he's picking up other people's."

"He works too many hours," I agreed, debating whether to tell her why. If Ros realized her choice was between Quentin's time and more jewelry, she might talk some sense into him.

"Do you think it's me?" she asked.

"Well. Actually—"

"Oh, no! What did I do? You have to tell me, Cassie."

"What? No." I sat down on my bed. "You didn't do anything, Ros. It's just . . . Quentin wants to buy you everything you're used to. And that's not going to happen on his allowance."

"That's why he's working so much? He's not tired of me?"

"He's absolutely not tired of you."

Trust me, I felt like adding.

"But that's crazy! I don't need him to buy me stuff!"

"Been there. Told him that."

"You have to tell him again."

"No, *you* have to tell him. And if you want him to listen, don't mention my name. Let him think you figured it out yourself."

"You're a good friend, Cassie," she said. "As soon as we hang up, I'm going to have Tess drop me off over there, to surprise him in his van when he gets off work. I'll bring some bread and cheese, and candles, and the CD he burned for me. If I fold the backseat down, it'll be like a little picnic."

"He'll love that," I said, bracing for the usual onslaught of jealous feelings.

But none came.

I poked around the old sore spots on my heart and couldn't rouse even a twinge. I honestly didn't care if Quentin and Ros made out in his van all night.

"You know what he really likes? Pie," I offered, high on

my own relief. "Blueberry, if you can find it. With whipped cream, not ice cream. And a spoon. He likes it in a bowl with a spoon."

"I know exactly where I can get one, too. What are you and Kevin doing tonight?"

"Nothing," I admitted. Definitely nothing involving candles and whipped cream.

"He's probably saving up for Valentine's Day. Have you guys made plans yet?"

"No, but that's still a week away."

Nothing to worry about.

Right?

"Hey, you know what you should wear to school on Monday?" she asked. "That gauze top you wore to Bonfire with the skirt you wore to my party. That would make a cute outfit."

That *would* make a cute outfit—if the top in question weren't wadded into a damp, molding ball at the back of my closet.

"I'm kind of done with that shirt," I told her. "Bad associations."

"No, it's cute. All the girls said so."

"Really?" Was Ros giving me *social* pointers?

"You know what else would be cute? A headband. Your hair must be long enough now. Try one and see."

"All right, I will." I had nothing to lose in the hair department.

"Thanks again!" she said, clicking off.

I sat on my bed long after her call, just thinking about

everything. She must have appreciated my help with Quentin, and that wardrobe advice was her way of returning the favor.

Not that she owed me. Quite the reverse. But the mistake I'd made with Quentin clearly wasn't on her radar.

Because she trusts her boyfriend, I realized. *Exactly like she told you to do.*

I could learn a lot from Ros. And not just about my hair. If I'd been smart enough to take her advice, who knows where Kevin and I would be now?

At least no one got hurt but me, I thought gratefully.

It was weird, but up until that moment, I'd never worried about Ros's feelings. All right, yes—I'd imagined her angry and wreaking revenge. But I'd really only cared how her learning the truth might hurt me, and Kevin, and Quentin.

Sitting on my bed that night, the phone still in my hand, I realized there was one more person I didn't want to see hurt.

I didn't want to hurt Ros.

Love Lessons. Not.

"This is going to be fun," Grandma said, easing Dad's Corolla into a metered spot downtown. Personally, I prefer the mall, but since Grandma was buying I could afford to be flexible. And it *was* going to be fun—although I couldn't help feeling sorry for Mom, missing all the shopping by working on a Sunday.

"I wish Mom hadn't gone to the office," I said as we started down the sidewalk. "I'm pretty sure she's only there to make a point."

Grandma chuckled. "Pretty sure? Your mother has always been headstrong. As long as things go her way, everything's fine. But your father taking off on this tangent she never expected or approved of . . . well, she's not going to take that lying down."

"I don't think it's *all* about getting her own way," I ventured. "There's other stuff going on. It's complicated."

"And you're very mature to recognize that. This looks like a fun store. Want to go inside?"

"Okay."

We flipped through the racks in a boutique that turned out to be more her taste than mine. Grandma considered a blazer before we decided to keep moving.

"How was your date with Kevin yesterday?" she asked when we were back outside again.

"I wouldn't call it a date. We just hung out at the park."

"Hung out?" Grandma raised a skeptical brow. "I helped your father pretreat grass stains on your shirt this morning."

My face went redder than a radish, which, as we all know, is not an attractive vegetable. "It's just . . . we were, you know . . . sitting on the grass."

"Which explains the grass stains on your *pants*," she allowed.

"Grandma! We were only—"

"Relax," she said, chuckling. "Gray hair doesn't make a person forget what it's like to be young and in love."

I stared at her, speechless.

"What?" she asked. "You two are in love, aren't you?"

I hesitated, then shrugged. Somehow it seemed safe to confide in Grandma. "I think Kevin feels like I do, but he won't say. We had this stupid fight and now it's like we're starting over. All I want is for everything to be perfect between us. I have no idea what he wants."

"Well, that's the age-old problem, isn't it?"

"What is?"

"Falling in love is easy. Being in love is hard."

I'd never heard it put that way before. "I guess," I said uncertainly.

"Trust me," Grandma said. "Why do so many fairy tales end with the first kiss?"

"You may be on to something."

"I'm way past on to it. You don't live with a man forty years without hitting a few snags. And you don't stay together without working them out."

"Do you miss Grandpa a lot?"

"Every day, like he never passed. My brain knows he's gone, but my heart won't give up. Love is complicated that way. Not that you need me to tell you love is complicated," she said with a wry grin. "You're getting a world-class lesson from your parents right now."

Which reminded me of something.

"Grandma?" I asked nervously. "Are you going to tell them about those letters I wrote?"

"I won't have to."

What does that mean? I worried. *Does she think they'll find out on their own?*

"Your folks will get through this," she added reassuringly.

"And I'm going to stay as long as it takes to help them figure out how."

"Are you going to stay until Friday? I need to sell one more ticket to our school talent show."

"Of course I'll buy a ticket. Oh, Cassie, look at that darling dress!" she cried, pointing to a mannequin in a window. "Do you still like pink?"

"I *love* pink," I assured her, beelining for the store.

"Oh, wait. Never mind. That shade won't look good with grass stains."

"Grandma!"

She laughed. "Let an old girl have some fun."

The Second Time Is <u>Not</u> the Charm

Monday morning I walked into Conway's room and nearly had a heart attack. A white-haired woman was camped out at the front of the class, burying Conway's usually pristine desk under piles of books and what appeared to be a jumbled assortment of sweaters.

"What happened to Mrs. Conway?" I blurted out in a panic. The last time we'd had a substitute, Mr. Conway had gone in for chemo.

The woman gave me a startled look, but didn't take offense. "I'm Mrs. Harrier. You must be Cassie."

In my experience, it's rarely a good thing when an adult knows my name before I introduce myself. "How did you guess?" I asked cautiously.

"That hair." She smiled. "It's hard to miss, isn't it?"

I touched my new headband self-consciously, wondering if a hat might have made an even bigger improvement.

"Wait, your teacher left you a note." She patted down the pockets of the sweater she was wearing, then turned to the backups on Conway's desk, eventually extracting a folded slip of paper. "Here you go."

All my inner alarm bells were going off, but I made myself walk back to my seat, where I could get some privacy.

"Why were you talking to the sub?" Kevin asked.

"Mrs. Conway left me a note," I said, sitting down and unfolding it.

"She did? What does it say?"

"I'll tell you in a minute."

"Excuse me, class," Mrs. Harrier called. "I'm filling in for Mrs. Conway this week, so if you'll all please take your seats, I'll call the roll and we'll get to know each other."

"Score!" Jeff Mann exulted, probably envisioning another supervision-free week in the library's computer lab. People traded excited whispers all over the room, but I barely heard them as I read Mrs. Conway's note:

Dear Cassie:

Something important has come up and I'm going to be out for a few days. While I'm gone, I have complete confidence in your ability to direct the talent show. Please hold all our rehearsals as planned, and talk to Principal Ito if you need help with anything. He's aware of the situation and will serve as faculty advisor in my absence.

Thanks for your help and understanding. I know I can count on you.

Mrs. Conway

P.S. Make sure Sterling sings this week. No more excuses!

I stared at that note long after I finished reading, like I thought its message might change if I just wished hard enough. Was Mr. Conway sick again? Did Mrs. Conway honestly expect me to run the talent show? And how did a mere mortal make Sterling Carter do anything?

Could things possibly get any worse?

Why, yes. As a matter of fact, they could.

The Blind Leading the Grind

"You can do it," Hayley insisted in the auditorium, trying to psych me up. "You've *been* doing it."

"Not alone! Mrs. Conway was always here for backup before," I whispered nervously.

"If I were you, I'd hurry and get things started," Ros advised. "If you hesitate, you'll just look scared."

I *was* scared. Obviously.

That was when Principal Ito walked in.

"Why are these people just sitting around, Miss Howard?" he asked, stalking down the center aisle with that perpetually worried expression of his.

"We were, uh . . . just getting started," I lied.

Principal Ito clapped twice. "Listen up, people! Mrs.

Conway is out for a few days and she's left Cassie Howard in charge of the show, under my supervision."

Groans filled the room.

"Nobody planned it that way," he assured them. "But since it can't be helped, we all have to do our best. I'll be popping in and out to check on progress. Between visits, I trust you to act like mature individuals."

Which was his way of saying he didn't trust us at all.

Particularly me.

"All right, then, Miss Howard. I'll be just down the hall. And I can hear you people from my office," he warned on his way out. "I want these doors left open."

He stopped long enough to kick down the doorstops on a couple of the auditorium's main entrance doors, gave us one last anxious glance, and disappeared.

"Thanks for the vote of confidence," I grumbled.

"At least he left," Hayley said.

Gathering my courage, I moved to the spot in front of the stage where Mrs. Conway always stood. "I guess we'd better get started. Sterling, you're supposed to sing today. Are you ready?"

She was in a back row with Tiffi again. "I'd rather save my voice," she said.

"Save it for what? Christmas?"

A couple of people snickered. Sterling gave me a hostile look.

"It's just that Mrs. Conway specifically said you're supposed to sing and I don't want to let her down," I pleaded. "Besides, you have to practice, right?"

"I'll practice with my coach," she snapped. "You can just skip me today. Cut straight to the part where you and Hayley humiliate yourselves."

Forget about my cheeks, I could feel my ears turning red. If I didn't make Sterling rehearse, I'd lose any minor credibility I had as a director.

But if I tried and failed, that would be even worse.

"Whatever," I said. "Hayley, you're up."

"We're up, you mean," she corrected.

"Just go on without me today. I can't perform and run things too."

She stopped halfway up the stage stairs. "You've been doing it."

"This is different." If Sterling wasn't performing, my taking the stage would only give her more of the upper hand.

Unfortunately, Hayley didn't get that. "Can I talk to you a minute?" she asked, glaring.

"Sure. After rehearsal. Gregor, get up there too. You're behind Hayley. And find your own basketball—it's backstage somewhere."

He gave me a blistering look as he stalked past.

And that was just the beginning.

Our fourth act, the unicyclist, was still absent, and no one knew if she was ever coming back. The next few acts didn't want to rehearse because the act in front of them hadn't. Our quartet from band *did* want to rehearse, but no one wanted to hear that endless piece of music again. There was chaos in the seats by the time they finished playing—people laughing and flirting and throwing paper airplanes.

So of course Principal Ito chose that moment to show up again. "What's going on in here?" he demanded.

"Nothing!" I chirped, rushing out to the edge of the stage. "Our, um . . . our next act is Julie Evans."

Julie walked onstage with a leash in one hand and a long silver whistle in the other. My heart skipped as I suddenly remembered the little detail I'd let slide.

Raising the whistle to her lips, Julie blew a long silent blast. Silent to people, that is. Her scruffy white dog heard it perfectly and charged out of the wings.

"We have a dog in here?" Ito bellowed. "Why wasn't I informed of this?"

Julie turned to me, wide-eyed. Her dog belly-crawled across the boards to cower behind her legs.

"I, uh . . . I was supposed to ask you about it, but . . . I kind of forgot," I admitted.

Ito shook his head. "Does your dog bite?" he asked Julie.

"No! Of course not."

"Then carry on. For now. But come to my office the moment you're done. I'll need your parents to sign some papers."

"Okay," she said meekly.

Julie tried to pick up where she'd left off, but her dog wouldn't venture out of her shadow after that. No amount of coaxing could make him do a trick.

"It's Bucky's first time on a stage. I think he got freaked out," she told me back in the wings.

"Yeah, sorry about the yelling."

"He'll do better next time," she said uncertainly.

I nodded and spent the next several acts desperately

pretending our whole show wasn't going down the drain. Finally, I got to Fitz.

"You don't have any birds here, right?" I asked. "If you do, don't let Ito see them."

Fitz shook his head. "I'm going to rehearse my new mind-reading trick today."

Fitz is my friend. Which is why I'm not going to describe his mind-reading trick. Let's just say it involved Hayley pretending to be surprised when he "randomly" picked her out of the audience and channeled the answers to her "unrehearsed" questions. People were groaning in their seats before he finished. Not magic, believe me.

"Maybe I won't do that one in the show," he ventured when he came off.

I forced a smile as he walked away, reminding myself that we still had two more practices before the actual show.

"Okay, you girls are on," I told our final act. All three sisters were wearing their dancing shoes, but not one of them moved.

"Is there a problem?" I asked.

"You just saw it leave the stage," the tapper told me snidely. "We don't want to follow that."

"Why? Afraid he'll show you up?" I joked weakly.

"When is Mrs. Conway coming back?"

"I don't know. Can we discuss this after rehearsal?"

"We're not staying in the show if Mrs. Conway isn't directing," the modern dancer said. "We won't let you make us look like fools."

"Even if she comes back, she's not going to cut Fitz. Besides, if you look like fools it's on you, not anyone else."

All three of them glared at me.

"Not that you will," I said quickly. "It's just . . . the other acts don't matter."

"*What* other acts?" the ballet dancer asked. "Basketball dribbling? Stupid pet tricks? We thought this was a *talent* show."

"Not everyone is lucky enough to get a glory talent. It doesn't mean they're not talented in their own way."

"Yeah, right," said the tapper. "You know what? I don't want to be in this show anymore."

"That makes three of us," said the ballerina. "It's official. We quit."

They all stalked off before I could argue, a single set of taps clicking out their indignant departure.

"Okay, that's a wrap," I called from the stage, not bothering to explain our lack of finale. "See you people on Wednesday, and don't forget dress rehearsal Thursday."

I could only pray Mrs. Conway would be back by then.

Ticket to Ride

"I've been asking around about ticket sales," Ros reported, running up as I came off the stage. "Looks like we'll have a full house Friday."

Was that supposed to make me feel better?

"Where's Hayley?" I asked.

"She left with Fitz."

Great. She was still mad at me, then.

"I'm going to find Kevin. I'll see you tomorrow," I said.

"Oh." Ros seemed disappointed. "Okay."

Sterling and Tiffi were still hanging out at the top of the auditorium. I was about to tell Ros she should go make up with Sterling when Bryce Tate swaggered in, dangling a long key chain.

"Got it!" he crowed triumphantly.

Sterling squealed and ran at him, jumping into his arms. "Really? The Porsche?" she cried deliriously.

"Come and take a ride," he gloated.

He was carrying her out caveman style when Tiffi ran up to join them.

"Hey, can I bum a ride with you guys?" she asked. "Just to my house, okay?"

"Sure. Why not?" Tate said magnanimously. "But it's only a two-seater. You'll have to squeeze in back."

"I'm little," she assured him, showing off her jutting hip bones.

The three of them walked out, all hanging on each other. When I turned back to Ros, the look on her face was just short of tears.

"You're getting a car too," I reminded her lamely.

She nodded sadly. "Yep. Next week."

I knew what she was thinking: Sterling wouldn't be riding with her.

"Things change. Stuff blows over," I said awkwardly. "Hey, if you want to tell Sterling that we fought and you hate me now . . ."

Ros shook her head. "But thanks for the offer. See you tomorrow, Cassie."

She headed up the center aisle, utterly dejected. I watched her as far as the doors before Kevin tapped my shoulder.

"Hey, what's the matter?" he asked.

"What *isn't* the matter? Hayley's mad, Ros is depressed, our grand finale just quit. I'd say this show is going to the dogs, except that even the dog won't perform. How am I going to pull this off if Mrs. Conway doesn't come back?"

Kevin made a face. "It wasn't that bad."

"Did we just see the same disaster?"

"So we had a few hiccups today. It's not worth getting worked up about."

"I am not worked up, Kevin! I'm just saying we have problems."

"Okay, I'm sorry. Calm down."

Calm down?

"You could be more supportive," I told him sullenly.

He blinked with disbelief. "I'm working the lights, aren't I?"

"Right, so what more can I ask for?"

"Listen, Cassie, if—"

"No, just forget it. My bad. I'll see you tomorrow," I said, giving him a quick hug before I traced Ros's dejected steps up and out the doors.

Me running the show?
I can't direct my own life!
Someone get the hook.

$(Cell)^2$

"How exciting!" Grandma said at dinner. "My grand-daughter, the director!"

"Yeah, exciting in a bad way," I muttered.

"Don't be ridiculous," my mother said. "Responsibility builds character."

She tossed my dad a significant glance, which he pretended not to see, miffed by her refusal to compliment his pot pie's flaky crust. Trevor continued sullenly plucking peas out of his gravy.

It would have been a relief to discuss how worried I was about what might be happening with Mr. Conway, but since I'd kept my teacher's secret at home as well as at school, I couldn't just suddenly bring it up. Besides, with that much tension at the table, the smartest thing to do was make a quick escape.

Dad apprehended me carrying my plate into the kitchen. "Here," he said, reaching into his pocket. "I want to give you this."

I held out my hand on reflex. I almost fainted when I saw what he put there.

"Your cell phone?" I squealed. "Do you mean it?"

"I'm proud of you, taking on such a big job. Having a phone will help you keep on top of the show."

"It will! It'll be a huge help!" I assured him. Not to mention its other, more attractive uses. I'd been begging for a cell forever, but Mom had always shot me down. "Are you sure?"

He nodded. "I don't need it around the house. No one calls me anymore." His gaze wandered off. "I really ought to start getting out. . . ."

"But about the phone," I prompted. "I can keep it? For good?"

"You bet. Congratulations, Spielberg."

Wheel of Misfortune

I thought Mrs. Conway was tough, but Mrs. Harrier is some sort of grammar overlord. *Modern English Grammar?* Too easy. Sentence trees? Child's play. We spent the entire class on Tuesday doing these horrifying timed punctuation drills. She started out by telling us that every score we were about to earn would count toward our final semester grade; then every five minutes she smacked one of those silver restaurant bells, just to up our stress levels.

At lunch I gave everyone my new cell number, but that was a big letdown. The guys don't have cell phones yet, and Hayley was still sulking. The only one who made a fuss was Ros.

I got even in PE by purposely missing easy shots. Hayley and I were still acting weird to each other when I left the gym and headed for home.

Dad and Grandma were in our kitchen. Again. I heard raised voices when I walked in—something about whether it ought to be illegal to melt paraffin into chocolate—and made a quick dodge down the hall to my room. I could have used a snack, but I definitely didn't need more drama.

Which was why I wasn't happy to find Trevor at my desk.

"What are you doing in here, you little snoop? If you touched anything, I swear I'll—"

"I didn't! The carpet's wet in my room is all. Grandma made Dad shampoo it."

"Then why aren't you studying in the den?"

Trevor cocked an ear toward my doorway. The paraffin debate was still raging. "Do you really have to ask?"

I could appreciate his dilemma, but I didn't need him bugging me. "Look, I have homework too, and I want to use my desk."

"Okay. So I'll read on your bed."

"Why can't you read on your own bed? You can jump that far from the hall."

He sighed as he gathered up his papers. "Remember this tomorrow, when *your* carpet is wet."

On his way out, he hesitated in my doorway. "Has Julie done her act yet?"

I groaned, remembering. "She tried. I don't want to talk about the show."

"Fine. It's just . . . well . . . I could help you. If you want."

"How's your whistling?" I asked.

"Oh, forget it," he said irritably. "It was a dumb idea. I just thought . . ."

I knew exactly what he'd thought. On the other hand, Trevor was the one person I wasn't afraid to direct. And if

Mrs. Conway didn't come back, I'd need all the help I could get.

"I could use a hand with the props," I admitted, taking pity on us both. "That is, if you promise to do what I say and not to bother Julie."

"Please! I don't even like her anymore."

"Right. You're just suddenly filled with charitable urges."

"Not like *that*, Hal!" Grandma scolded from down the hallway. "You have to dry the lettuce first."

Trevor shrugged. "Maybe I just want to get out of the house."

Who could argue with that?

What Goes Around (at Cucina Howard)

Antipasto salad
Ravioli with meat sauce
Fettuccine Alfredo
Chocolate-dipped biscotti

"You know, Hal, I think you're putting on weight," Grandma said at dinner that night. "All this good eating is catching up with you."

Mom snorted but shut it down quickly.

"I don't see how," Dad replied through a tight smile. "I certainly ought to be working it off."

"You get on the scale and see if I'm not right," Grandma said. "Tomorrow, I'll teach you my exercises.

You'll be amazed how well you can keep yourself up in just a few minutes a day."

My grandmother exercises to an ancient Jack LaLanne video every morning wearing pink hot rollers and a bright purple leotard. The mere idea of Dad joining in made me laugh out loud.

"Good health is nothing to laugh at, missy," Grandma said, her mouth crinkling suspiciously at the corners. "Now if you'll all excuse me, it's time for my bubble bath."

"Mine too," Mom said, getting up and exiting in the opposite direction.

"Leave the dishes, Trevor," Dad said. "Cassie will clear them tonight."

"Hey!" I protested as Trevor took off. "I'm already helping wash up!"

"I want to talk to you. Alone." Dad's expression made arguing seem like a bad idea.

"Did I do something wrong?" I asked nervously, following him into the kitchen.

"You might as well admit it. I know you're the reason your grandma is here."

"What? How?"

How? Had I just said *how?* I froze to the sticky floor, my eyes going huge while my lungs shrank to nothing. Have I mentioned I'm not a good liar?

"Aha!" Dad exclaimed. "I knew it! Process of deduction!"

Which meant that he hadn't known anything until I opened my mouth.

"Don't tell Mom," I begged. "It was an accident—this

stupid school assignment. I wrote Grandma some letters but I had no idea what would happen."

"Family business is family business," he told me sharply. "We don't spread our personal matters around."

"Grandma is family," I said, seriously hoping he wouldn't drag Mrs. Conway into it.

"That doesn't mean we tell her everything. Do you tell me and your mother everything?"

"Well . . . um . . ."

"Take the Fifth," he advised with heavy irony.

"She would have found out anyway. Besides, you invited her, right? You were *glad* to have her help."

"That was before."

"Before what?"

"Before I started suspecting that her real plan is to drive me crazy. Jack LaLanne—is she nuts?"

"It won't be that bad. I'll lend you a leotard."

I had picked a bad time to joke around.

"Don't think this is over," he warned. "Your mother hasn't lifted one finger around here since your grandma stepped through the front door. Meanwhile, I'm killing myself and no one appreciates it. Somebody has to pick up the slack, and I'm thinking that someone is you."

"I have rehearsal!" I whined. "I've got rehearsal for the next two days, and then the show!"

Dad's smile had a hint of evil about it. "What are you doing right now?"

Drama Queen

Wednesday's rehearsal was a nightmare. Only about five people cared enough to write down my cell phone number, a third of our acts didn't show up, and the ones who did all complained about rehearsing without Mrs. Conway again. Sterling refused to set foot onstage, Julie didn't bring her dog because her mom forgot to sign Ito's papers, and the dancing sisters stayed away, leaving us without a finale. Hayley was still sulky and, to add insult to injury, Principal Ito informed me there had better be less horsing around than he'd heard on Monday.

And then there was Trevor. He showed up at the side exit and waved me over frantically.

"I'm here, but I don't want anyone to see me," he said, lurking behind the door. He'd ridden his bike over from the middle school, and honestly, he smelled like it.

"Explain to me how you're going to handle props while nobody sees you," I said.

"Well . . . I'll be backstage."

"And so will everyone else. Look, Trevor, do you want to do this or not?"

"I . . . but . . . Just don't introduce me or tell people I'm your little brother."

"With pleasure," I said, pointing him toward the stage

stairs. "Go on up, and if we ever get started, I'll come show you what to do."

I have to give Trevor this: he busted his butt learning those props and organizing them better. There was only one awkward moment, when Julie's act was called. She couldn't rehearse without her dog, but she brought up a stuffed monkey to add to her things. I honestly thought Trev was going to pass out. I'm positive he stopped breathing.

"I should be able to bring Bucky for the dress rehearsal tomorrow," she told me.

"Okay, good."

She glanced at Trevor, who immediately turned his back. She gave me a questioning look. I sighed.

"Julie, do you remember Trevor? He heard we needed some help, so he's taking over on props."

It was obviously killing me not to make some crack about how he'd love to be her monkey boy, but I restrained myself, simply tapping him on the shoulder and handing him the toy. He added it to Julie's other props without ever looking her way, but after she left, his face was so tragic I had to feel sorry for him.

We ran through the remaining acts—the ones that were cooperating, anyway—and finally I called up Fitz.

"Listen," I told him. "How would you feel about being our new finale?"

"Me?" he said, flattered. "You think I'm good enough?"

"You're as good as anyone here," I said, which barely even required stretching the truth. "Plus, we need something flashy to end with. Maybe your trick with the doves?"

"Perfect!" he agreed. "I'll do it!"

Considering that I hadn't actually seen his dove trick yet, I wasn't as relieved as I might have been. But at least we had a finale.

"Don't forget dress rehearsal tomorrow," I shouted as people started leaving. "And turn in your ticket money to Ros." With Mrs. Conway out, Ros had become the de facto bank.

Kevin was retrieving his backpack when I came down the stage stairs. "Gotta bail," he said, heading for the exit. "I have a ton of homework tonight."

"Kevin, wait!" I called. "How do you think it went today?"

He shrugged. "Fine."

"Fine?" I gave him a disbelieving look.

"What do you want me to say, Cassie?"

"Forget it. Have fun with your homework."

"What?" he exclaimed as I walked away. "*Now* what did I do?"

But if he didn't know, how could I tell him? All I wanted was a little sympathy. All right—a lot of sympathy. But either he didn't get that or he just didn't care.

How could he say it went fine? I sniffed. *He should have said that they were mean, but I did fine. Even if I didn't.*

No, especially if I didn't.

The Pizza Man Always Rings Twice

The streetlights were coming on as Trevor and I walked up to our house, Trev pushing his bike listlessly. But despite the darkening sky, we were both surprised to see Mom's car in our open garage. She had gotten home early compared to the hours she'd been working lately.

"Mom's home," Trevor said.

"Uh-huh."

Neither one of us said what we were thinking, that all those gourmet meals weren't worth the strained silences we ate them in. Instead of coming around to having Dad at home, Mom seemed more unhappy every day. She barely spoke to him or Grandma, and when she did it was usually to say she was leaving.

I opened our front door a crack and stuck one ear inside, making sure the coast was clear before I took the plunge.

"Sounds quiet." But as soon as we walked in, I realized something was off. "I don't smell dinner."

Trevor sniffed the air. "Me either."

We headed for the kitchen. Grandma was sitting alone at the counter, flipping through a cookbook.

"Home so soon?" she asked, surprised.

"It's not soon, Grandma. It's dark out."

She checked her watch. "Oh, dear. Your father and I

were going to make Swedish meatballs, but we haven't even started yet."

"Where is Dad?" I asked. "We saw Mom's car."

"They're having a little chat in their bedroom. I'm sure they'll be out soon." Grandma closed her cookbook. "I'll tell you what, why don't the three of us whip up something quick for dinner?"

"I know the perfect recipe," I said. "555-0214."

She shook her head, not getting it.

"Pizza delivery," Trev explained. "Let's get sausage and mushrooms."

"Pepperoni," I said. "And *no* mushrooms."

"Sausage and no mushrooms," he countered.

"Done." I reached for the phone at the end of the bar.

"Surely we can think of something healthier than that," Grandma protested before I could dial. "Or, if it's pizza you're craving, we can make our own."

"This place is really good and really fast," I whined, too hungry to wait for a pizza from scratch. "We can make a salad."

"All right," she said, giving in. "If that's what you kids want."

I dialed Bongiovanni's and ordered before she could change her mind. We were putting the finishing touches on Grandma's elaborate gourmet salad when a sudden boom made the house shudder. I barely realized the sound was a door slamming before it was followed by angry voices.

"Maybe you could be more dramatic," my father said sarcastically. "Make some holes in the walls."

"If I make them, you and Mother will just turn it into another project," Mom fired back.

"Why don't you admit this is all about status? You don't care what I want—you're embarrassed to have me home because of what your lawyer friends might think!"

"Why don't *you* admit it's about you checking out and dumping everything on me?"

"How can you say that, with all the stuff I'm doing here?"

"No one asked you to do it. In fact, I'm pretty sure I asked you not to."

We ran out from the kitchen in time to see Mom storming down the hall, an overnight bag in one hand and Dad hot on her heels.

"So you're just running off to hide?" he demanded.

"You know exactly where I'll be—at the office. Someone has to support this family."

"Andrea," Grandma intervened. "Surely you're not going to sleep at the office? That seems a little dra—"

"Stay out of it," Mom snapped. "You've already done enough."

Grandma stepped back, clearing Mom's path to the garage. That was when she spotted me and Trevor. Her eyes dropped closed. She faltered a step, blind.

And then she just kept going. The kitchen door slammed behind her, followed by the sound of her car roaring out to the street.

"Well!" Grandma said into the silence. "That was unpleasant."

Dad looked dazed. He peered around at us as if he'd just woken up from a very bad dream.

"I'll go after her," he said shakily. "I should go, right?"

"Definitely," I said. "Go."

But Grandma shook her head. "The best thing you can do right now is give her some time alone."

"Are you sure?" Dad asked.

"Don't worry—she'll cool off. And in the meantime, there are plenty of ways to keep busy. There's the carpet to finish shampooing, for one, and I've been thinking we ought to repaint the living room—that cream is looking dated."

"Mom will have a cow if you change the living room," I said, feeling like somebody had to stick up for her. "She likes that color."

"She liked it when she chose it," Grandma corrected. "And we won't do anything drastic. I'm seeing a soft pale yellow, just to freshen things up."

"Yellow *would* look good with the furniture," Trevor said. "Plus, the drapes would really pop."

I shot my sibling traitor a dangerous look, only to find my father aiming a similar glare my way. Grandma continued smiling, oblivious.

The doorbell rang.

"I'll get it!" Trev and I both yelled at once.

"Who's at the door?" Dad asked, confused.

"The pizza man. Oh, yeah—we need some money."

"No one told me we were ordering pizza," he griped, fishing out his wallet. "I don't even know if I have enough cash."

The bell rang again.

"Let me get this, Hal," Grandma said. "It's the least I can do, since I didn't get to teach you my meatballs."

She and Trevor scurried off, leaving me alone with Dad.

"Remember what I did last weekend?" he asked me. "Chore-a-palooza?"

"Yes," I said uneasily.

"Put it this way: if I end up shampooing and painting all weekend, I'm going to need a *responsible* helper."

Show or No-Show?

Our dress rehearsal was chaos. You might think having half of our acts pull a no-show would make things move more quickly.

You'd be wrong.

I'd just walked up front to get things started when Trevor ran out from backstage in a panic.

"Did you move our props?" he asked me.

"They're not where you left them?"

"No! Yesterday I put everything in that big dressing room with the mirror. I had it all organized and now it's gone!"

"Maybe Principal Ito moved stuff," I said, trying not to hyperventilate. "Are you sure you looked in the right room?"

"Cassie! There's only one room with a mirror."

"Which is why using it for props was so completely moronic," Sterling said, walking up to break into our conversation. "It's called a *dressing* room for a reason, you know—not to mention that people need someplace to warm up their voices. Your toys and whatnot are in the costume room. Where they belong," she told Trevor. "Tiffi and I moved them for you."

He just stared at her, speechless.

"You're welcome," she added sarcastically before turning to me. "Are we wearing our costumes today or what? I thought this was a *dress* rehearsal."

"Does that mean you're rehearsing?" I asked, astonished.

"Are we dressing?"

"Everyone, get your costumes on!" I shouted over the noise in the auditorium. "Let's get going, all right?"

My cell phone rang.

"Cassie? This is Principal Ito. I'm in a meeting and can't leave now. How is everything there?"

"Um . . . same as usual."

"Well, if something comes up, see my secretary. She knows how to reach me."

I had just said good-bye when my phone rang again. "Yeah, this is Gregor. I couldn't get my costume, so I won't be there."

"You're still coming tomorrow, though, right?"

He had already clicked off.

I found Kevin, Hayley, and Ros sitting in the front row, looking bored.

"Where's Fitz?" I asked.

"Putting on his costume," Hayley said. "Isn't that what you wanted?"

"Oh, right. Good. So . . . you don't have a costume?"

"Do you?" she countered.

I hadn't even thought about that. "Just clothes. It doesn't matter."

"Are you doing our act or not?" she demanded. "Because if you're bailing, why shouldn't I?"

"Hayley, you have a talent—I don't. Plus, all you have to do is whistle. Meanwhile, I'm running around like a decapitated chicken trying to keep track of the whole show."

"So you *are* bailing."

I sighed. "Would that be so wrong?"

Glaring, she got up and walked out the side door.

"Do you think she went to change?" I asked Kevin.

"Probably," he said.

"You can't be serious!"

"Why do I even try?" he griped, heading off to the sound booth.

"She'll be back," Ros assured me. "Hey, is Principal Ito coming today? I need to give him more ticket money."

"Just hold on to it," I said, fighting the urge to run after Hayley. I wanted to tell her not to be mad, but how could I leave when I was supposed to direct the show?

"We need a towel!" Trevor shouted, reappearing at the edge of the stage.

"What for?"

"Julie's dog just made a pud—"

"Paper towels. Bathroom," I said, holding up a hand to cut off his explanation. "And I know nothing about this."

All I needed was for Principal Ito to get wind of a dog accident in his precious auditorium. Or, wait—does getting wind of something mean you smell it? Because that would be even worse.

"Use *lots* of towels!" I shouted after Trevor.

Performers were crowding the wings when Sterling finally emerged from the big dressing room wearing her Snow

Queen tiara and a strapless, floor-length, silver-sequined formal. People gasped as she walked by—probably because she looked more ready to participate in the evening gown portion of the Miss America pageant than a student talent show—but Sterling loved the attention.

"I'm ready," she informed me haughtily. "You can introduce me now."

I bit my lip, walked into the spotlight, and addressed the empty seats. "Ladies and gentlemen, please welcome our opening act, Miss Sterling Carter!"

Her music started and Sterling pranced out. For a moment I actually believed she was finally going to sing. Then she looked around, threw up her hands, and started yelling, "Cut!"

Trevor and I both walked out to see what was the matter.

"Where's my microphone?" she demanded before I could say anything.

"You said you were bringing your own."

"It's on the prop list," Trevor added, backing me up.

"Well, I didn't get it yet. You should still have the regular microphone out here."

"You specifically told me you didn't want it," I reminded her testily.

"Not at center stage. Duh! It should be on the side, for backup. Do I have to think of everything?"

I took a deep breath and held it until the urge to slap her passed. "Trevor," I said, in an uncanny imitation of my mother's fake-calm voice, "would you mind getting the microphone?"

"Don't bother *now*," Sterling snarled, stopping him. "I can't sing after that."

"After what?"

"Just forget it, Cassie. You can't do anything right."

She stomped off the stage in a blinding flash of silver, leaving me and Trevor slack-jawed.

"Is she always so obnoxious?" he asked.

I shook my head. "Sometimes she's worse."

"Have you tried throwing a bucket of water on her?"

We both started laughing—it was either laugh or cry.

"I'm melllllllllting," Trevor mocked, shimmying his hips like Sterling on his way back to the wings. "Mellllllting . . ."

A burst of backstage giggling suggested I wasn't the only one who'd caught his performance, but I didn't care anymore. If someone told Sterling and she quit over that, I'd just put Hayley first. Unless Hayley didn't come back, in which case Gregor would be our first act. Unless he didn't show up either, in which case I'd just have a nervous breakdown and thank the audience for paying to see it.

That ought to be worth ten bucks, right? It's not every day you see an orange-haired lunatic being strapped into a straitjacket.

Kiss and Tattle-Tell

I followed Trevor out to the bike rack after rehearsal, thinking we'd walk home together again, but he decided he'd rather pedal than push, leaving me on my own. I didn't mind. After that nightmare in the auditorium, I could have used a little peace.

Unfortunately, my visit to my happy place lasted all of sixty seconds. That was how long it took me to run into Fitz and Hayley on our school's front lawn.

The two of them stopped talking when I walked up.

"Hey, what's up?" I asked. "You guys waiting for a ride?"

"No," Hayley said huffily, still mad about doing our act alone.

"Why? Do you need one?" asked Fitz.

I shook my head. "I'm walking."

"Alone? It's nearly dark." He glanced at his watch. "If you wait a couple of minutes, Quentin can probably give you a lift. He's getting off work early to come pick up Ros."

"Yeah, that's okay," I said.

"Oh," Fitz said heavily. "Right."

Even now I'm not sure which of us actually blew it, but I'd like to believe it was Fitz. The way he said "right" was a dead giveaway.

Especially to Hayley.

"What's going on?" she asked suspiciously, looking back and forth between us.

"Nothing!" we both said at once.

He grimaced. I shut my eyes.

"Fiiiiitz?" she asked, stretching his name into a question.

"It's just . . . Nothing."

Tell me this isn't happening, I thought. *Fitz is an even worse liar than I am!*

"It must be something," Hayley prodded.

"Cassie kissed Quentin," he blurted out.

My eyes flew open. "Fitz! You promised!"

"Well, I'm sorry, but I hate being in the middle of this. Besides, why shouldn't Hayley know?"

"*Nobody* should know!"

"You kissed Quentin?" Hayley obviously couldn't believe her ears. "When?"

"The day after Ros's party. I thought Kevin had dumped me for Tiffi . . . and I ran into Quentin and . . . It's embarrassing, all right? I made a stupid mistake."

Hayley looked at me as if I were a stranger. "I can't believe you didn't tell me."

"I can't believe Fitz did."

"Don't you try to blame this on Fitz!"

"It's just . . . You've never done something stupid you didn't want me to know about?"

"No. And if I did, I'd tell you anyway. Because we're best friends, Cassie. At least, I thought we were."

"Don't go there," I groaned. "That's not how it is."

"I don't know how it is, do I?" she retorted. "Because you won't tell me. Come on, Fitz. Let's go."

Glancing over one shoulder, Fitz gave me half of an apologetic shrug. Hayley never looked back.

Queen Bee-Ha!

I spent most of Thursday night crying and I couldn't even have told you why—there were too many reasons to choose from. Hayley was mad at me—again—and this time she had a good reason. Her reaction had made me even more ashamed of the way I'd treated Kevin. And Ros. And even Quentin. I just wanted the whole mess to go away. Better yet, I wanted a time machine so I could zip back to Ros's birthday and start over.

And then there was the talent show. If Mrs. Conway didn't come back on Friday, I'd have to direct, and there wasn't any question that I was failing there. How had I ever deluded myself into thinking I could be a Queen Bee? No one in the show even respected me anymore, let alone liked me. Being universally loved was a ridiculous, distant dream.

I couldn't even make my own boyfriend love me.

I'm just not the Queen Bee type, I admitted, tossing miserably on my damp pillow. *I was stupid to think I could be.*

I had finally discovered the flaw in that misguided fantasy: queens are born, not made. And I was born for second place. Every time I stuck my neck out, I learned that all over again.

My only hope of saving face was if Mrs. Conway

miraculously appeared to direct and announce the acts herself. At least then if the show failed it would be on her.

Mostly.

Plenty of people would still blame me.

And even her taking over there wouldn't fix the mess I'd made of the rest of my life. Hayley would probably forgive me. Eventually. But Kevin . . .

What if Kevin and I just weren't meant to be together? He obviously didn't understand what I needed, and I had let him down worse than he knew. It might be a relief to walk away.

Or it might cause permanent psychological damage.

I didn't know anymore.

I sure didn't know who to ask.

Meanwhile, Mom still hadn't come home from the office, and Dad had started pretending he didn't care. . . .

You know what I hate about being me? I never have only one problem. It's always this supersized barrel of worms that I can't begin to untangle. I could maybe cope with one thing at a time, but put them all together and . . .

Oh, who am I fooling?

Coping is not my strong point.

> If worms have a queen,
> Accept my application.
> Clearly, I'm no bee.

Horror Show

Don't try to pretend it's a coincidence that today is Friday the thirteenth. I'm not superstitious, but even I can't overlook something that blatant. What was Mrs. Conway thinking? What kind of genius schedules anything major for Friday the thirteenth?

On the other hand, if you're not going to be there, it doesn't matter, right? Mrs. Harrier handed me this e-mail at the end of second period:

Dear Cassie:

Principal Ito tells me you held all our scheduled rehearsals and that show tickets have sold out. Congratulations! If you hit a snag or two tonight, please don't stress—that's just show business. You should be very proud of what you've all accomplished.

Break a leg!

Mrs. Conway

I stood in the hall rereading those words while my guts tied themselves into macramé. It sounded like she wasn't coming. She didn't actually say that, though, so maybe she'd still show up. I would have asked Kevin's opinion, but after the past few days of rehearsal, I wasn't his favorite person— he'd already disappeared down the hall.

I had just set out for third period when my cell rang. As much as I'd begged for that phone, I was already starting to hate it. All it ever brought me was bad news. Pulling it out of my pack, I reluctantly flipped it open.

"Hey, listen," Ros said, the intense tone of her voice throwing me into a guilty panic. "Fitz wanted me to tell you that one of his doves is sick."

I took a breath and reassured myself that no matter how mad Hayley was at me, she would never squeal to Ros.

"What does he expect me to do about that?"

"He just wanted you to know."

"Well, is it going to be okay?"

"I hope so. Can you imagine how sad he'd be if it died?"

I could. Which is why the fact that I'd actually been asking if the bird would still be able to perform made me feel like dirt. All the worries of the night before came rushing back to overwhelm me . . . and with no warning whatsoever, I started crying in the main hall.

"No, I didn't say it *had* died," Ros corrected worriedly. "I'm sure it's going to be fine, Cassie."

"I have to go," I choked out.

Switching off my phone, I dropped it in with the other junk in my backpack. I was fumbling with the pack's zipper when Ito stepped out of his office and I almost mowed him down.

"Miss Howard!" he said, jumping back. "Is something wrong? You look a little . . . bleary."

I shot him a wounded look, and to my immense embarrassment, kept right on crying.

"Miss Howard. Cassie." He waved me into his office and

pointed to a chair. "I can't help you if I don't know what the problem is."

I plopped down heavily. "I doubt you could help me if you did."

"We won't know until I hear it."

He held a tissue toward me across his desk. I grabbed it and blew, grateful for the tactful way he edged the whole box closer.

"Everyone's quitting the show," I said. "Mrs. Conway isn't coming. I barely slept last night. My life is a disaster. And I might be having a nervous breakdown. What can you do about that?"

He smiled, just a little. "What class do you have this period?"

"Geometry." The bell was ringing too.

"And next?"

"Art."

"I'll tell you what," he said, taking out a pad. "I'm going to write you a pass for the next two periods. I doubt you'll learn much math in this state, and directing a talent show is simply another form of art. Go down to the auditorium and work on your introductions, the sets, whatever. Maybe catch up on that missed sleep. Or just sit there and breathe. I promise you, this is all going to turn out fine."

Sniffing hard, I helped myself to more tissues. "You really think so?"

"You'll see a whole new attitude from people tonight, when it counts. And don't forget, you're not on your own. If things get out of hand, I'll step in and run them."

I wiped my eyes, not sure which was freakier—that I'd just spilled my guts to Principal Ito, or that he'd actually helped me.

"You head on down to the theater now," he instructed. "I'll swing by later to see how you're doing."

I walked out of his office feeling measurably better. But once I hit the auditorium, I started stressing again. The place felt so empty and cold, but imagining it packed with a sold-out crowd of five hundred people was worse. I could only pray for massive audience no-show, beginning with my own family. I had begged Dad and Grandma not to come over breakfast, and with Mom still MIA at least I might avoid being humiliated in front of my parents.

Being humiliated in front of my peers?

That seemed inevitable.

Crimes and Kissdemeanors

Lunch was halfway over when Kevin showed up in the auditorium. I was still sitting down front by myself, so totally zoned out that I barely even blinked when his backpack hit the floor.

"Is there something you want to tell me?" he asked, annoyed. "Because you've been acting weird all week."

There were a *lot* of things I wanted to tell him.

Just none that I could.

"It's just . . . the show is tonight. And nobody's helping me except Trevor. We're not even going home after school—we're both coming straight here."

Kevin shook his head. "What's left to do? By now it's either going to happen or it isn't."

"What about my introductions, Kevin? What if I get up in

front of five hundred people and can't remember what to say? Or worse—what if I get so freaked out I can't even talk?"

"That's not going to happen."

"That could totally happen!"

"Then don't let it."

Was he serious? Maybe he could just tell cancer patients not to get sick too, and we could all go home.

"Really, Cassie. I want to know what's going on."

"I told you. Plus, my parents are fighting. And I don't think Conway is coming tonight. If Sterling refuses to sing again, that leaves me and Hayley as the opening act. Hayley's all ticked off at me. She might not even show up. And then what?"

"Way to think positive." He finally cracked a teasing smile, but that only made me feel worse.

"You saw the dress rehearsal. Everyone's going to laugh at us and say that we're pathetic."

"They won't laugh at me, because I'll be hiding in the sound booth."

"See?"

"I'm kidding! Come on, lighten up."

"It's not funny," I forced past the lump in my throat.

"It's just a stupid talent show. What do you care if a few people laugh? What difference does it make?"

I swallowed hard, but I couldn't stop the tears from welling into my eyes. "Because people *always* laugh at me! I'm always doing something lame, or something outright stupid . . . I didn't want to be that girl anymore. I wanted to be cool."

He looked amazed. "You *are* cool."

My tears overflowed. "No, I'm not. I'm so not."

Kevin pulled me into his arms, resting his cheek on my hair while I cried. I felt his chest rise and fall against mine and wondered how I could even pretend I still deserved to be there. Maybe he hadn't always done exactly what I wanted, but he'd always been a good boyfriend. I, on the other hand . . .

"I can't do this anymore," I heard my voice say. "I have to tell you something."

He leaned back to face me, obviously expecting something bad. And, for once, I didn't let him down.

"The day after Ros's party, when I thought you were with Tiffi, I went out walking. I swear I wasn't looking for Quentin—we just ran into each other. He was worried about me, and I was ripped up about you. I started crying on his shoulder and . . . it just kind of happened."

"What did?"

"We were hugging and . . ."

"He kissed you," Kevin guessed in an oddly frozen voice.

"No." I took a deep breath. "I kissed him."

He rocked away sharply, breaking off contact.

"Whatever you think about me and Quentin, it was honestly never like that," I pleaded. "But after that party, I was sure you and I were over. I didn't think you cared about me. And I thought . . . I don't know. For a second I thought maybe Quentin could."

"Does he?" Kevin asked coldly.

"Of course not. He's madly in love with Ros. And I didn't want him either. Not like that. I wanted you, but you were with Tiffi. Except that you weren't, which makes me even dumber."

Kevin looked away.

"Nothing's been the same since that night in the pool house and it's all my fault," I said. "I'm so sorry. I can't believe I screwed this up."

It felt like he sat there forever, gazing at the floor.

"Does Ros know?" he asked at last.

I shook my head.

He stood up and scooped up his pack. "It's gotta seem ironic now, you not trusting me."

"Please don't go," I begged. "I just want us to be like before again. Remember before, when everything was perfect?"

"Things change," he said, heading up the aisle toward the exit. "They change whether you want them to or not."

I watched, torn, as he walked away, but I didn't run after him. Until I actually heard him say we were through, I could keep believing that maybe it wasn't over, that maybe he'd give me another chance. . . .

The worst thing about keeping secrets is, nobody believes you when you finally tell the truth.

Very Badminton

I was late getting to PE, but Hayley didn't even glance at when I walked onto our badminton court. Her profile remained petrified, like she wouldn't give me the satisfaction of catching her blink.

Somebody threw us a shuttle.

"Do you want to serve?" I asked her, holding out the bird.

Her gaze never wavered my way.

"I'm guessing that's a no."

I fired a shot into the net. Meri Sparks retrieved the shuttle from underneath and backed up to serve for her team.

"Listen, Hayley," I said. "I'm sorry. I didn't want to tell you that stuff because I was embarrassed. I never meant to hurt your feelings."

"Service," Meri called.

Hayley crouched into her stance. I didn't move.

"I screwed up, all right? Could you possibly cut me some slack? You can't imagine the day I'm having, and tonight—"

"Service!" Meri interrupted impatiently.

"I heard you the first time!" I snapped back. "Can you see we're busy here?"

Hayley finally looked at me. "If you wanted to apologize, you had plenty of time before now."

"Hayley—"

"Serve it, Meri," called Hayley, cocking her racquet back.

The bird sailed over the net and landed in the corner where I was supposed to be standing. "One–love!" Meri gloated.

"Can we at least talk about this?" I asked Hayley.

She gave me a snooty look. "I didn't think we did that anymore. Are you going to throw back that shuttle, or should I?"

"Knock yourself out," I told her.

She stepped past me to pick up the bird.

And without even excusing myself to Coach, I turned and ran out of the gym.

Showing Up

"Here's the list of everyone who showed up," Trevor reported backstage, handing me a crumpled sheet of paper.

I grabbed his list, my hands shaking. With only twenty minutes until showtime, the names on this piece of paper would determine my social future. All my other problems were forced to the back of my mind as I read.

Kevin . . . Sterling . . . Hayley . . . Gregor . . . They'd all come! The fourth act, our unicycle, was still MIA, but we'd given up on her anyway. My eyes skimmed to the bottom, where the program still ended with Fitz.

"Did Fitz bring his birds?" I asked.

"In a couple of big cages. He's got way more stuff than anyone here."

"Do me a favor, all right? Make sure he—"

"Cassie!" Principal Ito called, his voice booming through the auditorium. "Cassie Howard, where are you?"

"Here!" I shouted, running out of the wings and onto the stage. I nearly wet my pants the next second. There were people in a few of the seats. Audience people.

Principal Ito walked closer. "How are things going back there?"

"We're not ready!" I said urgently. "We still have twenty minutes!"

Ito checked his watch. "Fifteen. And we've got a lot of people out here waiting to be seated. Where are your ushers?"

Ushers! The stage tilted beneath me. I'd completely forgotten about ushers.

And then, like a vision in a navy sports jacket, Quentin appeared at the top of the aisle, Ros shimmering on his arm. She was wearing her silver Snow Ball formal, but I was so glad to see them that I didn't stop to question her fashion sense.

"There!" I said, pointing. "Quentin is my usher. And Ros can help him."

"Two ushers?" Principal Ito looked annoyed. Then he noticed my desperate expression and threw me another break. "We'll just do a little recruiting," he said, hustling Quentin and Ros back up the aisle.

I was still watching them leave when I realized pandemonium had broken out backstage—and if I could hear it, so could the audience.

"Hey! Hey! Let's keep it down," I said, running back into the chaos. "They've started seating people."

"There's no place to get dressed back here," Kara Jenkins complained. Wearing jeans and a glitter-spangled tank, she carried a plastic-sheathed baton-twirling outfit over her arm. "Someone's been hogging that dressing room for an hour."

Kara pointed at the closed door of the one dressing room with a mirror. It didn't take a psychic to guess who the "someone" was.

"Listen, Kara," I said. "I'll try to get Sterling out of there. Meanwhile, she's up first and you're on eighth. So if you could maybe get dressed in the bathroom . . ."

"Whatever," she said, stalking off in a snit.

I waited until the coast was clear, then tried the dressing room doorknob. Locked. I rapped gently, afraid to knock any louder with our audience so near. Nobody answered.

"Sterling!" I hissed, pressing my ear to the door. "Hey, Sterling!"

I could hear her banging around in there, ignoring me. Losing patience, I pulled a bobby pin out of my hopeless attempt at a hairdo and pushed it into the knob's center hole, popping the lock open. I waited, expecting her to go off on me, then eased the door open a crack and stared in horrified disbelief.

Showstopper

Sterling was dressed in her sequined gown, her gorgeous hair piled on her tiara-topped head like a princess's. Her back was angled toward me, revealing the low bulge of her new microphone's power pack. Headphones filled her ears, which explained why she hadn't heard my entrance. But what froze me to the floor were the sounds coming out of her mouth.

Was that supposed to be *singing*? She sounded like someone suffering from a cross between a sinus infection and constipation, with a dose of nausea thrown in for good measure.

Or wait, maybe the nausea was mine. The room had started spinning in a deeply uncomfortable way.

She's just warming up, I reassured myself. *That's some sort of weird voice-coach exercise.*

Because it definitely wasn't the wind under anyone's

wings. Plus, she was mouthing the words so softly I hadn't even heard her until I opened the door.

Just warming up. Stay calm. Try to breathe.

Sterling threw her arms theatrically out to her sides.

"Did you ever knooooooow that you're my heeeeeerooooo?" she suddenly burst out in full voice.

I shut the door as fast as I could and leaned against it, heart pounding.

We were doomed. Worse than doomed. We were dead.

Sterling's voice assailed me through the wood—loud, proud, and more off-key than one of those yowling cats my dad used to chase from under my window. Couldn't she hear how dreadful she was?

Maybe if she took those headphones out of her ears . . .

Or no. Maybe if Kevin played her music really, really loud . . .

Oh, who was I kidding? I couldn't let her open the show with that caterwauling. I couldn't even let her go onstage.

But how was I going to stop her?

I was plastered to that door, wondering exactly how a person goes about starting a new life in Mexico, when Fitz ran up and grabbed me, shaking me in a panic.

"My cape!" he blurted out, waving a length of black fabric in one fist.

I struggled to tear my ears away from Sterling. Mercifully, she stopped singing, making that possible.

"What happened to it?" I asked.

"I was warming up and Gregor stepped on it and ripped

the ties out!" Fitz pantomimed being choked as his cape got caught, then ripped free. "I can't do my act without my cape!"

"Fitz, you're our finale," I said, in what I hoped was a reasonable voice. "And you look just swell in your tux and top hat. Do you actually *need* a cape?"

He took a deep breath. "What I'm about to say stays between us. Do you promise?"

I nodded.

"When I make my doves disappear, well . . . A magician employs certain *illusions*. The doves aren't necessarily *disappearing* so much as they're changing locations. Behind my cape. Do you follow me?"

"You can't make the doves disappear without your cape?"

"Bingo."

"Then we have to fix it." Grabbing it out of his hands, I took a closer look at the damage. "Tape?"

"You can't tape these on," he said, dangling the ties like black shoelaces. "They have to be sewn."

Inspiration struck. "Has anyone seen Trevor?" I cried, running farther backstage.

Julie and her dog were standing in the hallway outside the costume room. "He's in there," she told me, pointing, "trying to find a costume for Bucky."

"A costume for your dog? Now?"

"Just a bandana or something," she replied sheepishly. "I thought it would be cute."

"Here you go!" Trevor ran out wearing his best dress pants and the same ratty T-shirt he'd had on when he biked over. "What do you think of this?" he asked, handing Julie a triangle of striped blue fabric. I gasped as I recognized the scissored remains of the shirt that went with the pants.

"I guess that could work," she said, with an obvious lack of enthusiasm. "You don't have anything cuter?"

"This isn't a fabric store," he told her. "There aren't a lot of choices."

She tied the scarf around Bucky's neck. "Does it look all right?" she asked me skeptically.

"Fine. I need to borrow Trevor."

Julie took the hint and wandered off with her dog.

"She could have said thank you," Trevor grumbled. "She's as stuck-up as the rest of these girls."

"She doesn't know that was your good shirt, Trev."

"Dude! You cut up your shirt for her?" Fitz gave Julie's back a second look, to see if he was missing something.

"You're just lucky Mom's not here. Look." I shoved Fitz's cape and its ties at him. "Didn't I see a sewing machine in there? Can you sew these back on?"

Trevor blanched. "A sewing machine? What are you asking *me* for?"

"For Pete's sake, Trevor, cut the act. Fitz won't tell your secret if you don't tell his. The doves don't actually disappear, you know."

"Hey!" Fitz protested.

"Consider us even," I told him.

Shoving them both into the costume room, I slammed the door and held it shut. "Fix the cape!" I begged Trevor.

Trev gave the knob a halfhearted pull, then sighed heavily. "There is a sewing machine," I heard him tell Fitz.

"It's old, but I can probably figure out how to use it—if you swear you won't tell anyone."

"Who am I going to tell?" Fitz asked.

"Okay, let me see it. . . . Aw, man! I hate this cheap polyester! No wonder it ripped—this stuff practically unravels on its own."

"Can you fix it?"

"I can fix anything. Not that anyone appreciates that. I don't even know why I'm here."

"Just fix it, Trevor!" I yelled through the door.

I was headed to the wings when I ran into Julie walking back, Trevor's sacrificed shirt in one hand.

"Is there a problem?" I asked, stopping her.

"I'm still not sure I like this. Maybe if he let *me* look through the costumes . . ."

"Listen up," I said, spinning her back around. "If there was anything better in there, I'm positive you'd have it. Since there wasn't, Trevor cut up his favorite shirt for you. Give that back and you might as well slap his face."

"He . . . cut up his own shirt?" Julie asked with disbelief.

"Come on, Julie! Wake up! He's in eighth grade and he thinks you're a goddess. You're lucky he didn't give you his pants." There's a horrifying thought, but I was so stressed-out I barely knew what I was saying. "I realize you don't like him. You don't have to tell me he's a pest. But haven't you ever had a hopeless crush?"

"Well . . . but . . ." She blinked. "I feel awful."

I was about to suggest that she simply thank him for the shirt when Hayley stalked past with her nose in the air.

"I have to go," I told Julie, starting after Hayley.

But before I could catch up, Ros stepped out of nowhere and grabbed my arm. "Three minutes to showtime!" she squealed. "Isn't this exciting? The auditorium's completely full!"

Three minutes? I stared at her in a panic, then charged to the edge of the curtain, where I could peek out into the house. Nearly every seat was filled, and people were actually standing in back. My heart didn't know whether to race or stop altogether. I scanned the upturned faces, desperately hoping to spot Mrs. Conway's.

And that was when I caught a sight that nearly gave my poor heart its final shock. My mother was in the house—sitting next to Dad and Grandma. An empty seat beside her was presumably for Trevor, or maybe it was the buffer zone for the innocents on its other side. I yanked my head back to safety before they spotted me, trying to make sense of their unexpected appearance.

And then, right when things couldn't get any worse, Principal Ito dimmed the lights, signaling the start of the show.

* * *

Hey, wait! Isn't this is where you came in?

Hallelujah! You're all caught up.

Again.

Showtime!

Curtains

The auditorium has fallen into a nerve-rackingly expectant hush. My heartbeat fills my ears as I hesitate at the edge of the curtain, my eyes glued to the pool of light on an otherwise dark stage.

Just go. Just go. Just go, pumps through my brain in time to my pulse. But my feet aren't part of that loop. They stick stubbornly to the boards, refusing to move.

A murmur starts in the seats. The audience is restless.

"Will you get out there already?" a nasty voice whispers behind me.

Sterling.

Oh, no! I forgot to talk to Sterling!

I start to turn around just as her hand pushes me hard. I stumble backward onto the stage and the house breaks into applause.

They've seen me. There's no turning back.

My knees are weaker than wet noodles. Somehow I force them to support me as I totter into Kevin's spotlight and grip the microphone. So many faces, all looking my way . . . If I don't start breathing soon, the first act will be me blacking out.

Leaning closer to the mic, I take a big gulp of air. "Ladies and gentlemen, please welcome our first act of the evening . . . Sterling Carter!"

Carrying the microphone stand back with me, I drop it off at stage right. Sterling bursts out of the wings as I put it down, her arms stretched overhead in her trademark soc-y wave. Compared to her, I'm a peasant in a plain white dress.

The audience erupts into genuine applause.

Poor, ignorant lambs. They don't even know they've just entered the slaughterhouse.

Shaken, Not Ster-ed

"This is so exciting!" Ros whispers as I duck back into the wings. She and Quentin are both standing there, totally in the way. Technically, they should be down in the audience now, but I'm way past worrying about technicalities.

"You have no idea," I mutter.

Sterling's music starts. She hits her opening pose and the spotlight turns her sequins into glittering liquid silver.

The introduction swells. She takes a breath and opens her mouth. I grab the nearest hand—Quentin's—and squeeze till I feel bones crunch.

"Ohhh, oh, oh . . . ," Sterling sings.

Is it me, or is she barely making a sound? Hysterical deafness—that's a real thing, right?

"I can't hear her," Quentin whispers, and now I know there's nothing wrong with my ears. "Is her microphone working?"

"Run to Kevin," I beg, letting go of his hand. "Make sure everything's on."

Quentin takes off like a shot.

"It must have been co-co-co-coooooollllld there in my sha-doooooooooow," Sterling gets out.

The painful truth is now clear.

Her microphone *is* on.

"Wait!" I call, but it's too late. Quentin's gone. I should have told him to have Kevin turn her microphone *off*. Why, why, *why* can I never think in a crisis?

"She's a little nervous," Ros confides.

Yeah, that's the problem. Except that now I'm looking harder and Ros is almost right. Sterling isn't nervous—she's petrified.

Where did this sudden stage fright come from?

Unless . . . does Sterling *know* she can't sing?

Maybe so, because she's stopped. Her music plays on, but she's just standing there. Has she forgotten the words? Should we start the song over? My brain is self-destructing as Ros steps past me out of the wings, picks up the spare microphone, and crosses the stage to join her best friend. The spotlight illuminates them both—is all that silver a coincidence? Ros smiles at Sterling and opens her mouth, and my jaw drops to my knees.

Rosalind Pierce is singing. Singing diva style. Belting it out like she was born to sing this song, like Bette was just warming it up for her. The audience is rapt, spellbound.

And what's even more amazing is, she has Sterling back on track. Or on track for the first time. Sterling is singing backup now, as if this has always been a duet.

"Holy cow!" Hayley creeps up to whisper, finally speaking to me. "Are you hearing this?"

I nod, unable to answer.

"Did you ever knooooooow that you're my herooo-oooooo?" Ros's voice comes straight from her soul. Every one of us feels those words.

And it's cheesy, but I'm choking up. I can't help it. I wipe my eyes on the cuff of my dress as Ros continues carrying Sterling through her song.

"You can't buy that kind of loyalty," Hayley whispers. "Too bad Sterling doesn't deserve it."

Which is completely true. But that doesn't make Ros's performance any less moving. I'm pretty much jelly inside and they're only halfway through.

The audience sways to the beat as Sterling and Ros break out a few dance steps, the same ones Sterling's been rehearsing alone for weeks. They move in synch effortlessly. This was so clearly meant to be. Sterling hits a clinker, but it doesn't matter anymore. We're all swept up, thrilled to be seeing this, feeling the undeniable pull of something larger than ourselves.

Talent.

Big-time, God-given, natural-born talent.

And friendship. And love. Faithfulness.

Forgiveness.

"Get ready," Hayley warns as I sniff into my sleeve. "You have to introduce me in a second."

Ros and Sterling sing their last phrase, Ros lingering over the final note. And now she's blinking into the spotlight as if she can't believe what just happened.

Trust me, no one can. The audience is cheering like they've already gotten their ten bucks' worth. People are clapping in the seats, in the wings, everywhere. I let their adoration subside before I venture back onto the stage.

"That was amazing, wasn't it?" I ask, edging in on Ros's microphone.

The crowd cheers again. Ros and Sterling wave shyly.

"Sterling Carter and her *best* friend, Rosalind Pierce," I add as they walk off.

Let Sterling sue me for my emphasis on *best*. If she doesn't know I'm right, she's even dumber than she acts.

Second Act

I glance over my shoulder and see Hayley at the edge of the open curtain, waiting to come out and give a performance she never signed up for. Literally. Which is even more decent of her, considering the week we've just had.

The obvious hits me like a sucker punch: Hayley is every bit as loyal as Ros.

And I'm as undeserving as Sterling.

Remorse turns my mouth to cotton. My voice comes out a rasp. "Now please welcome *my* best friend, Hayley Johnson."

The crowd applauds. Hayley walks out. I yield the microphone.

But I don't leave.

Hayley puts one hand over the mouthpiece. "What are you doing?" she whispers.

I shrug.

"You're not . . . are you staying?" she asks, stunned.

"If you still want me to."

"I'll whistle slow," she promises. "I'll keep it simple."

"No. Don't," I say, sucking it up. "What would be the point of that?"

Hayley smiles. Really smiles. And suddenly I don't care anymore if people laugh at me.

What the heck? It's for charity.

Showing Off

The audience is *still* laughing. Honestly. Shouldn't they be clapping for Hayley instead? Because she can really whistle and I just made some faces. When I get home, I'm going to pucker up in front of a mirror and see what's so hysterical about it.

Or not. If I'm as funny-looking as these people think, I might never be able to kiss anyone again.

Assuming there's anyone left who wants to kiss me.

A basketball bounces in the wings. Raising my hands for quiet, I speak over the dying chuckles.

"And here's our very own Harlem Globetrotter, Gregor King!"

I run off as Gregor dribbles on. He's actually smiling, for once. It occurs to me that after tonight I'll never have to deal with him again and I smile too.

"That was great!" Ros congratulates me and Hayley backstage. "So funny, you two."

"Us? What about you!" Hayley gushes. "Where's Sterling?"

"In the dressing room. She didn't want to wear that dress anymore."

Ros is still wearing hers and Sterling is hogging a room other people could use, but I take a deep breath and let it go.

I have a show to run.

Gregor's getting cocky. He tosses the ball up behind his back and tips it off his head. He's going to lose it if—

Oh no! It just bounced offstage!

A guy in the front row tosses it back. Gregor tries to cover by pretending it's all part of his act, but honestly, the audience doesn't seem to care. They're into it now, clapping in time to his dribbling. I guess they don't expect perfection.

Or wait—maybe it's more fun if everything *isn't* perfect.

I'm so absorbed by this possibility that I don't even notice Gregor taking his final, bouncing bow. Hayley nudges me from behind and I trip into the spotlight again.

"Our next act is Mario Zapata, performing a monologue from *King Lear*."

People applaud. Mario walks on with an old man's limp, decked out in more faux velvet and painted gold plastic than I wore on Halloween. I run back into the wings.

This talent show stuff is cake! What was I freaking out about?

Act five sings a cappella. . . . Act six is our juggler. . . . Act seven dances hip-hop. . . . Kara Jenkins marches on with her baton.

Cake!

Trevor rushes up behind me, loaded down with folding

chairs. "Can you grab the music stands?" he asks. "The quartet is on next, and they have to carry their instruments."

I rush back to the costume room, where the musicians are warming up. "We need you people on deck!" I say, gathering up their metal stands. "Let's hustle!"

No one even gives me a dirty look. Instead, they adjust one another's collars and follow me into the wings.

Kara's act ends. The audience applauds less loudly; they might be getting tired. Not to worry. I'm about to give them a nice, long break.

"Here we go!" I say, stepping out in front of Trevor and the musicians. Putting the stands down quickly, I head for the microphone.

"Our next act is truly talented," I tell the audience. "Four members of our Hilltop High Concert Band have formed a string quartet specifically for tonight. . . ."

I'm stretching it out to give Trevor time, but he's already got the chairs unfolded. I hear a faint scraping of metal legs as the musicians take their seats. The cello hits a tuning note. The other strings join in.

". . . so without further ado," I say, relieved, "please put your hands together for the Hilltop High String Quartet."

Trevor and I bail under cover of the resulting applause, hurrying back toward the wings. Trev clears the edge of the curtain first. I dive in behind him and *wham!*

I slam right into his back.

We fight to catch our balance, grabbing each other to keep from tumbling backward onto the stage.

"Why did you stop right th—?" I begin indignantly.

Trevor's expression begs me to hush. His eyes roll farther backstage.

Julie Evans and Bucky are waiting on deck.

Puppy Love

Bucky is on his leash, Trevor's blue shirt tied jauntily around his neck.

"Are you guys ready?" I ask Julie.

She nods nervously. "I think so. Boy, that's a huge crowd."

"You'll do fine," I assure her. "Do you have all your props?"

She turns to Trevor. "I have my dog whistle. You're going to throw out the toys as I need them, right?"

"Don't worry about a thing," he tells her. "You'll say something like, 'Bucky, where's your monkey?' and I'll pitch it right out there. No one will even see me."

Julie smiles. Trevor beams. I've lost him to another of his futile Julie fantasies. I poke him subtly in the ribs.

"I'll, uh . . . I'll get the toys," he says, coming back to earth. One last, longing glance and he's gone.

"Your brother's a piece of work," Julie says.

"Excuse me?"

"No, I mean that in a good way. It's just, when I met him at Ros's party, I never would have guessed how much more to him there is."

Luckily, this piece of music is longer than a week of geometry, because now I'm intrigued. "Such as?"

"At the party he was acting all macho and tough, like he

thought he was so cool. But he's not tough at all. He's lucky Rex didn't kill him."

"Yeah," I say, embarrassed by the memory. "Thanks for saving his life."

"Don't tell Trevor this," Julie whispers, "but when I first met him, I thought he was kind of sad. I mean, I'll bet he can't even skate. But he's been killing himself to help with this show. And you know what else? I went back to the costume room after you told me about Bucky's scarf. I was going to thank him, but I heard him and Fitz in there, so I kind of listened at the door . . ."

I can guess what's coming. I let her tell me.

"Your brother was sewing Fitz's cape back together!"

"Yeah. He's good at stuff like that. Can you keep a secret? He made my dress for the Snow Ball."

Julie's eyes pop. "The pink one?"

"He wouldn't let me tell anyone because he thinks if people know, it will ruin his manly rep. He makes a mean breakfast casserole too."

Julie shakes her head. "He's not a bit like I thought. He's actually kind of cute."

"Please don't let him hear you say that. Not if you don't mean it."

"What? Oh, I don't mean *that*," she says, startled. "He's way too young for me. But he's still cute. For an eighth grader."

Trevor runs up, his arms overflowing with well-chewed stuffed animals, tennis balls, and a Frisbee. The monkey is clutched in one of his hands, his prop list in the other.

"Everything's here," he tells Julie. "I double-checked against the list."

He squats down to drop the toys on the floor and stays to scratch Bucky's ears.

"Hey, Bucky," he whispers. "Hey, boy. How're you doing? You're going to be great, don't worry."

I look up from Trevor and Bucky . . . and catch Julie watching them. The expression on her face knocks me sideways. Didn't she just tell me that Trevor was too young?

"Hey, Trev," I say. "Who's on after Julie?"

"Emmy Wilkins. You know that."

"Why isn't she up here? Can you go find out?"

He's not happy, but he goes, running at full tilt to make sure he gets back.

"Listen," I tell Julie. "Don't break his heart, all right?"

"What are you talking about?" The guilty look on her face proves she already knows.

"I'm just saying—it wouldn't be hard. And I have to live with the guy."

"I don't plan on breaking his heart."

"You won't need a plan, so just watch it, okay? He's my brother."

She's offended now. But if she had any idea how much pain she'd already caused . . .

"Emmy is on her way up," Trevor reports breathlessly, skidding to a stop. "And the quartet is almost done. Are you ready, Julie?"

"Ready, Trevor," she says, smiling sweetly.

Fitz of Panic

How can we be preparing for Fitz's finale already? And how can one single act have so many props? The wings are already packed, and Trevor and Hayley just ran back for more things. Fitz paces nervously in his tux and top hat, his newly repaired cape fluttering out behind him.

"How is your dove?" I ask him.

"Good. All better. I think it was just preshow jitters."

On whose part? I wonder. But the way he's wringing his hands makes it seem unwise to ask.

I peek out of the wings. Rick Nichols, our rapper, is winding up. "You're nearly on. What are you starting with?"

"The scarves. The scarves are good. Right?"

He is seriously nervous. He's starting to freak me out.

"The scarves are perfect. Everyone likes the scarves."

"Yeah. Plus, they're foolproof. I never mess up with the scarves."

"Of course not. You don't mess up any of your tricks."

Fitz gives me a desperate look. I gulp. He's not exactly filling me with confidence.

The audience applauds. I peek around the curtain to see Rick headed our way. His rap is over.

Fitz is on.

"You're going to be great," I say, trying to pump him up. "I have to introduce you now."

"Where's Trevor?" he asks anxiously.

"Here!" Trevor sprints up with Hayley and the final props. "We're ready. Go ahead."

I give Fitz one last, worried look and run out onto the stage.

Fitz of Genius

"Ladies and gentlemen! Please welcome our last act of the evening. He's quick with a trick . . . he's the cat in the hat . . . he's the Amazing Fitz!"

I just made that up. Right this second. I'm pretty pleased with myself too as the audience applauds and Fitz steps into the spotlight.

Hayley's still in the wings, watching anxiously. I cram in next to her as Fitz's music begins.

Fitz brandishes his wand in circles, grabs it at both ends, and pulls. It morphs into a black handkerchief.

"That's new," I murmur, but Hayley doesn't answer. She's soaking up Fitz's every move, trying to help him along by sheer force of will.

He waves the black cloth through the air before balling it up in his palm and closing his fingers around it. He shakes his closed hand up and down three times . . . and opens it to reveal three new scarves: red, purple, and blue.

He's getting good at this stuff!

Removing his top hat, Fitz lets the audience see that it's empty. Red, purple, and blue go in. He reaches into the hat, stirs things around, and pulls out his wand! A wave of his wand over the hat and Fitz reaches in again. The colored scarves come out tied into a long chain with the black one on the end.

The audience applauds. Fitz whips his cape around with a flourish, feeding off their approval. Throwing the scarf chain into the air, he points his wand at it. People gasp as the scarves flutter to the ground, untied.

"He's doing great!" I exclaim.

The second curtain opens behind him, revealing more equipment. Fitz snaps his cape again and circles two large black crates. Rolling one out toward the edge of the stage, he spins it so the audience can see every side. He does the same with the second crate and pushes them together, covering them with a black tablecloth.

Turning to face the wings, he stretches his hand toward us. I freeze, but to my surprise, Hayley bolts out to join him. Fitz shows off his lovely assistant before gesturing for her to lie on the table, where he flips another cloth over her, covering her completely.

This is creepy, really, Hayley lying there like she's dead. The shape of her body shows through the cloth, but I can't see her breathing. Fitz walks circles around the table, waving his wand, his arms, his cape. . . .

All of a sudden, Hayley starts to move. Just a little, like a shudder. And now a little more . . . Is she *floating*?

She is! Her body rises higher to delighted gasps from the crowd. Fitz grabs a hula hoop and runs her draped form through its center while she hovers motionless. He waves his wand again and Hayley sinks gently to the table. With a flourish of his cape, he whips the cloth off her. She sits up to mad cheers.

Fitz helps Hayley to her feet. She takes a bow and runs back to me, exhilarated.

"Wow!" I exclaim. "That was so cool!"

"Just wait," she says happily.

Reaching into his jacket, Fitz removes an egg and sets it on the black tablecloth. He puts a scarf over the egg and taps it with the wand. The scarf goes flat. The egg reappears in Fitz's free hand.

Closing his hand around the egg, he taps his fingers with the wand before opening them. The egg has disappeared again. The audience laughs as Fitz raises his hat, revealing the egg on top of his head.

He sets the egg back on the table and places his hat over it. A few waves of his wand, a flourish of his cape . . . Fitz lifts the hat and uncovers a live dove!

The crowd oohs and ahs as he holds the bird up to view. The dove goes back on the table. His top hat goes over it. Abracadabra . . .

Two doves emerge from underneath!

But Fitz isn't done. Lifting a bamboo cage onto the table, he puts both doves inside it, the birds still visible through the bars. He moves closer and covers the cage with his cape. Waving his wand above the cage, he snatches the cape back off.

Four doves!

I clap like crazy, not caring how much noise I make. The way the audience is going off, they can't hear me anyway.

"Go, baby!" Hayley calls, completely carried away.

Fitz covers the cage with his cape again. He waves his wand over the top. One . . . two . . . three . . .

A sudden, frenzied flapping erupts. I hear it a second before Fitz's cape comes alive from underneath, attacked by a flurry of beaks and wings. It looks like he's holding a sack of live cats . . . until the birds burst free and streak up into the lights.

The audience squeals as the doves fall into formation and fly circles over their seats.

"Tell me this is part of the act," I beg Hayley.

"Uh-oh," she breathes.

Fitz looks dumbfounded. He rushes to the edge of the stage, his cape fluttering behind him, his eyes on the doves. My eyes are on them too as I brace for the first sign of poopage.

The birds loop and swirl overhead. Fitz looks desperately back toward us, clearly without a plan. His music ends. The silence is broken only by flapping wings.

Fitz takes a breath, wraps his cape around himself, and bends into a dignified bow.

"Go!" I exclaim, pushing Hayley. "Get out there and bow with him! Everyone, out for a bow!"

I run through the wings shooing people onstage. Joining the cast last, I squeeze in between Fitz and Hayley, impulsively taking their hands. Hands link up away from me in both directions—a spontaneous chain reaction.

And we bow, Fitz's doves wheeling overhead like a declaration of our impending freedom.

Talent Shows

The audience is on its feet. Even my parents are clapping. No one cares that Fitz's doves are still on the loose, strafing up and down the aisles. The birds seem as giddy as the rest of us, flapping their wings double time. We bow again, happiness, relief, and gratitude welling up together.

And suddenly it hits me. All this time I've been so worried about being humiliated that I abandoned my own philosophy:

1. Everyone has a talent, and
2. Gifts shouldn't be judged by their glory factors.

Not everyone on this stage has discovered their best gift yet—and I sincerely hope I'm one of them—but there was talent here tonight. The audience knows it. The performers know it. Even those silly birds know it. That's where the giddy comes from. That's the rush we're all feeling.

There's this weird kind of urge in people, a yearning we all share to see something extraordinary, something that makes us sit up and wonder what else human beings are capable of.

Beethoven or badminton—in the end, it doesn't matter. All talent lifts us up. The gifts of others give us hope.

Why?

Because you never really know where talent is going to show.

Principally Pink

The curtains close. With the audience out of sight, it's pandemonium backstage. People are running and jumping and hugging each other. Fitz snatches up a cage and enlists Trevor's help to catch his birds.

"I can't believe we pulled it off!" I tell Hayley as they disappear.

"Too bad Mrs. Conway wasn't here. I wonder what's going on with her?"

But I don't want to think about that—the possibilities are too scary.

Principal Ito appears with a large, cellophane-wrapped bouquet. "Congratulations, Cassie. I told you there was nothing to worry about."

The flowers he hands me are gorgeous—pink lilies, carnations, and roses. Unfortunately, there's something extremely wrong about getting them from Principal Ito.

"Thank you," I mumble, embarrassed.

His cheeks turn as pink as the flowers. "Those came to my office for you this afternoon," he explains brusquely. "There's a card."

"Oh!" I gasp, relieved.

Finding an envelope among the ferns, I open it eagerly:

For Cassie,
With congratulations and thanks,
    Emily Conway

I can't believe she sent me flowers—it's completely un-expected. Unexpected to me, anyway, because if they ar-rived this afternoon, she must have already known she wouldn't be here. I glance over my shoulder. Hayley is talk-ing to Ros now and no one else is nearby.

"Is Mrs. Conway okay?" I ask in a low voice. "I mean, is everything . . . okay?"

Principal Ito seems surprised. "People get sick. There's no reason to believe she won't be back soon."

Either he doesn't understand my question or he doesn't want to answer it.

"Right," I say. "Okay."

"I'm sure she'd want you to enjoy the evening. You worked hard to make this happen. Go ahead, bask a little."

"Yeah. Thanks."

He's already walking away when I think of something else.

"Um, Principal Ito?" I call. "Do you think you could write me one more of those passes, for PE? I mean, *running* a show . . . that's exercise, right?"

A Whole New Light

I spot Sterling emerging from the big dressing room and abruptly realize she wasn't onstage for our bows. She's wearing jeans and a sweater now, a wardrobe bag draped over her arm.

Detaching herself from Quentin, Ros runs over to greet her. "There you are! Why didn't you come out to bow?"

Sterling gives her a disgusted look. "I'm sure you bowed enough for both of us. Why not? You hogged up my whole song."

"What?" Ros gasps, stunned. "I was only trying to help you."

"Well, you didn't. You ruined everything."

"You're kidding, right?" I break in. "Ros saved your butt out there!"

Ros looks relieved, but Sterling doesn't back down. "I didn't need her to. Now people will think I can't sing."

"You *can't* sing!" I exclaim. "Haven't you ever heard of a tape recorder?"

Sterling glares at me and there's violence in her eyes. I'm wondering if I could have broken that news a safer way when a voice simply oozing sociness rings out across the stage.

"There you are, darling!"

We all turn to see a mom-aged woman and a college-aged

guy headed toward us. The woman's hair is frosted platinum, and her swollen lips and breasts look even less natural. She clips forward on stiletto heels, her cleavage rigidly upright in a leopard-print camisole.

This can only be Sterling's mother and her latest trophy boyfriend.

"Sterling!" she reproaches, in her soc-y nasal drawl. "You were supposed to sing a solo! Isn't that why I bought you that expensive microphone?"

Sterling casts a baleful look at Ros.

"Oh, hello, Ros," Ms. Carter says dismissively. "What happened?" she asks Sterling.

"Well—" Sterling begins.

"We had people here to see you tonight! The Winstons and the Mastersons . . . You didn't exactly impress them, Ster."

I can't help cringing. No one wants to hear that from her mother—even if it's true.

"Ros wanted to sing," Sterling forces out, and none of us calls her a liar.

"Ros could have done her own act. You won't get anywhere in this world letting people steal your spotlight. Do you understand how embarrassing that was for me, watching you sing *backup*? People have certain expectations of my daughter."

Sterling shrinks before my eyes. She hangs her blond head. "I know."

"Those voice lessons aren't free," her mom continues relentlessly. "If you're not going to make better use of them, I can find other things to do with my money."

Her boyfriend smirks as if he's got a few ideas of his own.

"Well, come along," Ms. Carter says. "Robbie and I are meeting friends at the club. We'll drop you home on our way."

"I can find a ride," Sterling says without glancing up.

"Good. I hate to drive that loop for nothing." Reaching forward, she plucks the wardrobe bag off Sterling's arm. "I'll just hang my dress in the car, where it's safe."

Turning on her stilettos, she walks away, her hips swaying exactly like Sterling's. "Come on, Robbie," she calls over her shoulder. "We have to say good-bye to the Mastersons."

But Robbie lags behind. "I could talk her out of cutting those lessons," he offers in a low, suggestive voice. "Or maybe I should let her. Free your time for other things."

Sterling finally looks up, her eyes filled with loathing. "Don't bother. I'll never have *that* much time."

Robbie's grin creeps me out from my hair to my heels. "It only takes a few minutes, princess."

"Keep your hands off me," Sterling spits.

"You know where to find me when you change your mind."

I can't even look at Sterling's face. Robbie's eyes rake her body one last time before he finally walks away, his amused backhanded wave infuriating her even more.

"Don't let him get to you, Ster," Ros soothes. "The guy's a total pig."

Pig? I could suggest a few stronger words if I weren't still in shock.

Ros touches Sterling's arm. "Come out with me and Quentin. We'll go wherever you want."

Sterling's eyes are glassy with unshed tears. Turning to face Ros, she spots someone over her shoulder.

"Bryce!" she cries happily.

Sprinting across the stage, she launches herself at her boyfriend, wrapping her legs around him tight. "Take me out of here," she begs. "Let's get lost somewhere."

"Some of the guys are headed to Last-Chance Pizza," he says. "Wanna go?"

"Yes, anywhere," she says, kissing him. "Anywhere but here."

The Upside of Reincarnation

"Wow," Hayley says as Bryce stumbles off with Sterling. She shakes her head like she's trying to clear it. "Wow."

Ros and Quentin whisper to each other. "We're gonna bail," Quentin tells me.

I watch him slip his arm around Ros's waist, pulling her close as they walk away, and I swear my heart nearly breaks. It's not jealousy. Not anymore. It's just hard, seeing what those two have when Kevin and I are so—

"Sterling's mom is a nightmare!" Hayley exclaims.

"Yeah. Well. The tree doesn't grow far from the apple, I guess."

But suddenly I can't help remembering all those things Ros told me at Bonfire. With a role model like her mother, no wonder Sterling's such a pain. Not to mention that Tate the Great looks like Man of the Year next to Robbie.

"It was cool what Ros did, wasn't it?" Hayley asks. "Jumping in and singing with Sterling like that? I doubt Sterling would have done as well without her."

"You have no idea," I said.

"But that's what friends do, right? Come through for each other? Be there when they're needed? Stick together, no matter what?"

Is she being sarcastic? I can't tell.

"Um, yeah. Thanks for whistling tonight," I say uneasily. "Especially after . . . well, you know."

Hayley shakes her head. "You and I, we're getting older. Stuff's bound to change between us, and maybe that means we *will* have some secrets. But seeing Ros out there for Sterling, after all their ups and downs . . . You're my best friend, Cassie. I never want *that* to change."

"Yeah," I say, choking up. "Me either."

She hugs me and I hug her back hard.

"Friends for life?" she asks.

"And the next life, too."

What's Luv Got to Do with It?

Fitz runs up to me and Hayley. I sigh with relief to see his cage full of doves again.

"Never work with animals," he gripes. "They always steal the show."

Hayley hugs him. "No way. You were brilliant!"

Fitz smiles. "I was kind of brilliant, wasn't I?"

"Yes, you were." She aims a peck at his cheek, but he turns his head and her lips land on his. There is nothing buddy-buddy about this kiss. My heart thumps. My face turns crimson. I gaze at the floor, the ceiling, my fingernails . . . anywhere but at Hayley and Fitz. Let me just take back everything I've ever said about them needing to act more romantic—this is embarrassing! I'm backing away like a jewel thief when someone taps me on the shoulder.

"Hey," Kevin says. "I locked up the sound booth. Here's your music, Fitz," he adds, holding out a CD.

Romeo and Juliet come up for air, but I'm so blown away by the fact that Kevin has just spoken to me, I barely even notice.

"Your act was cool," he tells Fitz. "And even though your birds got loose . . . that part was cool too."

"I told you!" Hayley cries, poking Fitz in the chest.

He looks ridiculously pleased. "I'd better go put these bad boys in the truck before they escape again. I have my dad's pickup tonight. I'd offer you guys a ride, but it only seats two, especially with this cage wedged in."

"That's okay," Kevin says. "I want to talk to Cassie anyway."

My lungs shrivel. He's going to break up with me. What else can he need to tell me in private?

"So," he says as Hayley and Fitz walk away. "I thought it went well tonight."

"Yes. Surprisingly well," I force out.

"It wasn't all perfect, but it was all good. There were some real good parts."

This is torture.

"Just say it," I beg. "Do what you have to do."

"What?"

"You're going to break up with me, right? Do it fast, like a Band-Aid, before I start crying."

But it's too late for that. I'm already crying.

Kevin shakes his head. "I've never met anyone like you for jumping to conclusions."

"Huh?"

"I talked to Quentin earlier. I believe you guys."

It's like a steel band snaps from around my chest—suddenly I can breathe again. I gulp down big, steadying breaths.

"So . . . does that mean . . . you're not mad anymore?"

"I'm not *happy*." He shrugs. "But yeah. I'm not mad." He pulls a small gift-wrapped box from his jacket pocket. "I brought you something," he says, pressing it into my hands.

I want to protest that I don't have anything for him, but that's probably pretty obvious. Instead, I yank off his gift's silver ribbon. Under the lid is a layer of cotton, and under that . . .

"A bracelet!" I gasp, lifting it out.

He points at one of two silver charms dangling from a linked chain. "Do you know what that is?"

I hold it closer to my face. "One of those squawk-talker things?"

Kevin smiles. "If you mean a megaphone, you're right. It's an exact copy, right down to the little trigger."

"Okay . . . ," I say, not getting it.

"Because directors use them. When I saw that in the store, I knew you needed it, as a souvenir of tonight."

"That's so sweet!"

"I'd have bought you the real thing, if I'd thought of it sooner. Maybe then people would have listened to you."

"Yeah. I seriously doubt it."

"Look at this other one." He lifts the second charm with his fingertip. "See? It's your Snow Queen crown!"

"Kevin!" I protest, blushing. "I didn't win Snow Queen."

"You would have if I'd been the judge. So I'm giving you my crown now. A little late, but I hope you still like it."

It's kind of a second-place crown, then. Could anything be more perfect?

"Here," he says. "Let me put it on for you."

I hold out my hand and he fastens the bracelet around my wrist, its crown and megaphone dangling. "We can add more charms to it later," he says. "Those are just the first two."

We? Later? There's a big lump in my throat and suddenly I'm blinking way too much. "Does that mean . . . well . . . ?"

Kevin's eyes are shiny too. "I don't want us to be over. Not if you don't."

"I don't," I choke out. "I've missed you so much."

I wriggle into his arms and he holds on tight. This is where I belong, where I always want to be. I tilt my face up to his, needing to tell him so, but before I can, he kisses me.

Our lips melt together. It's impossible to describe all the emotions surging through me. I couldn't stand to lose him now. I don't know what I'd do.

Kevin's kiss goes deeper and I kiss him back, not caring

who sees. Everything feels so right again, like we're going to last forever.

He breaks off suddenly. I look up. A tear sparkles in his lashes.

I can't breathe. I close my eyes, spilling my own tears down my cheeks. He kisses them one by one.

He *does* love me.

He doesn't have to say it anymore. I just know. I know it down to my smallest bone.

He loves me.

And I love him.

Party Pooper

Life ought to stop after moments like that. There ought to be some sort of time-out you can take until you feel like rejoining the human race. Unfortunately, life doesn't stop, and my proof is that Trevor and I are on our way out to the parking lot now to pick up his bike and ride home with our parents.

In fairy tales, this is *not* how it works.

"What a cool night," Trevor says as we exit the auditorium. "You know what? Julie thanked me for Bucky's costume."

I'm about to demand details when I spot Principal Ito lurking in the hall.

"Cassie!" he says, handing me a sheet of paper. "Is anyone else left in there?"

"No, we're the last ones out."

"Good, because I'm locking up. See you tomorrow," he says.

"Tomorrow?" I repeat, confused. "Tomorrow is Saturday."

"It's all there on your invitation. Good night."

I don't know what to say. I'd be talking to his back anyway. I look at the paper in my hands:

IMPORTANT MEMO

To: All Talent Show Participants
From: Principal Ito
Subject: Mandatory Saturday Cleanup and Wrap Party

Congratulations on a successful show! The effort you put in and the money you raised for charity are a credit to you all.

We just have a few loose ends to take care of. I assume Mrs. Conway told you that since the show was an extracurricular event it would be the responsibility of the participants to clean up the auditorium and return the backstage area to its original neat condition (all props removed, sets dismantled, etc.). Since she's left me in charge of this, I expect the entire cast to meet me at the auditorium at 10 a.m. tomorrow.

With everyone pitching in, we'll finish our cleanup quickly and have time to enjoy a job well done.

Is he kidding? Ten o'clock in the morning? On a Saturday? On Valentine's Day!

And I was almost starting to like him.

Waffling

"Don't tell me you kids aren't hungry either," Dad whines unhappily. "What's the matter with everyone?"

I don't know why Trevor's picking at his strawberry heart-shaped waffles. Speaking for myself, I'm too annoyed to eat. My very first Valentine's Day with a boyfriend and I'm about to spend it cleaning the school auditorium.

Yippee. Way to completely ruin the most romantic day of the year.

At least I can hope my valentine will be at Ito's "party." Which puts me a step ahead of Dad.

"Should I take Andrea a tray?" he asks Grandma a second time. "Maybe just some tea and strawberries?"

Grandma shakes her head. "If she wanted to eat, she'd come out of the bedroom."

Dad looks around at his elaborately festive food and decorations and sighs with disappointment. Apparently Valentine's Day isn't an official holiday either.

"Can you give us a ride to the high school, Dad?" Trevor asks. "I don't want to show up there all sweaty."

"Yes, because you'll stay daisy fresh cleaning the auditorium," I say. "You don't even have to go, Trevor. What's Ito going to do to you?"

He ignores me, though, and I know why. He thinks Julie will be there. "Will you, Dad?" he asks.

Dad looks longingly down the hall. Still no sign of Mom.

"I guess so," he says with a sigh.

Show Us the Money

The auditorium is fuller than I expected. Not only is the whole cast here, but some of them brought friends, presumably for the rides. Sterling sauntered in with Bryce and Tiffi, and Ros could have sat with them—especially since Quentin's at MegaFoodMart this morning—but instead, she's up front with us, pretending her feelings aren't hurt by the way Sterling's ignoring her. I glance from Kevin on my one side to Hayley on my other and feel truly grateful despite this sad waste of a day.

Principal Ito walks in with Mario, the two of them carrying a huge cooler. Together they lug it up to the edge of the stage.

"Thanks for coming, everyone," Ito says, as if we had a choice. "I know it's Saturday, and we're all in a hurry to get out of here, but I want to take a second to say what an excellent job you did last night."

Reaching into his pocket, he pulls out a slip of paper. "Four hundred ninety-three tickets sold at ten dollars apiece. That's four thousand nine hundred and thirty dollars. I'd like to chip in an additional seventy, which means we'll be handing Mrs. Conway an even five thousand dollars to donate to cancer research."

People give themselves a hand. Hayley unlooses a whistle that probably makes him sorry for bringing it up.

"Um, yes. Now, does everyone know what to do?" he asks. "We need to get the programs, trash, and ticket stubs cleared out of these aisles. Props and sets need to be taken apart and taken home. The costume room needs straightening. I have a few things to do in my office, and then I'll be back with some cookies. In the meantime . . ."

He opens the cooler's hinged lid, revealing an assortment of jewel-colored sodas in glass bottles. "Enjoy," he says, dropping a bottle opener next to the cooler.

He's no sooner gone than people start grumbling about the job ahead. I pick up a trash bag while Kevin walks off in search of a broom. Trevor heads straight for the cooler and pries the caps off a drink for each hand.

"I'm going to go help Fitz load up the rest of his props," Hayley tells me.

"Do me a favor on your way: tell Trevor to take it easy on those sodas. They're supposed to be for everyone."

"I could ask him to straighten up the costume room."

"Okay."

"Unless you'd rather he just keep standing there looking studly."

"Don't encourage him!"

"Back in a few," she says, winking as she walks off.

Faith, Hope, and Even More Charity

The auditorium is about half clean. Kevin and I are sitting next to the cooler, taking a break. He pops the tops off a couple of sodas, their caps dropping into the growing pile on the boards.

"Cassie!" Hayley squeals, running up and grabbing me by the arm. "Come on! You've got to see this."

"See what?" I ask, in no mood to move.

Handing my drink to Kevin, she hauls me to my feet. "Just come on."

"I'll be right back," I promise as Hayley drags me off across the stage. "Where are we going?" I ask her.

"Shh!" she whispers. "You'll see."

We're headed for the costume room. "Oh, no," I moan. "What did Trevor do now?"

"Shhhhh!"

Creeping down the hall, Hayley stops outside the room's open door, motioning for me to do the same. I sidle up and hear Trevor talking inside.

"It's no big deal," he's saying, his obvious pride contradicting his words. "Anyone can run a sewing machine."

"*I* can't," counters a flirtatious female voice.

Julie!

I do a double-take at Hayley. She claps both hands over her mouth to keep from laughing.

"Sure, you can," he says. "I'll, uh . . . I can teach you. If you want."

I can't stand it. I have to peek. Trevor and Julie are standing back by the racks of costumes, oblivious to everything but each other.

"I don't know," Julie teases. "Maybe."

I pull my head back and give Hayley a disbelieving look. She's squatting on the floor now, helpless with suppressed laughter.

"Why didn't I know you were like this before?" Julie asks. "When I met you at Ros's party—"

Trev groans. "I was a butthead. I know. I just thought, all those older guys . . . I felt like I had to compete."

Julie laughs. "Want to hear something funny? If you had been yourself, I'd have liked you a million times better."

"Really?"

Hayley finally has her giggles under control. She hauls herself up off the floor to resume eavesdropping. But suddenly there's nothing to hear. We exchange puzzled glances as the silence stretches out. I peek around the doorway again and nearly faint on the spot.

Trevor and Julie are kissing! Has he ever even kissed a girl before? *Eew!* This is just wrong.

I yank my head back before I go blind. Hayley takes one look at my face and hits the floor laughing again.

"I wish you weren't in eighth grade," I hear Julie say.

"Only till the end of the year," he reminds her.

"Yeah, but . . . that's a long way off."

"Not so long," he whines. "Four months."

"I guess. If you don't count summer."

"No one counts summer. Would you ever . . . I mean, would you want to go to a movie with me?"

"Oh, Trevor," she sighs.

I can tell she's about to say no. Of *course* she's about to say no—if Trev understood anything about high school, he'd know she has no choice.

"Just sometime!" he adds desperately. "Whenever you want."

"Okay."

Okay? I look around the door in time to see Julie slip him one last kiss.

"Ask me again in September," she says.

Two Not-Wrongs Do Make Me Right

"What were you doing?" Kevin asks me as I walk up. He's still hanging out by the cooler, waiting.

"Don't ask. Please."

Reclaiming my soda, I take a long drink, trying to wash away the hideous memory of my brother kissing a girl.

Ros climbs the stage stairs to join us. "Hey," she says. "Has either of you seen Sterling?"

"She's not backstage," I tell her. "Did she leave with Tate and Tiffi?"

"No, I saw those two headed this way. You didn't see them?"

"I did," Kevin says. "Maybe Sterling's in the bathroom."

"Maybe." Ros starts back down the stairs just as Sterling walks in the auditorium's side door.

"There you are!" Ros exclaims. "I've been looking for you."

"What for?" Sterling asks ungraciously.

"Just because . . . last night . . . How was it when you got home?"

"Could we maybe not talk about this here?" Sterling asks with a significant, hostile glance in my direction.

"Sure. I just—"

"I think I left my hairbrush in my dressing room. You can help me look for it if you want."

If I were Ros, I'd tell her to pound sand. But Ros is way more patient than I am. I shake my head as they walk past us.

"After what Ros did for her, Sterling ought to be kissing her butt," I tell Kevin.

"That's not really Sterling's style."

"I know that. What I don't understand is why Ros lets her get away with it."

Which is to say, I kind of get it. Now. But lots of people have problems and we still have to act human.

A hair-raising shriek splits the air. I leap to my feet, heart pounding, not a clue what's going on.

"What—?" Kevin begins.

"You bastard!" Sterling cries. "You two-faced, back-stabbing slut!"

I start running and find Ros and Sterling in the hall outside the big dressing room. Sterling's face is purple as she yells at someone through its open door. "Get out! Come out of there right now!"

Bryce saunters out, an amused grin on his face. "You're overreacting," he says condescendingly.

Sterling points to the exit, enraged.

He shrugs. "Have it your way."

"You too!" she demands back through the doorway.

Tiffi Hughes slinks out, her top twisted halfway around and her long curls all messed up. "Stop screeching," she says. "It's not how—"

"Shut up! You disgust me."

Tiffi straightens her shirt and smiles coldly. "I don't disgust your boyfriend."

They lock eyes and Sterling lunges. Ros grabs her from behind.

"Don't, Ster. She's not worth it," Ros begs.

"Just get out of here," I tell Tiffi. "You too, Bryce."

He laughs. "Are you going to make me, Red?"

"Do it, Tate," Kevin says behind me.

Have I mentioned that Bryce Tate is huge? By ourselves, Kevin and I wouldn't stand a chance. But a crowd is gathering now. And Bryce has no reason to stay.

"Don't get your panties in a wad, Matthews," he says. Putting his arm across Tiffi's shoulders, he steers her toward the stage stairs. "Like we *want* to hang out with these losers."

Sterling breaks free from Ros.

"You're both scum!" she shouts at their backs.

Tate turns and rolls his eyes. "You're always so theatrical, Sterling. Too bad you can't sing."

Sterling recoils.

"Don't listen, Ster," Ros says loyally. "You sang great last night."

"You did!" I jump in. "You were good!"

Okay, I can't believe I just lied about that. But catching your boyfriend with your supposed new best bud . . . that calls for some support.

The rest of the gathered performers all start talking at once, filling each other in on the parts they missed. Sterling glances around like she can't believe we're there and runs out to the edge of the stage alone. Tiffi and Bryce are headed up the center aisle. Sterling's eyes land on the cooler. She bends down and grabs something.

Oh no, I think, envisioning shattered glass and Technicolor stains. *Ito will kill us all if she throws one of those sodas.*

But instead, she comes up with a handful of bottle caps. Taking one between her right thumb and middle finger, she snaps it off like a miniature flying saucer. It sails through the air and hits Bryce in the back of the neck.

"Ow!" He lets go of Tiffi to cover the spot with his hand. Sterling snaps another cap and hits him in the butt.

"Ow! Knock it off!" he says, turning to face her.

"Oh, I'm sorry. Does that hurt?" Sterling asks sarcastically. She lets fly again and hits Tiffi in the knee.

"Stop it, Ster!" Tiffi says. "You're acting pathetic."

"Don't you call me Ster."

"Let's just get out of here, Tiffi." Bryce starts walking again. Glancing back over his shoulder, he dishes out one last insult: "Sterling Carter—what a letdown! You don't live up to a tenth of what's written about you in the toilets."

Sterling gasps. She'd obviously love to strangle him and she looks just about mad enough to succeed. Scooping up another handful of caps, she starts firing nonstop.

Sterling tags Tiffi in the back of the head, the small of her back, and both calves. Bryce's butt is one big target. She's snapping them off like machine-gun fire, hitting every time.

"Ow! Hey! Knock it off!" Bryce and Tiffi whine.

Ros runs to the edge of the stage and picks up more caps. "Here," she says, replenishing Sterling's ammunition.

All the way up the aisle, Sterling keeps up her barrage. When Bryce and Tiffi finally disappear, she tosses her head, triumphant.

"Skank!" she declares.

"Loser!" Ros agrees.

"Who needs them?"

Ros shakes her head. "Not us."

"Exactly. Not us."

I see the look Sterling gives Ros, like she's just realized she was about to throw away the winning lottery ticket.

Gregor King ventures out to join them. "That's the coolest thing I've ever seen. Can you teach me how to do that?"

"What? Snap caps?" Sterling shrugs. "You have to practice, that's all."

"Just show me how you do it," he persists as people crowd around. "Can you hit that trash can?"

He points to a small metal wastebasket near the wings. Sterling rolls her eyes.

"There's a challenge," she says sarcastically.

She lets a bottle cap fly. People clap as it pings against the trash can.

"Put one *inside* the can," Ros suggests.

Sterling smiles and shoots again, hitting the sliver of

exposed back rim in just the right place to bounce the cap into the basket.

"Unbelievable!" Gregor exclaims.

Everyone starts talking excitedly, pointing out new targets. Sterling hits them all.

"Don't you ever miss?" I blurt out, astonished into forgetting who I'm speaking to.

Sterling looks my way. Our eyes meet. My insides freeze.

But Sterling only shrugs. "Not very often. Practically never."

"But . . . that's not natural!" I persist foolishly. "How did you learn to do it?"

"Just have the knack, I guess. My parents used to throw these endless parties. Imported beer . . . lots of caps . . . deadly boring when you're a kid. A bartender showed me how and by the end of the first night I was hitting better than he was."

"Ster's the Annie Oakley of bottle caps," Ros brags.

"Shoot something else," Gregor begs.

"Geez, you guys. It's not that big a deal."

But she's wrong. It's a very big deal.

Sterling Carter's true talent has finally been revealed.

Right This Second

Ito's wrap "party" is finally over. Ros called Tess to come get her and Sterling, Hayley and Fitz left in his dad's pickup, and Kevin and I are walking across the school library's lawn.

"Let's hang out on the grass for a while," he says, tugging on my hands. "Look how nice it is out here!"

He's right. The sun is shining, the birds are busy, and the clouds overhead look like white cotton candy. Despite Ito's attempt to ruin it, it's a perfectly gorgeous day.

"Yeah, but wouldn't you rather go somewhere else?" I ask. "I'm so sick of school."

"We'll just stay a while," he says, dropping to the grass.

I sit so close beside him our legs are pressed together, not sorry to have the final stragglers from the auditorium seeing us so tight again. Not that that type of thing matters to me anymore. I am so over worrying what other people think.

That's my newest resolution.

"Happy Valentine's Day," Kevin says, surprising me with a tiny red box.

"Another present?" I exclaim. "I left yours at home!"

"Go ahead. Open it."

I smile and give the box an exploratory shake.

"Hey, no guessing," he says with a laugh.

I can't take the suspense anyway. Ripping off the paper, I find a third charm: an open silver heart.

"Ooh," I breathe. "It's beautiful!"

"Here, let me add it on. You just have to . . ." He manipulates the charm's connector around a link on my bracelet and lets the ring spring closed. "There. It looks good there, don't you think?"

"It looks perfect." I hold my wrist up into the sun, letting the whole bracelet sparkle in the light.

"I love you, Cassie," he says.

"You . . . what?"

I must have heard him wrong. But the instant our eyes meet, I know this is for real.

"I love you," he says. "So much."

Remember before, when I decided I didn't need him to say that anymore? I was wrong. Finally hearing those words feels more incredible than I ever dreamed.

"I love you too," I say.

"You do?"

"Kevin! Yes! You have no idea how long I've been waiting for you to say that."

"I just . . . I wanted to say it before, but I was never sure how you felt. And then things got kind of weird . . ."

"Yeah."

He grins. "Of course, things with you are always weird, so I guess I shouldn't have worried."

I try not to smile, but I can't help it. I slap his arm, charms jangling. He catches my hand. Our gazes connect. And suddenly nothing else matters except that the two of us are together, closer than we've ever been.

"I love you, Kevin," I say, falling into his arms.

Running a hand through his hair, I slide my fingers down his cheek to trace his lips. "I can't believe I thought today wouldn't be romantic!"

Why worry now, when
right this second I can fly?
Let the future wait.

Okay, This Is Starting to Scare Me

"She still hasn't come out of the bedroom?" I exclaim. It's Saturday afternoon and I've just said good-bye to Kevin. Dad's in the kitchen with Grandma, and Mom is nowhere in sight. "What's the matter with her? Is she sick?"

Dad keeps rubbing spice on a hunk of beef, getting it ready to roast.

"I'd imagine she's just tired from working so hard," Grandma says. "I wouldn't worry about her."

But I am worried. I'm *very* worried. My mother has never spent an entire day lying around in my life—not even that time she had pneumonia.

Dad washes his hands and shoves the roast into the oven. "Dinner's in a couple of hours. Not that anyone cares." He gives us a demoralized look as he walks out of the kitchen.

"What's the matter with *him?*" I ask Grandma.

"I think your father's a little depressed. He wanted to make this a special day for Andrea, but she's not cooperating."

"She's probably sick! Has anyone checked on her?"

"Of course. He's been in and out of there all day. I promise you this is nothing to worry about. Your mother's just feeling blue."

"Because they're both being stupid. If either one of them would give an inch . . ."

Grandma chuckles. "Very true. But we're almost there now. Try to keep the faith a few more days."

Eat Your Heart Out, Juliet

It's dark and the temperature outside has reverted to February. My blinds are open anyway, and so is my bedroom window. Kevin has promised to ride by after dinner so I can give him his Valentine's present.

I hear a faint squeak of pedals and the low hiss of tires against the sidewalk. Jumping up, I run to the window with a huge cookie tin, a handmade Valentine taped to its top. Kevin coasts up and ditches his bike on our grass.

"Hey," he says softly, picking his way through the bushes to my window. "I missed you."

"I missed you more."

I lean out and he kisses me—another perfect moment.

"I can only stay a minute," he says. "My mom wasn't thrilled about letting me ride over here in the dark."

"Then open your present." I hand him the enormous heart-shaped tin, eager to show off the batch of cookies I was miraculously allowed to make all by myself. Even better, I've hidden a new surf T-shirt and two CDs beneath them.

"I *could* open this now," he says thoughtfully. "Or I could open it later and spend my time here kissing you."

"Open it later," I say.

Official Holiday

Is there anything better than Monday off? Besides Monday through Friday off, obviously. Trevor and I lounge at the breakfast bar, eating seconds on eggs Benedict like there's all the time in the world.

"What are you kids doing today?" Grandma asks, washing the egg pan. Dad stands beside her at the counter, scooping leftover hollandaise sauce into a plastic tub.

"Kevin and I are going to the movies," I say before Dad can enlist me to help with his chores again, like he did all day yesterday. Mom is back at work today (Presidents' birthdays? So what?) and the last thing I want to do is stay home and suffer with Dad. "You guys ought to take the day off too," I suggest. "Make it an official holiday."

Dad turns a defeated expression my way. "That living room won't paint itself."

"It won't take more than three hours, though," Grandma tells him, "and we need to start our spring planting. We'll knock out our painting first, then head down to the garden center."

I give Dad a pleading look. *Don't make me do that with you!*

"Whatever," he says with a sigh.

"Can I have my allowance, Dad?" Trevor asks. "I'm going to the mall too."

"Not with me, you aren't!" I say.

"Relax," he says scornfully. "Like I really want to hang out with my sister. Bill and I are hitting the food court, to see who else is there."

He can't keep the smug grin off his face. I'm not sure he's even trying.

"Pace yourself, Don Juan," I say. "September's a long way off."

Trevor drops his fork. "Wha . . . ? Did Julie tell you that?"

I raise my brows mysteriously, preferring not to confess to eavesdropping.

"Aw, man!" he cries, thrilled. "She digs me!"

Dad slaps some bills on the counter. "Have fun," he says dully. "Somebody ought to."

Right and Ros

"Cassie!"

The voice I hear calling my name is not the one I'm expecting.

"Cassie!" Ros shouts again. "Hey, over here!"

I spot her near the front of the huge crowd outside the movie theater, smiling and waving her arms overhead. Quentin is standing with her, digging through his pants pockets, and Kevin is beside them, waving as hard as Ros. I hurry over, not sure what to make of this unexpected encounter.

On the one hand, we'll definitely get tickets.

On the other, does this mean we're sitting with Quentin and Ros? Because I kind of wanted to be alone with Kevin. Not to mention that if we *were* going to double, Quentin and Ros wouldn't be my first choice of couple—for obvious reasons.

"Look who I found," Kevin greets me. "It's a lucky thing, too, because this place is crazy."

"Yeah, I noticed. Hi."

Quentin starts checking his jacket pockets. "How could I have lost that coupon? I swear I had it when I left the house."

"Free small popcorn," Ros tells me, amused.

"Hey, let us buy the popcorn," says Kevin. "It's the least we can do for these cuts in line. I'll get a giant tub and we'll all share."

"If Quentin's sharing, it had better be giant," I say.

Oops.

Was that too much information? Because it could make someone suspect I've eaten popcorn with Quentin before. Which I have. Lots of times. But not recently. My cheeks take on a life of their own as I peek from Kevin to Quentin to Ros.

They're all checking showtimes, oblivious. I take a few deep breaths and wonder if this is how it's going to be from now on. Now that Kevin knows, and Ros never will, am I doomed to live in constant fear of saying something stupid?

Okay, fine, if you have to get technical, I already live in fear of that. But this is different. Someone could get hurt.

I fidget nervously while the guys buy our tickets. Inside the lobby, we head for the candy counter.

"Extra butter," Quentin tells Kevin.

"Better make my soda diet, then," Ros says.

"What do you want, Cassie?" asks Kevin.

"Whatever you're having. Red Vines are good."

He smiles and inches closer to the mobbed counter. This crowd is making me claustrophobic.

"I'm going to the bathroom," I blurt out. A few too many heads turn. "Better now than later," I add, embarrassed.

"I'll go with you," Ros offers. "You guys get our seats and we'll meet you inside."

"Okay," Quentin says, distracted. "No, dude—the *Mega*Tub. With extra butter."

"I heard you the first time, dude." But Kevin doesn't seem to mind. If anything, those two are getting along better than ever.

I, on the other hand, am being escorted to the bathroom by my guilty conscience and Little Miss Trusting.

How much would Ros hate me if she knew? I wonder, feeling a sudden urge to tell her. But it's not a good urge. It's more like standing on the edge of a cliff and randomly thinking *What if I jumped?*

The ladies' room isn't as crowded as the lobby, but all of the stalls are full.

"What did Kevin give you for Valentine's?" Ros asks as we wait our turn.

I show her my new heart charm. "What did you get?"

"I got a heart too—but mine was filled with chocolates."

Candy? I'm surprised Quentin didn't go bigger.

"I gave him a spending limit," Ros says, reading my mind. "And guess what? He's cutting back his hours to three afternoons and Saturday mornings. No more extra shifts!"

"How did you make him agree to that?"

"I told him if he wants a girlfriend, he needs to spend time on her, not money."

She's obviously delighted with the way things worked out. I'm happy for her. She deserves it.

And suddenly I know what I have to do. I have to jump off that cliff.

"There's, uh . . . there's something I ought to tell you, Ros. The day after your birthday, I saw Quentin at MegaFoodMart. I was upset about Kevin and Tiffi, and what happened was . . . well, Quentin gave me a shoulder to cry on and . . . it's just . . . I'm embarrassed about it now," I end lamely.

I can't take this leap after all.

"Why?" Ros asks. "Because you kissed him?"

The air rushes out of my lungs. "You knew?"

"Quentin told me the Wednesday after it happened. He didn't want me hearing it from someone else and getting the wrong idea." She smiles ironically. "Good thinking, huh?"

"But, but . . . you're not mad?"

Ros grimaces. "I was. But you and Quentin go back. There's history there. . . . I get that. Do I wish it hadn't happened? Yeah. But it's not going to happen again."

"It's not! I swear!" I assure her. "It was a stupid, stupid mistake. Quentin totally loves you."

"Yes, he does," she says, smiling for real.

"Why didn't you tell me you knew? Do you have any idea how hard I've been sweating this thing?"

"You don't think you deserved to? Besides, I'm not real big on direct confrontation. I thought you knew that about me."

She's right. I *did* know that about her.

"Anyway," she says, "I knew you were on my side the night you gave up the pie."

"The pie?" I repeat, confused.

"Blueberry? In a bowl with a spoon? No girl gives up a tip that good if she's trying to keep a guy for herself."

"Right. The pie," I say, dazed. "So you and I . . . we're still friends?"

Ros nods. "But if something like this ever happens again . . ." There's just enough steel in her eyes to let me know she means business.

"Nooooo! No way."

"Good. Because I really like you, Cassie, but this is a one-time amnesty."

I Might Be Getting Spoiled

Because oatmeal doesn't cut it when you're expecting pancakes.

"Where's Dad?" I ask Grandma as she puts my bowl down. She's alone in the kitchen this morning, and except for the sound of Trevor slurping milk on the next stool, the house is completely quiet.

"He has some important errands," she says. "He'll be back when you get home from school."

"Wait. We have to *walk?*" Trevor asks. He might be getting spoiled too.

"Better hurry." Grandma sets two brown bags on the counter. "Here, your father made you both Howard Hoagies for lunch."

"Awesome!" Trevor gulps the rest of his milk and slams

down his empty bowl. Grabbing his lunch, he jogs out of the kitchen.

I try to hurry too, but there's a lump down in my gut that has nothing to do with oatmeal. I miss my dad. I miss the way he used to be, back when the house was messy, and he was happy, and a Howard Hoagie was a once-in-a-lifetime experience instead of a brown-bag lunch.

I miss my mother, too. I miss hanging out with her after dinner and hearing her work horror stories. I miss telling her about school, and the takeout she used to bring home. . . .

Okay, I just miss takeout in general.

"You don't have to finish that oatmeal if you're not hungry," Grandma says. "Here, take an apple for later."

She adds the fruit to my lunch bag and hands it to me as I slide off my barstool.

"Have a good day," she tells me. "And try not to worry so much. I've got everything under control."

You Can't Take the Soc out of Sociopath

Poor Sterling. Everyone's talking about her. You can't walk down the hall without hearing the hiss of her name being whispered over and over. And not in a good way. The gossip du jour is how Tate the Great dumped her hard for Tiffi Hughes.

I have a pretty good idea who's spreading the story. Tiffi showed up here this morning dressed like a preppy pinup and oozing soc attitude. She and Bryce have been cruising the hall between periods acting like the newly crowned king and queen of popularity. And you know what? People are buying it. Honestly, it's sickening.

And I still haven't seen Sterling. I've heard rumors, though. I've heard some unbelievable rumors.

I hustle through the crowd toward the quad, hoping to get the straight story from Ros. Hayley waves from our usual table. I start jogging over and miss a step, stunned. Fourteen-Karat Carter is eating lunch with *us*!

Not that Sterling is looking so golden today. If you want the truth, she looks like the brainy girl in a bad music video, complete with glasses and greasy hair. And what is that outfit she's wearing? Sweatpants and her grandma's shawl?

Those rumors were dead right.

"Um, hi, everyone. Sterling," I say, sliding in.

She glances my way and nods once. Our eyes don't really connect before her gaze returns to the tabletop.

"Ster's not feeling well," Ros says, putting an arm around her best friend. "Some kind of vicious bug, but it will pass."

So that's their cover story. I have to admire them for trying.

"Don't worry. I'm not contagious," Sterling mumbles.

"We're not worried," Hayley says kindly.

The guys take the pizza order and clear out as fast as they can, leaving us girls alone.

Well.

This is awkward.

Sterling's staring at the table like she's going to burst into tears any minute. Hayley and I have no clue what to say. Should we talk about what happened with Bryce?

Should we talk about something else? Should we sit here in total silence?

Ros finally helps us out. "He's not worth it, you know," she tells Sterling.

"No," Hayley agrees.

"Not even," I chime in.

Sterling nods without speaking, too miserable to answer.

An eruption of giggles makes me turn my head. Tiffi and Tate are palling around with a bunch of Sterling's old crowd, and they're headed directly toward us. I give Ros a desperate look. She sees Tiffi and sighs.

"They're coming over," she warns.

"Of course they are," Sterling says bitterly. Her shoulders tense, like she's bracing for the knife in her back, but her eyes don't leave the table.

"Look who's here!" Tiffi's voice rings out. "The hot air beneath our wings! All those lessons and she still can't sing."

Giggles break out again. Tamara and Angie lean into Tiffi like the three of them are best buds. Tate and his friends strut behind them.

"Then again, she can't do much, can she, Brycie?" Tiffi taunts.

"You got that right," Tate says, with a scornful glance Sterling's way. He grabs Tiffi's long hair and pulls her backward like a Neanderthal, looping his arm around her neck.

His woman. Ug.

"Love the bedspread," Angie mocks as they walk past. "That whole homeless look is so fashionable now."

Tamara giggles evilly. "That's a *poncho*, Angie."

"Oh. So sorry."

The whole group howls with laughter as they pass us and keep walking.

I've just witnessed my first soc drive-by.

"What's the deal?" I ask Ros. "I thought Tamara and Angie were your friends."

Ros looks disgusted. "Tiffi thinks she's queen bee now, but this is Angie and Tamara's big chance to move up too. One false move and they'll eat that skinny girl alive."

"We can only hope," Sterling mutters.

"Just because she has Sterling's boyfriend and a couple of fickle groupies—" Hayley begins.

"He's not my boyfriend!" Sterling snaps, finally showing a little life. "I *hate* him."

"Good, because he's slime," I pop off. "Tiffi's not the first gir"—I hesitate as Hayley shoots me a warning look—"um, I mean, the last girl who'll find that out," I cover lamely.

Hayley's right. This might not be the best time to mention Tate's other indiscretions.

"You can do better than both of them," Ros says.

"Oh, yeah! All kinds of better," I say.

Sterling gives me a squinty look, like she's trying to figure out if I'm making fun of her.

Here's the amazing part: I'm not.

There's not a drop of joy in this for me. In fact, it's actually pretty awful, seeing my old rival brought so low.

I always thought Sterling was invincible.

Turns out she's only human.

(Showing Up)²

I've just finished my post-PE shower and am about to head over to Ros's house. Her new car is arriving any day, and we're all going to hang out and see the brochure. Wind ruffles my damp hair as I dash down the hall to my locker, needing to grab my psych textbook before meeting the gang at Quentin's van. I'm passing the office doorway when I hear a voice that brings my sneakers to a squeaking halt.

Mrs. Conway is back!

I jog into the office and find her leaning on the counter, talking to Ms. Masters, our school secretary.

"Hey! You're here!" I say.

"You're right." She looks tired, but she's dressed nicely.

"So how come we still have a substitute?"

"Mrs. Harrier has agreed to stay through the week. I'll be back on Monday."

"Is, um, is everything okay? I mean, at home and all?"

Mrs. Conway gives me an incredulous look.

"You know what?" Ms. Masters says uneasily. "I just remembered some filing I'd better finish." She disappears into a back room, leaving me and Mrs. Conway alone.

"So is it?" I ask recklessly.

"I'm not sure what you mean, Cassie."

I see what she's doing. She wants to act like everything's

347

normal. I might let her, too—if she hadn't just dumped a talent show on me. Flowers are nice, but the truth would be nicer.

"I mean is your husband okay?" I ask bluntly.

I'm fully prepared to take her on if she goes all Conway on me. But she hardly even flinches. She just studies me a long time.

"I won't ask how you figured that out," she says at last.

"You could have just told me," I accuse.

"I could have. But when you let something like that out into the world, you lose your right to control it."

"Huh?" Is it me, or does that make no sense at all?

"You'll understand someday. There was always a chance I wouldn't be able to finish the show—that's why I made you second in charge. And you did great, Cassie. I only wish I could have been there to see it."

"But why didn't you come? Is Mr. Conway sicker?"

"Not sicker." She sighs. "Not better. There was another surgery and it seems to have gone well. I'm hopeful."

"I'm hoping too. And don't worry—I'm not going to spread your business around. I just want you both to be okay."

Mrs. Conway gives me a genuine smile. "Thank you, Cassie."

"You're welcome. Emily."

Her eyebrows soar.

All right, over the line. Just checking.

"I mean Mrs. Conway. I'll see you Monday, then?"

"Monday," she agrees, smiling.

The Art of B-ing

"Stop it!" I squeal as Kevin tickles my ribs on our way into the school parking lot. I stumble across the asphalt slapping his hands away, laughing helplessly. "Hayley! Save me!"

She rushes in and begins tickling Kevin. "Come on, Ros!" she cries. "Help us."

Ros thinks half a second and starts tickling Quentin.

"Hey! That's not helping!" I protest.

"Helping who?" she counters.

"I've got your back, man!" Fitz declares, jumping in to attack Hayley.

"Fitz! You traitor!" She wriggles around to tickle him.

We're all laughing and slapping and begging for mercy. A car horn honks—we're blocking the aisle. We laugh even harder as we stagger out of the way.

"See what you started?" I tell Kevin.

"Everyone, just settle down," Ros orders, in a dead-on imitation of Ms. Carter's socialite drawl. "What if someone who matters sees us? Think of our positions!"

"You should have thought of that before you fell for me," Quentin teases her.

"Yeah, Ros," Fitz pipes in. "You'll never recover from that one!"

Ros sighs melodramatically and presses a hand to her forehead. "My stint on the A-list is over, I guess."

"Lucky you," says Hayley, and I couldn't agree more.

If this is the B-list, sign me up.

I've seen the A-list. Tiffi can have it.

Taking Out

The only light on in our house is in the dining room. I gulp and start walking faster. I'm home late for dinner, and the way tempers have been around here lately, that wasn't a real smart move.

"Hey! Sorry! I got held up!" I call, running the last few steps into the dining room. My family is sitting around a table littered with empty Chinese takeout containers.

"Man, you missed it," Trevor gloats. "That was the best Chinese ever!"

"I think there's some sweet-and-sour pork left," my mother offers.

Trevor peers into the nearest carton. "Nah. I picked out all the pork. There's just sauce and onion chunks."

"Sit down, Cassie," Grandma says. "Have some rice, at least."

She spoons fried rice onto the only clean plate as I take my chair and look around in a daze. My father is seated across from me, wearing a dress shirt and tie. My mother is wearing a smile, which is even more unexpected.

"What's going on?" I ask, pouring orange sweet-and-sour

sauce over the rice Grandma hands me. "Did I miss something besides dinner?"

"You tell her, Hal," Mom says. "It's your big news."

"Very big," Grandma murmurs.

Some people like suspense. I'm not one of them. "Tell me!"

"I got a new job," Dad says, grinning. "With the Hilltop Unified School District. I start tomorrow."

"Isn't that fantastic?" Mom jumps in.

"But . . . what will you do at a school?" I ask, confused.

"It's at the district offices. And I'll be accounting, same as before."

"With one big difference," Trevor chimes in.

"*Lots* of official holidays!" he and Dad cry together, slapping delighted high fives.

"Not to mention killer benefits and weeks and weeks of vacation," Dad adds. "That place is Disneyland compared to my old job."

"Isn't it wonderful?" Mom asks me, practically swooning.

It must be, to make everyone this happy. The only one without much to say is Grandma.

"What do you think, Grandma?" I ask.

"You know me," she says with a tired little sigh. "I just want what's best for my family." Pushing back her chair, she rises from the table. "I'd better start my packing if I'm catching that flight out tomorrow."

"What? You're leaving?"

"There's no reason for me to stay anymore."

"But . . . but . . ." I look around the table for an ally. Nobody speaks up. "Grandma!"

"Now, let's not have a scene. I had to go home sometime."

I'm starting to freak out. The way she's leaving so abruptly . . . She must be upset about Dad's new job.

I give her a desperate look as she passes my chair. I stand up to protest. . . .

And I'm the only one who sees Grandma toss me a big, sly wink.

Back in Black

Mrs. Harrier is still making us jump through punctuation hoops, but I don't care anymore. Now that I know Mrs. Conway's coming back, I can relax and take the ride. Besides, I've got these punctuation drills wired now. Even that obnoxious timer has stopped making me cringe.

The end-of-period bell rings. I pass my paper forward and lean across to Kevin. "Lunch in the quad today?"

"Of course," he replies, like he can't believe I need to ask.

The charms on my bracelet jingle as I hoist my backpack onto my shoulders. My smile stretches out till it hurts.

It's a good day to be Cassie.

We walk down the hall together, stopping to kiss goodbye at its end. Leaning forward lips first, I catch a sight that makes me gasp.

"No way! Do you see what I see?"

Sterling is walking—no, strutting—toward us down the hall like she's keeping the beat in her own music video. She's wearing black suede pants, black spike heels, and a little black top that definitely pushes the dress code. The glasses are gone, and her hair floats around her with every step, restored to the pinnacle of blond glory.

But that's not what's making me rub my eyes. What's dropping jaws all the way down the hall is the person she's holding hands with: Tate the Great.

Bryce lopes at her side like a smitten puppy, like Tiffi never happened. He can't tear his eyes off her. With every step they take, the gossip crests behind them like a wave.

"I'm officially shocked," Kevin says, speaking for us both.

"What is she doing?" I ask.

"She got him back, obviously."

"But *why*?"

He shakes his head, baffled.

In geometry, where I'm already concentrationally challenged, I spend the entire hour fighting the urge to text-message Hayley.

In art, where I could conceivably get away with it, I have to remind myself she won't be able to answer. Luckily, art is one big gab fest. The rumors start as soon as we break out our collages.

"I hear he *begged* her to take him back," Molly Greer reports.

"Because he knows he blew it," Courtney Haines weighs in. "Sterling Carter for Tiffi Hughes? Talk about trading down!"

"Has anyone seen her today?" Molly asks.

"I saw her," I pipe up. "She looks incredible."

"Smokin'," agrees Clint, the only guy in our group.

"No, I meant Tiffi," Molly says. "Has anyone seen Tiffi?"

Nobody has, which makes it that much harder to wait until lunchtime, when I can sort this out with my friends.

Ms. Lane finally tells us to start cleaning up. I leap out of my seat with a bottle of glue in each hand and hustle to the supply cupboard. Half the class is in a hurry, and I know why: if the scene in the hall was interesting, it was only a teaser for the show we expect in the quad.

The bell rings and I sprint halfway down the hall before I remember it's not cool to run. It's also not cool to be so eager to see Tiffi and Sterling meet up again, but let's be honest: this is better than free HBO.

Out in the quad, our table is already full, with one important exception. "Where's Ros?" I ask Quentin.

He tilts his head to one side. Ros is sitting a few tables over, with Sterling, Tate, and a full complement of upper-tier socs. Sterling is holding court, her suede-clad rear perched on the edge of the table instead of down in a seat, her head high enough to give the whole quad a view of her frequent hair tosses. It feels like looking into a time machine.

"What's going on?" I demand. "Why is Ros back over there?"

Quentin shrugs. "Something about supporting Sterling. Doesn't look like she needs it to me."

No, it doesn't. Not at all.

"I'm going to buy lunch," Fitz announces. He makes Quentin go with him, leaving me, Hayley, and Kevin alone at our table.

"I can't believe she's back with Tate," Hayley says. "The whole school is talking about it."

"You'd think she'd have more pride," I agree.

Kevin shakes his head. "I never got that relationship in the first place."

I did. Eventually. But I don't get this. I watch fascinated as people wander up and attach themselves to Sterling's group like yesterday never happened. She's so back on top again.

Queen Bee.

"Uh-oh," Hayley says. I follow her gaze to edge of the quad, where Tiffi has just appeared with Tamara and Angie. My heart starts beating faster as they head in Sterling's direction.

I have to give Tiffi credit. She keeps her chin in the air, working every inch of her limited height as she stalks across the quad. Like Sterling, she's dressed to thrill, relying on those jutting hip bones for what she lacks in cleavage. Her curls tumble perfectly down her back, but something about her rosebud lips looks more pinched than pursed. There's an injured air about her as she makes her way through the crowd, Angie and Tamara lagging behind.

"Those two wish they were anywhere else right now," Hayley guesses. "Serves them right."

I rip my eyes from Tiffi to take a closer look at her ladies-in-waiting. Second thoughts are written all over Tamara's pretty face. Angie looks ready to bolt.

"That's the danger of a mutiny," Kevin says. "The whole crew walks the plank."

I don't know about that. Tiffi doesn't look beaten to me. Down, maybe, but not out. Reaching Sterling's table, she strikes a pose with both hands on her hips.

"What are you doing with my boyfriend?" she asks loudly.

Sterling's group falls silent. So does half the quad. Grinning fearlessly, Sterling slides off the table and stands up to face her new rival. "Who? Bryce?"

"He's not yours anymore," Tiffi says.

Sterling's laugh is pure, tinkling soc. "Duh! Why would I even want him?"

"What?" Tiffi and Tate say at the same time.

"Take him," Sterling tells Tiffi. "Keep him with my compliments."

Tate's face is completely priceless. He can't tell whether she's kidding or not.

"Yeah, right," he laughs, looking around at his teammates until they all join in. "Good one, Ster."

She turns to him with a big Snow Queen smile. "You didn't really think I'd take you back?"

"Huh?"

His teammates' laughter takes a mocking turn.

"Please!" says Sterling. "Run along with Skanky and have a nice life."

Tiffi trembles with humiliation. "Come on, Brycie. Let's go."

Tate rises from the table, but instead of joining Tiffi, he gives her a loathing look. "Get lost, Hughes. I'm not with you."

He turns imploringly to Sterling, like he still thinks she might change her mind.

"Buh-bye!" she says, waving him on his way with just her fingertips.

"Ouch," Kevin mutters.

He's not the only one. Catcalls sound across the quad as Tate grabs his backpack and slinks off toward the gym. Tiffi turns on her platforms and marches in the opposite direction. Angie and Tamara freeze like a couple of dazzled deer. To follow Tiffi now is social suicide.

But what choice do they have?

They finally unstick their feet and move to join their new queen. Sterling's voice rings out before they take two steps.

"Tamara! Angie! Don't you want to sit with us?"

It's an official pardon, an act of royal mercy.

"Of course! Thanks, Sterling!" they say fawningly, running to join her group.

Sterling soaks it up, her power play complete. Climbing back onto her blue plastic throne, she smiles down at her subjects like the past few days never happened. "Life's too short to date one boy. Especially a loser like that."

The guys jump at the bait, vying for her attention, while the girls congratulate her loudly on her soon-to-be-legendary dumping of Tate. Ros glances over, catches my eye, and winks.

The show is over.

You know what? Sterling just may be an actress in addition to a bottle-cap snapper. Anyone who didn't know the truth would never guess that under that devil-may-care performance she's exactly like the rest of us—scared, lost, and fronting for all she's worth. I never realized before how much inner strength it takes to be such a witch.

Not that she couldn't put her energy to better use.

But still . . .

You have to admire a self-made queen.

Taking Off

"These stupid precautions!" Grandma complains. "What is this world coming to when an old lady can't even have her family walk her to the gate?"

We're standing in an alcove near the airport metal detectors, because that's as far as the rest of us can go without tickets.

"They just want to make sure you're not a terrorist, Grandma," Trevor says.

"They're letting me on the plane," she points out, a teasing glint in her eye. "It's obviously you they're worried about."

I'm still struggling to believe she's leaving any second. Stepping forward, I hug her hard. "I wish you weren't going! I'll miss you so much!"

"I'll miss you too," she says. "But we won't let it go so long before we see each other again. And in the meantime, we can write. I sure do enjoy those letters of yours."

I jerk my head off her shoulder. "Grandma!"

But it doesn't really matter. That cat is already out of the mailbag. Besides, Mom's in such a good mood tonight that nothing could possibly wreck it.

"Now, you be careful walking on that ice, Mother," she instructs. "There's no reason Roy can't salt your walks for you. I'm going to call him and Catie as soon as we get home."

"I'm perfectly capable of salting my own walks."

"Roy is younger. His bones heal faster. You let us kids work it out."

Grandma smiles. "All right, Andrea."

"And we want to see you at Christmas this year. Catie's had you too many holidays in a row."

"Or you Howards could fly out," my grandmother suggests. "Then we could all be together."

Mom hesitates. "We could fly to Ohio," she agrees, to my amazement. "Nothing like a few days of freezing to make a person appreciate California."

"I have that new boiler. It's toasty warm inside."

"Okay." My mother steps up and gives Grandma a hug. I'm surprised by how long she hangs on. "I get it now," she whispers. "The real reason you came . . . Thanks, Mom."

"You've got it," Grandma says softly. "Anytime, anywhere, till the day I stop breathing. You know I love you, Andrea."

Mom nods and steps back. There are tears brimming in her eyes. I'm choking up big-time. Trevor's sniffing. Even Grandma Smythe looks iffy.

Dad steps into the gap. "Thanks for coming, Arlene," he says. "I may not be a homemaker anymore, but I definitely learned a lot of your tricks."

The smile returns to Grandma's face. "You certainly did," she agrees. "Well, I'd better go. We don't want the plane taking off without me. You kids be good," she adds, giving me and Trevor one last kiss. "I'll see you at Christmas!"

We watch as she passes through the metal detector. Picking up her tote on the other side, she turns and waves to us.

"Bye, Grandma!" I call, waving frantically. "See you soon!"

She gets smaller all the way up the escalator. She waves once more from the top, and she's gone.

"We're really going to Ohio, right?" I ask my mom. "Because you can't just say that and then take it back."

"Well . . . we do kind of have to now," she says, looking for Dad's reaction.

"I have two weeks off at Christmas!" he tells us gleefully.

"Hey!" Trevor butts in. "Can we rent a snowmobile?"

"Not on your life," Mom says.

"Not even a little one?"

"You want to run a motor in the snow? I'll teach you to use the snow blower. You can spray snow all over the place."

"Cool!" he says, with a suspiciously evil grin in my direction.

"Don't even think it," I warn.

"All this talk about snow . . . Let's go to Udder Delights," Dad says.

"Ice cream? Now?" Mom protests as he leads the way to the exit. "We haven't even had dinner."

"Hey, it was my first day at the new job and I want to celebrate."

"I'm going to get that huge hot fudge sundae," I say. "The one I can never finish when we eat first."

"Ooh! I'll have the Banana Blaster!" Trevor says, targeting the biggest thing on the menu. "I'll finally get my name written on that wall!"

Mom smiles and shakes her head. "Don't expect to get used to this. It's not normal, eating ice cream for a meal."

"It's the new normal!" Dad declares, looping an arm around her. "And I like it!"

"I like it too," Trevor says.

Mom shoots me a pleading look, obviously hoping for backup.

I can't help her out. "What's not to like?" I ask.

She turns back toward my father and the last reservation leaves her face. "Nothing," she says happily, laying her head on his shoulder.

Let It B

Conway's back today! I'm giving her a new haiku, just to celebrate. She may have to work this one out, but you'll know what I mean.

E's don't define me.
I'm content to simply be
Maybe to B+.